# ARCHIE MEETS NERO WOLFE

# ARCHIE

## MEETS

# NERO WOLFE

*Robert Goldsborough*

MYSTERIOUSPRESS.COM

OPEN ROAD

INTEGRATED MEDIA

NEW YORK

To Barbara Stout and Rebecca Stout Bradbury,

whose support and encouragement have been

appreciated more than I can ever say

# CHAPTER 1

Even though September was barely half over, the wind off the Hudson made me wish I had worn my new fur-lined jacket. In the two-plus weeks I had patrolled the Moreland Import Company docks, each night seemed colder than the one before it. At this rate, I would freeze before Halloween.

I wouldn't have taken the job if anything better had turned up, but I felt lucky just to have work of any kind. I saw enough of those long lines on the sidewalks outside the soup kitchens to appreciate getting a paycheck, even a small one. Besides, I was not about to go back to Chillicothe, Ohio, with my tail between my legs.

Bates had told me to be especially alert, what with the big shipment of Swiss watches and fancy clocks on the boat that docked an hour before I came on duty. They would get unloaded tomorrow morning. "Probably nothin' will happen, kid, but we don't want to take no chances," he said, patting me on the shoulder. "Remember, if you see anybody messin' around, fire into the air. That'll bring the cops soon enough and scare 'em away."

I fingered the revolver nestled in the holster on my hip. Although I had hunted ducks with a shotgun along the rivers back home with my father, I had never used a pistol and figured I wouldn't have to on this job.

I had just finished my third circuit of the long pier and found myself staring at the lights of New Jersey across the river when I heard a sound like the scuffing of a shoe somewhere behind me. I flattened myself against the wall of the warehouse and pulled out my flashlight. Before I could turn it on, though, I saw a figure disappear around the bow of the ship.

"Stop!" I yelled, running toward the bow. I fired one shot into the air, startled by its report. I slowed as I got close to where I had seen the figure and was about to fire into the air again when another shot was fired—at me!

The shell buried itself in the wall of the warehouse just over my shoulder, which sent me into a fast crouch. Cold night or not, I started sweating as I crawled around the bow of the big freighter, gun drawn. Two men, silhouetted against those Jersey shore lights, began to shinny like monkeys up one of the hawsers that secured the freighter to the dock.

"Stop!" I shouted again. Both men fired this time, but their aim was bad because they struggled to hold on to both the rope and their guns as they swayed. My aim was better. I got off a pair of shots, and two bodies thudded onto the dock.

And they turned out to be bodies, all right, though I didn't know it yet. I approached them with my revolver still drawn, but relaxed when I saw that their guns were several feet from them and they were not moving. The realization began to hit me: I had just killed two people.

Suddenly, I found myself in a spotlight. "Hold it right there!" a voice holding an electric torch boomed. "Drop the gun. Hands in the air!"

I did both, fast.

"Lord Almighty, what have we got here?" a heavyset New York cop said as he shone his torch in my face and studied my uniform. "Are the piers so hard up they're hirin' teenagers as guards now?"

"Blame it on this cursed Depression, Murph," a second cop said as he ran up to us, wheezing. "They can get these young guys cheap."

"How old are you, son?" the first cop asked.

"Nineteen. And they fired at me first, after I'd given them a warning shot into the air," I said, gesturing toward the two prone figures with a shaking hand and then pointing out the bullet hole in the wall of the pier. "There's a big order of expensive Swiss watches and clocks on board," I added. "I was told to be extra-cautious tonight."

"Well, I'll be damned, it's Jake McCaffey," the second cop said, shining his light on one face, then the other. "And his two-bit sidekick, Rumson. This pair has been pulling heists, or trying to, on the docks along here for years. Well, they'll never do it again," he added without emotion.

"What's your name, son?" asked the one called Murph.

"Archie Goodwin," I said hoarsely.

"Well, Archie Goodwin, it looks like they shot first all right, but you'll still have to come down to the precinct. There's reports to file, questions to answer, like it or not."

I ended up spending three-plus hours at the Tenth Precinct, which I learned also was headquarters for Homicide West. For at least two of those hours, I got grilled by a surly lieutenant named Rowcliff, who had bulging eyes and a snarling voice that broke into a stutter when he got excited, which seemed to be much of the time.

He kept trying to get me to say that I fired at the robbers first. I was nervous, but when I wouldn't budge off my story, his stuttering got worse, which would have been funny under different circumstances. In the end, Rowcliff gave up with a growl, and I was told to go but to let the cops know where to reach me, which I did.

Back in my room, I went over the events of the night, asking myself what I should have done differently. No good answer popped up. Two men, bad men, were dead. Why wasn't I feeling better about it?

The next afternoon when I reported for work, I was met at the door of the Moreland Import office by my boss, Luke Bates. "Sorry, Goodwin, but we're going to have to let you go," he said with a shrug.

"Why? I was just—"

"I know, I know. You were just protecting the ship and its cargo, which we appreciate. But having a trigger-happy guard is bad for the company's image. That's just how it is."

"You know they fired at me first, after I had fired into the air," I said. "And that they'd been looting on these docks for years."

He shrugged again, as if to underscore his helplessness. "Tell you what, it's against regulations given what a short time you've been here, but I'll authorize a week's severance pay to go along with your two weeks' wages."

So it was that after my first month in New York, I had the equivalent of three weeks' salary in my pocket, along with no job and no prospects.

# CHAPTER 2

I trudged back to my rooming house on West Fifty-Second Street near Tenth Avenue, wishing I knew Manhattan well enough to find a speakeasy and get a drink, assuming they would even serve me, given my age. I had come to the city to get away from the dullness of small-town Ohio and find excitement. That had not taken long at all.

The first thing that caught my eye back in my small, tired third-floor room was the copy of *Black Mask* magazine on the nightstand. I had picked up the habit of buying the occasional detective magazine a couple of years earlier. Reading about fictional private eyes and their cases was okay, as far as it went, but I felt that if given a fair chance, I'd be as smart as any of the shamuses in those pulps.

I thumbed idly through *Black Mask* then set it down, making a decision. On a shelf next to the pay telephone in the hall outside my room sat Manhattan's fat classified directory. I turned to "detective agencies" and started down the alphabet, going past AAA Investigations and ACE People Finders as too slick-sounding. A little farther along, I stopped at the listing for the Bascom Detective Agency, which had an address only six blocks away from the rooming house.

A pawnshop with a half-dozen musical instruments behind its dusty windows occupied the street level of the run-down, narrow, four-story building. A sign over a door to the right of the shop listed the building's upstairs tenants: Madame LeBlanc—Reader-Adviser; Holman's Coin & Stamp Shop; The Bascom Detective Agency.

The open-cage elevator piloted by a bald, tobacco-chewing scrag in a sweat-stained shirt rattled its way to the fourth floor, depositing me across the hall from a frosted glass door that simply read BASCOM. I thought about knocking then decided to just push on in. A woman with a pinched face who could have voted for U. S. Grant for president looked up at me over rimless glasses from a small desk in a small anteroom. So much for the image of the detective with the voluptuous secretary.

"Yes?" she said, arching a painted eyebrow and giving me a look suggesting that I had wandered into the wrong place by mistake.

"I'd like to see … Mr. Bascom, is it?"

"Is he expecting you?" she said with a sniff.

"No, but I believe he would want to see me."

"Really?" She sniffed again. "Your name?"

"Archie Goodwin."

"And your business?"

"It's confidential. Very confidential."

She sniffed a third time and stepped to a partially open door behind her desk that had no name on it. She looked in and said, "Del, there's a Mr. Archie Goodwin out here who wants to see you. He says it's confidential. Very confidential."

The person inside must have said something like "Send him in" because the sniffer stepped aside, letting me enter the sanctum. To say the room was unimpressive did it a favor. The lone window looked out on the blank brick wall of the building next door. A single battered desk was piled high with messy stacks of paper. Behind the desk sat a fiftyish man with mottled skin, a double chin, unruly leaden-colored hair, and a four-inch scar on one cheek. So much for the image of the lean, square-jawed detective.

"Yeah, what can I do for you?" he muttered, pulling the stub of a cigar from his mouth.

"You are Mr. Bascom?"

"Del Bascom, that's me. What's so confidential, kid?"

"I need a job," I said, sliding uninvited into the scarred guest chair in front of his desk.

"So do millions of other Americans," Bascom said in a world-weary tone. "What makes you so special?"

"I've got the makings of one hell of a detective," I told him.

"That so? What kind of experience you got?"

"None yet. Give me a week to prove myself. I'll work free. How can you beat a deal like that?"

"Lemme lay out the situation for you, kid," Bascom said, planting both beefy hands palms down on his desk. "You're looking at the entire staff of this operation, other than Wilda out front, and I'm stuck with her—she's my wife's aunt, and I don't need trouble at home. I used to have a couple of operatives on the payroll, but business isn't exactly breaking down the door these days, and now I only use freelancers, which is almost never."

"It won't cost you anything to give me a try," I argued.

Bascom sighed. "You got any kind of work record at all? What were you doing before you walked in here?"

"I was a night guard at one of the North River piers."

"That so? I read a short bit in this morning's *Daily News* that a couple grifters got bumped off someplace along there last night. Helluva thing."

"I was the one who bumped them off."

Bascom's mouth dropped open. "The hell you say! Who were you working for?"

"The Moreland operation. I reported to Luke Bates."

"Geez, I know Bates. Did a job for him a few years back," Bascom said. "One of his dock crew was pilfering watches and jewelry. Didn't take us long to nail the stupe."

"Watches, that's just what these guys last night were after, and fancy clocks, so I was told."

"So you did Moreland a favor. You get tired of working for them?"

"They canned me. Said I was trigger-happy."

"Are you?"

"I never fired a pistol in my life until last night. And I got shot at first. I'm only walking around because their aim was lousy."

Bascom leaned back and stroked his stubble-covered chin. "The name's Archie Goodwin, right? Mind if I call Bates?"

"Be my guest," I said as he thumbed through a dog-eared notebook and picked up his phone.

"Hey, Luke, it's Del Bascom. How you been?"

"Yeah, things are plenty tight here, too. Understand you had quite a ruckus there last night. No kidding? Jake McCaffey caught it, huh? Well, he was lucky to have lived this long, the swine."

Bascom listened for another minute or so, then said, "Luke, I've got a guy here named Archie Goodwin. What do you think of him? Uh-huh … yeah … yeah, uh-huh. Okay. Yeah, we ought to grab a bite one of these days. Be good to get caught up."

He cradled the receiver and fixed his gaze on me. "Bates says you're a good man, as far as he could tell after two weeks on the job. He didn't want to sack you, but Old Man Moreland wouldn't budge. He thinks any publicity for his operation is bad publicity, never mind that you did them a big favor by getting rid of McCaffey and his lamebrained sidekick. Word on the street is those two knocked off a couple of guys some years back but never got fingered for it."

"They almost knocked off a third one last night," I said. "How about giving me a try on something? Like I said, it won't cost you a cent."

Bascom sat back and rubbed his chin again. "Tell you what, Goodwin, I've got this job I put a freelancer on, but he didn't get anyplace at all with it. It's a missing persons case—maybe." He went over to a filing cabinet and pulled out a thin file, handing it to me. "Wilda will show you the empty office that got used back when I had a staff. Take a look at what's in here, and see if it gives you any ideas."

I plopped down at one of the two desks in a windowless office next door to Wilda's anteroom and opened the folder, marked CHAPMAN. After twenty minutes, I had digested everything Bascom and his freelance operative, a guy named Phelps, had learned, which wasn't much. The client was one Muriel Chapman, age forty-seven, at an address on the Upper West Side. Her husband, Clarence, age fifty-one, had failed to return home from work as a salesman in the camera department at Macy's Herald Square store on the first Friday in September, now more than two weeks ago. She had heard nothing whatever from or about him in that time.

She had told Bascom her husband was "honest, hardworking, a good provider who neither smoked nor drank." The couple, native New Yorkers, had been married twenty-four years and was childless.

The police had been notified regarding missing persons and unidentified bodies, but nothing had turned up about Clarence Chapman. A snapshot in the folder showed him to be a middle-aged man with a handsome, angular face, a thin mustache, and dark, slick hair parted in the middle.

Bascom suggested to Mrs. Chapman that perhaps her husband wanted to lose himself, but she replied *vehemently* (so the report said) that "he was very happy here," and she quickly volunteered that "he never looked at other women, even really beautiful ones who passed us on the street." She added that none of his clothes were missing, other than what he wore the day he disappeared.

Phelps had talked to the manager of Macy's camera department, who told him Chapman was a model employee, never late, always well dressed, and that virtually every month, he led the department in sales. The manager had no idea why he hadn't shown up for work.

I took the picture of Chapman, closed the folder, and went into Bascom's office. "Okay, I've been through the stuff," I told him. "Anybody made a check of camera shops around town?"

Bascom threw me a disappointed look. "Now why would we do that?"

"Maybe he's selling cameras someplace else now. The guy's got to live."

"Think, Goodwin. The only way he could get a job with another camera outfit would be to use Macy's as a reference, and his new store would surely call Macy's to verify his service and his ability.

Chapman's boss would have told Phelps if somebody had called there checking on him."

"Yeah, I suppose. But I'd like to poke around anyway. Just call it a hunch."

"Go ahead," Bascom said, rolling his eyes. "What the hell, it's not costing me anything."

# CHAPTER 3

Tearing out the pages listing camera stores from one of the Manhattan classified directories in Bascom's office, I drew a frown from Wilda and grinned at her in response. I didn't bother to count the number of listings, but there were plenty. My knowledge of the island's street system and addresses wasn't very good yet, but I knew enough that I could put together a plan. Besides, I had bought a map of Manhattan, and I'm a quick learner.

I began by ruling out any shops within six blocks of Macy's, which I now knew was at Thirty-Fourth Street and Broadway. Too much chance of Chapman being recognized in that neighborhood. Same on the Upper West Side, specifically centering on the intersection of Eighty-Third and Amsterdam, where the Chapman apartment was.

That left the rest of Manhattan, plus Brooklyn, Long Island City, and the farther reaches of Queens, as well as the other boroughs. But I chose to focus on Manhattan, realizing that even so I might be setting out on a wild goose chase that would give Bascom something to laugh about with his fellow operatives.

The next morning, with the picture of Clarence Chapman and my newly purchased street map in hand, I started downtown, working my way through the Financial District, Chinatown, Little Italy, and

Greenwich Village. I stepped into each camera shop long enough to eyeball the employees and raise a few eyebrows, although I never stayed inside long enough to be questioned. I ran the risk, of course, that this, a Wednesday, might be Chapman's day off.

I hit what seemed like dozens of places on the big east-west thoroughfares like Fourteenth and Twenty-Third Streets. Most of them were small operations, one or two employees grinning and eager behind the counters. At a few minutes after noon, I stopped at a little café on Lexington near Thirty-Seventh and sat at the counter with a cheese sandwich and a glass of milk. I pulled out the telephone book pages and unfolded them, noting the shops I had visited and crossing them out. I was maybe 25 percent of the way through the Manhattan camera establishments. A long afternoon awaited, and very likely another day, or two, or three.

After lunch and a six-block sweep of both sides of Lexington, I walked north along Madison Avenue, which I learned was the heart of the city's advertising business. It also had numerous places selling cameras, including three in a two-block stretch. At the third of these, Devereaux Cameras & Film, I saw him through the window, showing a Kodak to a matronly woman wearing a flowery hat and one of those hideous fox fur wraps complete with the animal's head and sightless eyes.

I walked in and pretended to study the array of cameras in the display cases. A second salesman asked if he could help me, but I replied that I was just looking.

Much of my looking, at least surreptitiously, focused on the man I knew to be Clarence Chapman—no question. His dress was immaculate: a blue, pin-striped, double-breasted suit that looked new and a blue-and-yellow-striped silk tie.

His spiel went with his clothes: smooth, sharp, crisp, and the woman clearly was drinking it in. I contemplated waiting until after he had closed the inevitable sale and then approaching him, but decided to learn more about the man first. I left the shop, noting that its closing time was five p.m.

I had an hour to kill, so I parked at the counter of a little coffee shop just off Madison. By my second cup, I found myself on friendly terms with the counterman, a talkative little hunchback named Kevin. "I've been looking at camera shops around here," I told him. "I want to get one for my uncle; his birthday's coming up. You know anything about this Devereaux place up the street?"

"A little. 'Course their help don't come in here much. Too snooty for the likes of us," he sneered. "Rich dame owns the place."

"Really?"

"Yeah. Surprised you ain't heard of her, Alicia Devereaux. She's one of them society types who hasta have a cause."

"What kind of cause do you call running a camera store?"

"Ah, I can give you an answer to that," Kevin said with a grin as he ran a rag over the surface of the counter. "She bought the store half a dozen years ago or so, and she makes a big deal out of giving a percentage of its profits to some charity; I think it has to do with kids' orphanages."

"Sounds generous to me."

"I s'pose, but seems like her picture's on the society pages every couple weeks or so. I think she's in it to puff herself up."

"Married?" I asked.

"Divorced, twice. Good-looking stuff, if you like 'em middle-aged."

"Interesting. She ever work in the place?"

Kevin cut loose with a rasping laugh that caused the only other guy at the counter to look our way. "Nah, she wouldn't think of lowering herself. She likes to be seen as a benefactor, but she draws the line at anything resembling common labor, and that includes sales."

"Hmm. Any idea where she lives?"

"Park Avenue, where else? Reason I know is that the *Times* did a piece on her mansion in the sky a while back, with a batch of pictures. Looked like a palace. She gives lots of parties. All in the name of charity, so she says."

"Pretty fancy place, eh?"

"I'd say. It takes a whole damned floor of the Winchester, which is up around Sixtieth Street. Just about the toniest address on the avenue."

"A woman like that would be a good catch for someone," I observed.

"Talk is, she does the catching," he said. "Now I'm not suggesting that she's exactly a man-eater, but she likes to have male company close at hand."

"You seem to know a lot about her."

Kevin grinned. "Funny thing, the stuck-up society types give me a pain, but somehow years back I got into the habit of reading about 'em. Do you think I've got some crazy sort of love-hate relationship?"

"Maybe, although in a strange way I suppose these people are fascinating. See, now you've got me interested. In my case, maybe it's envy. This Devereaux woman have any current gentleman friends you know of?"

"There I have to say you've got me, pal. That's not exactly my crowd. From photographs I've seen in the papers, though, she seems to prefer the dapper type, smooth, you know. The kind with those thin little mustaches you see on actors like John Gilbert in the moving pictures."

"Well, thanks for the coffee and the conversation," I said, leaving a dime tip on the counter and stepping out into the sunny afternoon.

At a few minutes before five, I stationed myself across the street from Devereaux Cameras & Film. I could see through its plateglass window that there were no shoppers in the store now and that both Chapman and the other salesman looked to be getting ready to leave. My watch read 5:02 when Chapman walked out, popped a black homburg on his head, and walked north on Madison Avenue while the other man locked up.

I had never tailed anyone before but figured in this case it was a snap because the gent had no reason to think he was being followed. I stayed on the opposite side of the street as he turned east at Fifty-Sixth, going one block to Park Avenue.

As I expected, Chapman then went north, walking with a jaunty gait and looking like a man without a care in the world. We both were on the west side of Park now, with me a discreet distance behind him. Just north of Sixty-Second Street, he turned in at the green-canopied entry to a handsome brick-and-stone structure, where he and the splendidly uniformed doorman exchanged pleasantries before he stepped into the building.

I walked on by, looking at the gleaming brass plate next to the entrance that proclaimed the edifice to be the Winchester. That, I felt, was enough work for one day, and I headed in the direction of my rooming house.

# CHAPTER 4

The next morning, I got to the office of the Bascom Detective Agency at nine o'clock sharp, greeting Wilda, who answered with her usual sniff. "He in?" I asked, gesturing toward the closed door.

"Yes. Knock first."

I did, heard "Come on in," and went on in, dropping into the guest chair without being invited. Del Bascom put down a sheet of paper he'd been reading, took a puff on his cigar, and favored me with a smile. "Well, Goodwin, I suppose you didn't have any luck trying to find that missing husband, eh?"

"You suppose wrong. I've got the whole business figured out."

"Yeah, and I suppose you've seen this Chapman, too, huh?"

"This time you suppose right. How about I bring him by here for a chat around lunchtime?"

He took the stogie out of his mouth and gaped at me. "You're kidding, right?"

"No, I am not. I've never been much of a kidder. I'll see you in a few hours." I got up and walked out, assuming he was staring at my back with his mouth still open.

At 11:45, I stepped into the Devereaux shop, where the only customer was talking to the other salesman. "May I help you?" Clarence

Chapman asked with an ingratiating smile as he rubbed his palms together.

"Yes, I think you can. I have something here that I would like you to look at." I took a folded sheet of paper from my jacket pocket and handed it to him. He opened it, read it, then swallowed hard, looking at me wide-eyed. His expression lay somewhere between pain and panic.

He leaned across the counter and whispered, "Who are you?"

"I thought you would find this an interesting challenge," I responded in a normal tone. "I've heard many good things about this store and felt sure you'd be able to help me. I have to run off on some other business now, but would it be possible to discuss this further during your lunch break?"

"Yes, yes, that would be at, er … twelve." Beads of perspiration had formed above his eyebrows and on his upper lip. All of a sudden, he didn't look the least bit suave and debonair.

"Excellent; I will be back then, and we can go somewhere to talk," I said in a voice meant to ooze conviviality and good humor.

Exactly at noon by my watch and the chimes at St. Patrick's over on Fifth Avenue, I popped back into the store, but got nudged right back out by Chapman, who had seen me coming. "Not in here," he whispered as he steered me onto the sidewalk "Let's … let's walk."

When we got a few yards away from the store, he grabbed my arm. "What is this all about?"

"You read my note. I don't see how it can be any clearer."

"Who are you?"

"You'll find out soon enough. We're going to visit my boss," I said, this time taking hold of his arm gently but firmly.

"Are you some sort of hoodlum?" he said in a choked voice, trying to look irate.

I laughed. "Not in the least. But you are in some sort of trouble, Mr. Chapman, and you need to have a few things explained to you. It won't take long, and then you can be back in your store—if you will even want to go back."

He didn't say another word as we walked toward Bascom's

building, or even when we rode up in the open-cage elevator and stepped into the office. "We're going in," I told Wilda, who looked so surprised she didn't even sniff.

"This is Clarence Chapman. You may recognize him from his photograph," I told Bascom, whose eyebrows went halfway up his forehead. I steered our quarry to the chair and stood with my back against the wall.

"Well, well," Bascom said, recovering his aplomb and folding thick arms across his chest. "We knew we'd find you for your wife. What the hell did you think you were doing?"

I almost felt sorry for the guy as he put his hands over his face and sniffled. "Muriel ... she came to you?"

"That's right, pal. She thought something terrible must have happened to you. But you look like you haven't exactly been suffering."

With that, it all came out. A blubbering Chapman told us how Alicia Devereaux had gone into Macy's, checking out their camera department to get ideas on how to better display her own store's wares—or so she said. She and Chapman hit it off from the first—or so he said. He described it as "magic." They went to lunch, and before they'd finished the meal, he said he realized this was the woman he had been waiting for his whole life.

Under Bascom's questioning, Chapman told us he didn't return to Macy's after lunch but went straight back to the Winchester with the Devereaux woman. She bought him fine clothes, put him on the payroll at her store, and gave him a place to live that was far more luxurious than anything he had known or even imagined. And she seemed not to care anything about his past.

"So you lived a fantasy life for a while—now what?" Bascom barked.

"I ... I guess it's over, isn't it?" Chapman said between sobs. "What am I going to say to Muriel?"

"That is your problem, buddy," Bascom said, clearly disgusted with the man sitting across the desk from him. "But if I was you, I'd cook up a story about amnesia, or maybe kidnapping, although I don't know why anybody would kidnap you. You ain't exactly rich."

"Are you going to say anything about this to Muriel?"

"Of course I am! She hired me to find you, and I did ... with my associate's help." He dipped his head in my direction.

"Do you have to tell her ... where you found me?"

"Frankly, I don't know why I should save your skin," Bascom said, "but I don't have to tell her anything other than that we've found you. That fulfills my commission from her."

"What is she paying you?" Chapman asked as he dabbed his eyes with a handkerchief.

"That is strictly between me and my client," Bascom snapped. "I'm going to call her now and tell her you're coming home. And by God, if you don't go straight home, one, we will find you again, and two, your wife will learn all about you and the exotic and exciting Mrs. Devereaux of Park Avenue."

As we learned later, Chapman did go straight home, although what he told his wife remained between them. After he had left us, Bascom closed his office door and told me to sit down.

"Okay, Goodwin, you did one helluva job; I take my hat off to you. Now fill me in on just how you did it."

"Well, as you know, I started checking out camera stores, and—"

"Yeah, and I admit up front that I thought it was a lousy idea at the time. If the guy was trying to lose himself, why would he go right back to the same kind of job he had before? To say nothing of the risk he was taking by being recognized by somebody who remembered him from Macy's."

"People aren't always logical, particularly when it comes to love. I figured something made him disappear, and there was a good chance a woman was involved in the story. I felt he was susceptible to feminine—what do you call them?—wiles, from the way his wife said he never, ever looked at another woman. Sounds like a guy who's trying too hard not to seem interested."

"So you found him at this camera shop the Devereaux dame owned?"

"Yeah, I did get lucky there. He could have been off that day, or in the back room and out of sight when I walked by." I went on to tell Bascom how I learned about Alicia Devereaux's man-eating tendencies from Kevin the café counterman.

"I'd read something about her before all right, but I've never paid much attention to that social world," Bascom said. "One thing seems sure: we did that poor sap Chapman a favor by smoking him out. That woman would have chewed him up and spit him out within six months, a year at most."

I nodded. "And he never even thanked us, the ingrate."

"Here's another question for you," Bascom said, leaning back and clasping his hands behind his head. "How did you get Chapman to come over here with you?"

"Showed him this," I said, handing across the note that had shaken the guy up so much in the camera shop.

*Your wife misses you, Clarence, and she is worried sick. Do you want me to tell her where you are working and where you are living, or would you prefer discussing this with me on your lunch hour? The choice is yours.*

Bascom looked at the hand-printed note and shook his head, grinning. "For a kid, you act like you know what you're doing."

"Put it down that I'm old beyond my years. And as I said when I first walked in here, I can use a job."

"I got still another question for you."

"Shoot."

"I noticed that you recited all your conversations to me without looking at any notes and they sounded like they were word for word."

"They were word for word," I told him. "I didn't take any notes, none at all."

"No baloney?"

"No baloney whatever. Back when I was in high school, I got a perfect score on this history test. The teacher—Mr. Mason, it was—asked me how I did so well when I never seemed to write down any notes when he was talking. I told him that I never took any notes in any classes or when I read my textbooks, either, and I only went through the books once.

"That's when he told me I must have something they were starting to call 'total recall.' I felt like some kind of freak."

"Freak, hell, that's one great asset you got, especially in our game. Tell you what, Goodwin," he said, lighting a cigar. "I'll give you fifty bucks for the work you did on the Chapman business. That is a one-half of what the guy's wife paid me to find him. And I'll show you the woman's check so that you can see I'm not stiffing you. I haven't cashed it yet, but I called a friend at her bank. That money and more is in their joint account."

"Good, but what about—"

"I'm not done yet," Bascom said, holding up a hand like a traffic cop. "I can't afford much, as I told you before, but I'll put you on at a sawbuck a week to start with, and you can have the vacant office, which has a telephone in it. Also, if you crack a case the way you did today, you'll get twenty-five percent of the fee."

"Not fifty?"

"Not fifty," Bascom snapped. "That was a one-shot. Call me a softy. Remember, I'm supplying you with office space."

"Of course, I would like more than that, but, okay," I told him. "You just got yourself a deal."

"You're learning your way around town fast, Goodwin," the grizzled detective said, standing and pumping my hand. "I like that. And by the way, we're going to get you licensed in the State of New York as a private investigator. I'll help you get the paperwork going."

"I think that I'm liking this burg," I responded with a grin. "I might just stay around here awhile."

# CHAPTER 5

So I became a detective. I even had an office, albeit small and shabby. And Wilda started treating me like I wasn't some lower form of life. She even stopped sniffing when I walked in off the elevator.

My payment from the Chapman case and my regular check, small as it was, allowed me to get out of the dump I was living in and move into a modest but clean apartment hotel on the West Side in the Sixties. I still ate at places like the Automat and hole-in-the-wall coffee shops, although I wasn't complaining.

I liked Bascom. He seemed honest. He wouldn't touch divorce cases and all the spying on one spouse or the other that usually went with them, even when he was hard up for business, which was much of the time.

"A lot of people look down on our so-called profession, Goodwin," he told me, "and Lord knows there's plenty of joes around who give it a bad name. I try not to be one of 'em."

On slow days, of which there were too many, he'd regale me with cases he'd had, some of them sounding like they came right off the pages of pulps like *Black Mask* or *Dime Detective*.

"This Chapman business you did such a good job on, in a weird way it reminds me of something I worked on a few years back," he said one rainy morning as we sat in his office drinking coffee brewed by Wilda. "This natty swell named Fletcher—he was some sort of middle-level bank officer—shows up at my door one day and says his wife has disappeared. My first thought is that she's run off with some other guy, but I don't say so, of course. I listen.

"He tells me she's a perfect wife, that they been married eight years, no kids, have a nice apartment on the Upper East Side. He makes it sound like an ideal marriage, of which there is no such thing. He goes on about how wonderful and beautiful she is, blah, blah.

"I ask about her family, and he tells me she was an only child, came up from North Carolina, both parents dead. He's willing to pay big dough for me to try finding her, so I figure, what the hell, I'll give it a shot. I ask a bunch of questions about her habits, her friends, and he says she's pretty much a loner, reads a lot at home. Sounds fishy to me, especially when he gives me a snapshot of her. She's a real doll, and he tells me that she has flaming red hair, which you can't tell from a black-and-white shot.

"This looks to me like a skirt who should be out and around town, having good friends, enjoying life," Bascom says, then adds apologetically, "I guess I'm making this too long, huh?"

"Not at all, take your time," I said. "I like a good story."

"Anyway, I start by doing the usual, checking around the neighborhood where they live. I go into groceries, drugstores, dry cleaners, that sort of stuff. 'Oh yeah, that's Lucille,' they say when I show the picture. 'Nice lady, quiet, haven't seen her around lately. Has something happened to her?'"

"How do you answer that question?" I asked.

Bascom took a puff of his cigar. "I get vague and say I don't know her exact address and that I'm trying to locate her because a distant relative left her some money. Usually, somebody will give me her address then, which, of course, I already know, but at least it's a cover for why I'm asking about her.

"I get this hunch, don't ask me why, that she's left Manhattan. So I hang around the Staten Island Ferry docks, showing her picture to crewmen. No luck at all. Then I try the Hoboken Ferry, and one of the crew recognizes her, but only after I mention her red hair. 'Yeah,

I think she was on a westbound run a few weeks back. I remember the hair, and one other thing. It was a rainy day, but she was wearing dark glasses.'"

"Now I think I might have a hunch," I put in.

"You just might at that," Bascom said. "I start hanging around the business area of Hoboken close to the ferry terminal, asking questions in shops and restaurants. I show her picture to everybody and tell the same story that I had on the Upper East Side. Turns out several people know of her, and a waitress in a coffee shop says 'Oh, that's Lucille Jones, she comes in here often—a lovely woman, so refined, a real lady.' Before I can even ask, the waitress gives me the address where she lives, a small apartment building about three blocks away.

"Sure enough, there's an 'L. Jones' listed on a mailbox in the foyer. She's on the third floor, and I press the button. When she answers, I say into the speaker that I'm from the gas company investigating a leak, and she buzzes me in.

"She's waiting for me at the door to her place, and she looks great. Her husband hadn't exaggerated the red hair. It's spectacular. Once inside the apartment, I tell her who I really am and why I'm there.

"Damned if she doesn't collapse onto a sofa and start sobbing, her face in her hands. I sit across from her and wait for the crying to stop. When it does, she looks at me and says, 'I don't know what my husband is paying you, but I'll pay you more to say you can't find me.'

"I tell her I don't want her dough and ask why she doesn't want to go back home. That's when I find out that Fletcher was madly jealous of her, didn't want her going out when he was at work. Even worse, she says he beat her at least once a week, sometimes more often, especially when he'd had a snoot full. No wonder she stayed home so much of the time."

"So those dark glasses on the Hoboken Ferry ride were to hide a shiner?" I posed.

Bascom nodded. "And some other bruises; she even shows me one on her arm that hadn't quite healed. Then she gets almost hysterical, taking out a checkbook—she has her own account—and asks me to name my price.

"I tell her to forget it, that I'm already getting plenty from her husband. I also tell her I've already forgotten ever having found her. Then I leave."

"And that's it?"

"That's it," Bascom says. "Next I tell Fletcher that after an exhaustive search using several operatives, I am simply unable to locate his wife, although I keep every cent of his generous advance. And I don't feel guilty about that, not for a second."

"Did he ever find her?"

"Not that I know of. You have to remember that even though the Hudson—or the North River, as we old-timers call it—is only about a mile or so wide, it might just as well be fifty times that or more. How often do New Yorkers go to Jersey, other than those who work there? Sure, in addition to the ferries and the tubes, you got the brand-new Holland Tunnel for autos now, but still, it's another world over on that side of our old Hudson, as far away as Mars. Chances are if Lucille stays put in Hoboken, nobody she knows from Manhattan will ever see her."

I tell that story because it says a lot about Del Bascom, and also because it's been part of my continuing education as a detective. That education also included all manner of cases I worked on with Bascom, including the Morningside Piano Heist, the Rive Gauche Art Gallery Swindle, and the Sumner-Hayes Burglary, the last of which got both of us into hot water with the cops for a while.

Among the most memorable of those early jobs, though, had to be the one involving a warehouse over in Long Island City, which lies just across the Queensboro Bridge from Manhattan. Radios, phonographs, and bicycles had been disappearing from the building, and the security service guarding it—no surprise—was suspected. The agency got hired to investigate, and Bascom put me on the case with a freelance operative named Fred Durkin.

I had never met the man until he came into the office the day we were to begin our surveillance at the warehouse. Bascom made the introductions. Durkin was my height at five eleven, thickset and thin haired, and had a face like the map of Ireland.

"Nice to meet you, Goodwin," he said, smiling and shaking hands with a firm grip.

"Call me Archie."

"I will, and you call me Fred. Sounds like this warehouse thing is some sort of inside job," he told Bascom.

"Yeah, it sure does. I got the owner to send their guards home temporarily. He told the service he was going without any security, at least for a while, because of costs. You two will be on the premises for at least the next several nights, from nine o'clock until the sun comes up."

"Seems like the security outfit would be suspicious as to why they've been replaced," Durkin said.

"No doubt they are," Bascom replied. "That's not our problem; it's theirs. Seems like either their own people are sticky fingered or they're being paid off to let somebody else into the building. At least that's how I read it."

Durkin carried his own pistol, while Bascom gave me a .32-caliber snub-nosed revolver. This was the first time working for him that I'd been armed, and I knew he still had a deep-seated fear that I had an itchy trigger finger.

The first night on the job, nothing happened. The brick warehouse, all five stories, was quiet as a tomb. When we left around six in the morning, Durkin muttered about this being "a fool's errand." I was inclined to agree.

Night number two seemed like more of the same, until three a.m., when I heard noises coming from the direction of the loading dock. I was on the fourth floor at the time and made my way down three flights of stairs, avoiding the noise of the elevator. Durkin and I arrived on the ground floor together, each with flashlights on. He whispered that we should be on opposite sides of the loading dock doors about twenty feet away from them.

"Let 'em come on in, and we'll wait until they start trying to haul stuff out," Durkin said in hushed tones. "That way, we'll catch 'em red-handed." I was glad it was so dark he couldn't see me stifle a chuckle. I didn't know anybody actually used "red-handed" other than in the pulps.

We separated, shut off our flashlights, and crouched down. I drew my revolver as the big sliding door to the loading dock got rolled back with a subdued rattle. Light from an outside streetlamp silhouetted a figure in the now-open doorway who carried an electric torch. As its beam played around the vaulted room, I ducked for cover behind piled-high stacks of crates, but my foot kicked a loose wooden palette on the concrete floor, making a scraping sound that I felt could be heard all the way across the East River into Manhattan.

The beam from the torch lit me up as I dropped onto the floor and pointed my revolver in its direction. The click of a hammer cut the sudden silence. Before I could squeeze the trigger, a single shot cracked off, followed by a cry of agony. Fred Durkin?

"You son of a bitch!" That definitely was Durkin, but he hadn't been the screamer. "There's another one outside, Archie," he rasped as I rushed to the open doorway to see a tall, lean man in the parking lot, hands in the air.

"Don't shoot!" he pleaded. His own pistol, an automatic, lay on the ground at his feet, a sign of surrender. I jumped down from the loading dock and covered him as I picked up his gun and pocketed it.

The scream I'd first heard now became an extended groaning. I marched the lean man back into the building, prodding him with my revolver. I found Durkin standing over a writhing little weasel who clutched a bleeding hand. "The miserable bastard had the drop on you, Archie," he growled. "I had no choice. I hadda fire."

"You shot the revolver out of his hand?" I said, stunned. Durkin nodded.

"That's a great piece of shooting."

He shook his head. "Not so great, Archie. I was trying to kill him."

Several hours later, Bascom, Durkin, and I sat drinking coffee in Bascom's office and reviewing the events of the early morning. Fred and I had spent a couple of hours with members of New York's finest at the Tenth Precinct. Once again, I had the pleasure of a spirited conversation with Lieutenant George Rowcliff, although like the first time, he did most of the conversing.

"You're new to this town, Goodwin, and already I've s-seen more of you than I hope to see for the remainder of my life, which I hope is a g-good many years. Are you a trouble magnet?"

"I'm just a guy trying to make an honest living, Lieutenant. Seems I keep running into citizens of your fair metropolis who have guns pointed at me with intent to do harm."

I could give you more of our one-sided dialogue, but suffice it to say Rowcliff's stuttering increased as his ranting grew louder. Since I had not fired a shot, he didn't have much to go on, although he spent plenty of time with Durkin.

"What could the lieutenant do to me?" Fred posed. "After all, we nailed a couple of armed robbers for his department."

"True," said Del Bascom. "But you have to remember that Rowcliff was born angry. He needs to blow off steam or he'll explode. Did either of you see Cramer while you were at the Tenth?"

Durkin shook his head. "Who's Cramer?" I asked.

"Inspector Lionel Cramer, he runs Homicide West," Bascom said. "Tough but fair, and a damned sight smarter than Rowcliff. Of course, this wasn't a homicide case, which is why he didn't bother seeing either of you. For that matter, I don't know why Rowcliff stuck his nose in. He's a homicide man, too."

"All in all, I think it was a pretty good day's work," I said, "thanks to Fred here."

Durkin's Irish face reddened with the praise. "I just did what either of you woulda done in the same spot," he muttered.

"Maybe," I said. "All I know is, I was a bull's-eye for that sawed-off mug. Another couple of seconds, and I would have ended up on tomorrow's train home to Ohio packed in a pine box."

"Hell, he might have missed you altogether," Bascom said in an attempt to lighten up the conversation.

"Anything is possible," I conceded, "but I am sure glad that Mr. Durkin here is fast on the draw, even if he claims his aim was off."

Fred colored again, and we finished our coffee in silence, contemplating what had happened and what might have been.

"Well, I gotta get home," the stocky detective said, rising. "The wife will wonder where I am. See you both later. Thanks for the business, Del; I don't get enough jobs these days. It was good working with you, Archie. Maybe our paths will cross again sometime."

"It will be my pleasure," I replied, meaning it.

# CHAPTER 6

I worked on a lot more cases with Del Bascom after the Long Island City warehouse business, but they definitely weren't the most memorable ones. After I'd been on his payroll for about a month, Bascom came in late one morning and asked me to join him in his office.

"Close the door," he said after I'd walked in and started for a chair. This had to be something out of the ordinary, because the gumshoe didn't often shut his door.

I sat as he looked down at his desk blotter, frowning. "Archie, what I'm going to tell you is confidential."

"As you know, I have been known to keep a secret or two."

"Of course, of course. Okay, here's the deal: I've been invited to be part of a team investigating a kidnapping, and I want to bring you along on this."

I nodded. "Who's been grabbed?"

"Burke Williamson's kid."

The name meant nothing to me, and my face must have registered the fact, because Bascom slapped his forehead with a palm.

"Sorry, I keep forgetting how new you still are to this town. Burke Williamson has to be one of the ten richest men in New York, maybe even one of the five richest. He owns the Olympus Hotel Chain, the one with the slogan 'Every Day, Olympus Houses a World of Travelers.'"

"Now them I have heard of. That name is known even in the most off-the-beaten-track corners of Ohio."

"Their eight-year-old son, Tommie, got snatched from the big country place they have out on Long Island yesterday morning. There's been nothing in the papers about it."

"If they're as rich as you say, why wasn't the kid better protected?"

"Fair question," Bascom said.

"Also, given their piles of dough, why don't they just pay the kidnappers off?"

"Another good question, Archie. We'll have to ask Nero Wolfe."

"Who?"

"Nero Wolfe, the smartest private detective in town, and maybe in the world, for my money. It's his case, but he's asked me to be part of his team. He's got three operatives he usually works with, and occasionally he brings me in on his cases. This is one of those times, and I want you along, too."

"Fine by me. Nero, huh? Where'd he get that moniker?"

"I don't know, but you'll have the opportunity to ask him, if you don't care what kind of reaction you get. We're due at his place at eleven."

Twenty minutes later, we were in a Yellow Cab headed for Nero Wolfe's residence, which I learned was on West Thirty-Fifth Street over near the Hudson. "Be prepared for an experience," Bascom said. "This man is like nobody you've ever met, or will ever meet." We pulled up in front of an ordinary-looking brownstone that was part of a solid row of similar residences between Tenth and Eleventh Avenues on what seemed like a typical New York City block, if there is such a thing.

The door was opened by a short, white-haired man with a neatly trimmed mustache and wearing a waiter's white apron. "Ah, Mr. Bascom, Mr. Wolfe is expecting you," he said in what I took to be a French accent. "And you are Mr. Goodwin, I believe?" he added, turning toward me with the hint of a bow.

"In the flesh. But you can call me Archie, everybody does."

He smiled, took our coats, and hung them on a rack in the foyer, then led us along a carpeted hall to the second door on the left. We stepped into a big room that seemed inviting. In order, I noticed a cherrywood desk with no one behind it, a wall of bookcases, an Oriental rug that was mostly yellow, and the largest globe I had ever laid eyes on, at least four times the size of the one in Mr. Mason's history classroom back home in my high school.

Only then did I realize three people were parked in the room, one of whom I recognized. "Hi, Arch," Fred Durkin said from his spot on a sofa, giving me a salute and a grin. "Didn't take all that long for us to meet again, huh?"

The man next to Fred looked to be about four years older than me and was not bad-looking, if you could get past the smirk on his phiz. He looked like somebody who thought damned highly of himself and dared you to suggest otherwise. The third joe sat on a red leather chair at one end of the unoccupied desk. He had stooped shoulders, and his face seemed to be about two-thirds nose, but his dark eyes moved quickly, missing nothing.

"Hi, Del," he said to Bascom, then turned to me. "I'm Saul Panzer, and I see you already know Fred. That self-appointed God's-gift-to-women next to him is Orrie Cather. And you are …?"

"Archie Goodwin."

"Welcome aboard, Goodwin," Panzer said. "Mr. Wolfe should be down in about … one minute," he said after consulting his wristwatch.

Bascom took one of the yellow chairs facing the big desk, and I dropped into a similar one next to him. My back was to the hall doorway, so I did not see our host arrive until he came into my line of sight. And quite a sight he was.

Large does not do Nero Wolfe justice. I was not prepared for someone of his … *volume*, which at a glance I put at 250 pounds, minimum. He moved in behind his desk with surprising grace and placed a small bouquet of delicate, magenta-colored flowers in a vase on his blotter. They looked nothing like any of the blooms in my Aunt Verna's prizewinning garden back home in Chillicothe.

Our host got seated, adjusted himself in an oversized chair, and surveyed the room without expression. "Saul, Fred, Orrie, Mr. Bascom." He spoke crisply, dipping his head an inch to each. And to me, a look of mild curiosity. "You are the Archie Goodwin Mr. Bascom told me about on the telephone." It was a statement, not a question.

I nodded.

"Just so. He speaks highly of your capabilities, and he is not a man to dispense praise rashly."

I had encountered more than a few fat people back home, but they all seemed somewhat unkempt—not necessarily slovenly, just careless in their dress and overall appearance. Nero Wolfe was neither. He wore a pin-striped brown suit with vest, a starched yellow shirt, and a brown-and-yellow-striped silk tie. His large, square face was crowned with well-barbered dark brown hair, and his eyes had an intensity that made you feel he could see right through you.

"Gentlemen, we have a great deal to cover this morning," he said. "First, however, I would be a poor host indeed if I did not proffer refreshments. I am having beer. Will anyone join me? Or, given the hour, perhaps coffee? Fritz just brewed a pot." Fred Durkin chose beer, the rest of us, coffee.

I don't know how Wolfe did it, but within forty-five seconds, our greeter at the front door, whom I now knew to be named Fritz, wheeled a serving cart into the office. On it were three bottles of a Canadian beer, two frosted pilsner glasses, a pot of coffee, and three cups with saucers.

Fritz placed two bottles and a glass in front of Wolfe and opened the third beer, giving it and the other glass to Durkin. He then poured each of us coffee and placed the steaming cups on small tables next to our seats. All was done with swift but unhurried efficiency.

I watched as Wolfe popped the cap off one of the bottles with an opener he had pulled from his center desk drawer. He looked at me as he poured the beer.

"Mr. Goodwin," he said, "by your expression, you wonder how I come to possess what the United States government considers contraband. A man in Toronto feels he is in my debt because of a service I performed for him several years ago, and I have drawn freely and unashamedly upon his debt. He sends me shipments of beer regularly, using a channel I choose not to specify.

"If my possession and consumption of this beverage constitutes a criminal act, so be it. In my defense, which I concede no court would recognize, I point out that the Volstead Act is an egregious decree passed by misguided legislative bodies that feel the need to legislate morality. The disastrous results of this constitutional amendment are obvious to even the most casual reader of newspapers in New York, Chicago, or any number of major cities in the grip of organized crime syndicates that profit from the government prohibition of alcohol." With that, he drained half the beer from his glass and set it down.

"Now," he said, dabbing his lips with a handkerchief, "we come to the reason for this gathering. Yesterday morning shortly before he was to leave for school, Tommie Williamson, age eight and the son of hotelier Burke Williamson, disappeared from the grounds of the family's country estate in the environs of Garden City, Long Island. Within hours, the family received a ransom note asking for one hundred thousand dollars in exchange for the boy's return."

"Did Williamson call the police?" Orrie Cather asked.

"He did not. He feared his local constabulary would somehow endanger Tommie with what he called a 'ham-handed attempt' to free his son. He called upon me because I was recommended by a close friend of his, a man whom I once extricated from a difficult situation involving a blackmailer who now resides in one of this state's penal institutions."

Saul Panzer nodded. "You'll show them the note?"

"I will pass it around. Fritz has dusted it for fingerprints, and the only ones found on it were those of Burke Williamson. We took his prints when he was here yesterday afternoon."

The single sheet made the rounds. It had been torn from a pad of inexpensive paper, the kind available in any drugstore or five-and-dime. "The note came in a plain white envelope that also bore no prints other than those of Mr. Williamson," Wolfe continued. "It was delivered to the front door of their Long Island residence by a boy of about twelve, according to the butler, who had never seen the youngster before."

"And I suppose the kid turned tail and hasn't been seen since," Cather put in.

"You suppose correctly, Orrie. He dashed off after handing the note over," Wolfe said as I read the message, which was neatly printed in ink, all capitals:

MR. WILLIAMSON
YOUR SON IS SAFE. AND HE WILL BE RETURNED TO YOU SAFELY, TOO, BUT ONLY AFTER $100,000 IS RECEIVED. HE IS IN NO DANGER OF BEING HARMED. YOU WILL SOON GET INSTRUCTIONS AS TO HOW THE MONEY IS TO BE DELIVERED. UNDER NO CIRCUMSTANCES ARE YOU TO CONTACT THE POLICE.

"Isn't the boy watched when he's out in the yard?" Del Bascom posed.

"He is supposed to be," Wolfe grunted. "He has a nursemaid, named ..." he turned to Saul Panzer.

"Sylvia Moore," Panzer said. "I drove out to the estate first thing this morning. As you can guess, the place is in turmoil. I talked to this young woman, whose job it is to keep an eye on Tommie, help him with his schoolwork, that sort of thing. She's distraught, blames herself for what happened."

"What did happen?" Cather barked.

Panzer held up a palm. "I'm getting to that. Tommie goes to a pricey private school not far away, the MeadesGate Academy. The family chauffeur takes him and picks him up every day. Yesterday morning around eight, almost an hour before he was to leave for school, Tommie was out on the grounds, gathering different types of leaves from the grass and off trees as part of a school project. Sylvia Moore was with him. Then one of the other members of the household staff hollered from the house that Miss Moore had an urgent telephone call."

"Let me guess," I cut in, tired of being just a listener. "When she picked up the instrument, there was no one on the other end. And when she went back outside, the boy was gone."

"Bingo on both counts. He had disappeared just like that," Panzer said, snapping his fingers. "Williamson was at his office in Manhattan, but his wife, Lillian, and everybody on the staff combed the grounds—eight acres in all, and not a sign of him. And there's a six-foot wrought-iron fence encircling the property. The only break is the gates at the entrance off the main road."

"Did anybody check to find out where the call came from?" Cather asked.

"I did," Panzer answered. "No luck. The local telephone company out there doesn't have that capability."

Wolfe finished his first beer and opened the second bottle. "Saul, you were able to meet the entire staff of the Williamson estate this morning, however briefly. Please give everyone your impressions of them, as well as of the estate itself."

Panzer flipped open his notebook. "Okay, first off, the house is a real mansion, brick and stone, English style, three stories, slate roof, with a built-in five-car garage, tennis court, and a swimming pool. It's got outbuildings, too, a greenhouse and stables. Mrs. Williamson is quite an equestrian. That's a horseback rider to you," Panzer said with a grin, turning to Orrie.

"I know what it means," Cather shot back.

"As to the staff, there are eight in all," Panzer said. "The top dog is the butler, Waverly—just goes by one name, although his given handle is Earl. He's around fifty-five, stuffy, tall, almost bald, speaks with a British accent that I'm guessing might be affected. He's been with the family for twenty years, and according to Williamson, their trust in him is absolute.

"Emily Stratton is the housekeeper, a spinster, been on board about fifteen years. She's thin as a telephone pole and prim as a schoolmarm. I'd put her in her mid-to-late forties. Getting five words out of her is a challenge. Even you, Orrie, with your myriad charms, wouldn't be able to sweet-talk her."

Cather scowled. "Based on your description, I sure as hell wouldn't want to."

"The cook is Mrs. Price, although it's unclear as to whether she's ever been married. Short, white haired, sixtyish, and carrying at least twenty-five pounds she could easily do without. Like the butler and the housekeeper, she oozes with self-importance and acts like the entire operation would go to wrack and ruin without her. She is susceptible to flattery, though. When I suggested that she must be good to prepare meals for this family, her face turned as red as a Fifth Avenue stoplight and she got tongue-tied.

"The housemaid, Mary Trent, figures to be all of nineteen at most. She's slender, dark haired, and shy in a fetching sort of way. She comes from a blue-collar family in Yonkers, where her father runs a service station and auto garage. She has only been with the Williamsons for a year, since just after she graduated from high school. She does most of the housecleaning and waits on the table at meals along with Emily Stratton.

"Charles Bell handles the chauffeuring duties. He has been with the Williamsons for three-plus years and cuts quite a figure, strutting around in his uniform, cap, and polished boots. He doesn't seem to be particularly well liked by others on the staff, apparently because of his arrogance. The young man—he's probably around thirty—seems very pleased with himself. Maybe it's because of the cars he gets to drive. The Williamson fleet currently includes a Packard sedan, a Pierce-Arrow phaeton, and an Auburn roadster, which Burke Williamson likes to take out for weekend spins."

"Probably to impress his neighbors," Durkin mused.

"I don't think so, Fred," Panzer answered. "Most of his neighbors are probably almost as rich as he is, and besides, he seems like an all right egg, far more modest and self-effacing than several of his household staff."

"Well, look at who he is, though. He doesn't have to impress anyone," Bascom pointed out.

"True. To continue, there's Sylvia Moore, the previously mentioned nanny. And Orrie, this one you would like. She is twenty-six, slender, blond, and smart. Went to one of those classy girls' finishing schools up in New England. She got hired five years ago to look after little Tommie and tutor him before he started school, and she still works with him on his lessons, as well as helping Mrs. Williamson with her charitable work. I didn't have much of a conversation with her, though, because she's so devastated.

"There are two other members of the staff," Panzer continued. "Lloyd Carstens oversees the greenhouse and the grounds, including the flower gardens, which have won some local prizes. He's a crusty character, probably around fifty. He doesn't waste words and apparently keeps pretty much to himself.

"Then you've got the stable master, Mark Simons—I'd put his age as forty-five—who has worked with horses all his life. He looks after the three animals Mrs. Williamson owns, and I got the distinct impression he and Carstens don't get along. It has to do at least partly with who has the say over the maintenance of the half-mile bridle path that loops around the property. Each one thinks it's his responsibility."

"Do all these people live in the mansion?" Bascom asked.

"Everybody but Carstens and Simons," Panzer said. "They eat breakfast and lunch with the rest of the staff in a servants' basement dining room but go home every night. They each live only a few miles away."

"Anything else to report?" Wolfe asked.

"No, sir, that's pretty much it."

Wolfe glowered at his empty beer glass, then looked up, taking in a bushel of air and exhaling it slowly. "You all will go out to the Williamson house; the family expects you. Saul will direct the operation. He and Mr. Goodwin will talk to the Williamsons and Miss Moore, the—what did you call her, Saul?"

"The nanny."

Wolfe made a face. "Disgusting term. Orrie, you are to interview the cook, the butler, and the maid. Fred, your assignment is the gardener and the stable master, and Mr. Bascom, see the chauffeur and the housekeeper.

ARCHIE MEETS NERO WOLFE

"All these conversations should be one-on-one, with no one else present. You are to find out where each of them was between seven thirty and nine o'clock yesterday morning. I assume this house is run on a series of well-defined routines. Determine whether there were departures from any of those routines yesterday morning. Check out the work areas of all the employees and determine which of those areas has a telephone, either an extension or a separate line to the outside. Mr. Williamson seemed uninterested concerning this detail when he was here, but then, he was under a great deal of stress. Any questions?"

"We all will fit in your automobile, Mr. Wolfe," Panzer said. "May I assume we will be taking it?"

"You may," he said, rising and walking out of the room.

"So Wolfe isn't going out there himself to have a look-see?" I asked Bascom under my breath as we rose to leave.

"Who are you kidding? He almost never leaves this place, kid. He just sits behind that big desk of his and noodles things out. And damned if he doesn't get it right every time. At least that's been true whenever I've been around."

# CHAPTER 7

Saul Panzer wheeled Wolfe's big Heron sedan out to Long Island. Cather reached the car first after we left the brownstone, so he grabbed the front passenger seat, leaving Bascom, Durkin, and me to wedge into the back, there being no jump seat. The conversation on the way out naturally centered on the kidnapping.

"I can't figure out how somebody hustled the kid off the property so fast," Durkin said. "The nanny wasn't inside for much more than about three or four minutes at most, at least according to what we're being told."

"Yeah, and they had to somehow get the boy up and over the iron fence that rings the whole place," Del Bascom added.

"What I can't get is why Wolfe seems so casual about the whole business," Cather said. "If it was my kid, I would want faster action than this, and I'd probably call in the cops, too."

"As you should be aware by now, Mr. Wolfe always knows what he's doing, Orrie," Panzer snapped. "Other than my having a fairly brief conversation with the man, Wolfe is the only one of us so far who's talked to Williamson, and he has the best sense of the degree of urgency." I tended to side with Cather in this instance, but I was by far the low man in the pecking order, so I contented myself with watching the scenery as we headed east on the big island, leaving the city behind.

Saul Panzer did not exaggerate in describing the Williamson estate. We passed through an entrance of opened iron gates hinged to brick pillars that were capped by frosted electric globes the size of basketballs. The paved road passed over a small stone bridge, beneath which ran what I assumed to be the bridle path.

After we had driven about a quarter mile along a lane lined with flower beds, the house came into view—brick and stone, its width the length of a football field, three full stories, with gables on the top floor and a porte-cochere entrance under which arriving guests in their swank automobiles could disembark without rain or snow falling upon their wealthy and well-tended noggins.

We tumbled out, and before Saul could rap on its polished brass knocker, the elaborate dark wood front door swung inward, revealing a lean, bald uniformed man, obviously Waverly, the butler.

"Ah yes, sir, Mr. Panzer, greetings once again. Mr. Williamson is expecting all you gentlemen. Please come in," he said in a British accent or a reasonable facsimile thereof. We followed him through a vaulted, chandeliered entry hall big enough to hold a first-class dance band and into a paneled, windowless room with indirect lighting that turned out to be Burke Williamson's study. "He will be with you shortly," Waverly said, executing a crisp about-face and walking out.

"Quite the joint," Fred Durkin observed, eyeballing the rosewood paneling, the floor-to-ceiling bookcases, the fireplace, and the chromium bar built into the far wall. "I could get used to this."

"As if you'd ever get the chance," Orrie Cather snorted. "This is hardly your kind of a place to—"

He got interrupted by the entry of our host. Burke Williamson, who I put at somewhere between forty and forty-five, had the look of wealth about him, from his well-barbered brown hair with a tinge of gray to his herringbone suit and his polished wing-tip shoes. His face, however, bore the lines of strain.

"Gentlemen, thank you all for coming," he said in a deep voice like that of a radio announcer. "Please sit down. May I get anyone a drink?"

We all declined, taking chairs while Williamson remained on his feet. "I met Mr. Panzer earlier today, of course, and as you all know, I visited Mr. Wolfe yesterday. I understand you want to interview everyone on the staff, although I can't for the life of me imagine why. No one who works here is capable of this ... *thing*."

"Very likely you are correct," Panzer said with a nod, "but one of them may have seen or heard something that could help us find your son, something they're not even aware is a clue. Have you gotten a call from the kidnapper yet?"

Williamson swallowed hard, working to keep his composure. "No, and this waiting ... this damned waiting, has been hard on me, even harder on my wife. I keep expecting the phone to ring." He lit a cigarette with a shaky hand.

Panzer, whose diplomacy impressed me, said a few words of commiseration to Williamson, then he introduced all of us.

The hotel magnate nodded grimly. "I've told all the staff they would be interviewed—that is precisely the word I used, *interviewed*—because I did not want them to feel they were being interrogated. I hope each of you understands and appreciates that distinction."

It became Panzer's turn to nod. "We do, sir, and all of us will try our very best to make the conversations with your staff cordial and without confrontation. However, I know you want us to do everything we can to find your son, and that, not the possibility of offending a member of your household staff, should be our top priority—and yours as well."

"You are correct," Williamson said tightly, biting his lower lip. "I do not know what your specific assignments are, but Waverly can direct each of you to the proper individual." He pushed a buzzer on his desk, and within seconds, the butler appeared in the doorway, standing at attention.

"These gentlemen will need to be directed, Waverly." Then he turned to us. "Now if you all will excuse me, I must go upstairs to my wife," he said as the others filed out behind the butler.

"Mr. Goodwin and I are to talk to both of you," Panzer said quietly but firmly.

Williamson spun around, eyebrows raised. "Lillian and me? But why?"

"Mr. Wolfe requested that we interview everyone here."

Our host clearly was peeved but sighed in resignation. "Do you want us together or separately?" he asked Panzer.

"Separately would be preferable, sir."

"All right, you can start with me, then, right now. Let's get it over with." He dropped into the upholstered chair behind his ornate desk as his padded shoulders sagged.

"Were you here when your son disappeared?"

"No, no," he snapped. "I already told Wolfe that. I had gone to Manhattan, to my office in the Olympus Hotels headquarters on Fifth Avenue. Charles drove me to the village depot about three miles from here and I took the 7:35 commuter train into Penn Station."

"You also told Mr. Wolfe that the telephone company out here does not have the ability to trace calls, I believe."

"As a director of the local company, I am sorry to concede that is true," the hotelier said grimly, shaking his head. "If I have anything to say about it, and I believe I will, that condition will soon change, however. You must understand that we have only had dial instruments in this area for a little more than a year now."

"How many telephones do you have here?" Panzer asked.

Williamson frowned and looked at the ceiling. "Let's see … counting one each in the greenhouse, the stables, and the kitchen downstairs … we have seven—no, eight."

"All of them on the same number?"

"Certainly not! Each one of these instruments is on a separate outside line. It is my way of trying to promote greater telephone usage by getting people to have more than one line in their homes. In fact, a local newspaper some months back did a feature on all our phone lines here, which I encouraged. And I—" He stopped and looked sharply at Panzer. "Just why are you so curious about our telephone arrangements?"

Panzer squared his narrow shoulders, as if preparing for an argument. "It is possible, isn't it, that the call that brought Miss

Moore inside from the yard could have been made from elsewhere in the house or on the grounds?"

"Possible, yes. Probable, not at all! Not at all! As I told you before, sir, no one in my employ here is capable of this … this …" Williamson exhaled loudly and slapped a palm down on his desk as if to complete the sentence.

"Mr. Wolfe expects us to explore every avenue," Panzer said in a quiet but firm tone. "You hired him because he is widely known to be thorough, and he expects those of us who work for him to be thorough as well."

"Yes, of course," Williamson said in a whisper. "Sorry, but my nerves are raw."

Panzer nodded. "Certainly understandable. Have there been any previous attempts to kidnap your son?"

"None, although my wife and I would be irresponsible if we did not make every effort to protect Tommie," he said as his voice started to crack. "He has been driven to and from school each day, and he never plays out in the yard alone, except for …" He didn't have to finish the sentence.

"Do you have any theories as to how Tommie disappeared from the grounds here?"

Williamson scowled. "We are again going over ground I already covered with Nero Wolfe. No, I am completely baffled as to what happened."

"Are the front gates to the property always kept open?" I asked.

"Yes. There is no reason to keep them shut. We have a lot of deliveries—tradesmen, grocers, and the like. And Tommie never plays in front of the house."

"Have you, or anyone on your staff, noticed anyone on the grounds or in the neighborhood who appears to have no business being there?"

"No, I haven't seen or heard of anybody unusual or out of place hanging around. Other than the boy who delivered the ransom note, of course."

"Thank you, sir," Panzer said. "May we talk to Mrs. Williamson now?"

"I'll go up and get her," Williamson replied, rising with effort and walking stiffly out.

"Too many darn phone lines in this place," I said after he had left. "Not only is Williamson a hotel baron, he seems to be a telephone tycoon as well."

"And a tycoon who's determined to show off the product," Panzer said.

"So, like me, you figure it's an inside job?"

"Sure seems that way," he answered, scratching his oversized nose. "But maybe the other guys will come up with something to point us in a different direction." He didn't sound convinced, though.

"Well, I think—" I stopped because a tall, elegant woman in a mauve housecoat had entered the room. She reminded me of many of the ladies I used to see at our country club back home where I caddied as a kid. I could see how she would look regal atop a horse.

"I am Lillian Williamson," she said in a quietly cultured tone as we both rose and introduced ourselves. "Please sit." She took a chair and clasped well-tended hands in her lap.

Panzer thanked her for seeing us and asked if she had any thoughts at all about who might have kidnapped her son.

"None whatever," she said, starting to tear up.

"Does your son have a lot of close friends at school?" I asked.

She shrugged. "Not terribly close. Oh, there have been a couple of boys here to play once or twice after school. In each case, a parent or chauffeur came along as well. We're all pretty protective of our children around here."

"Has Tommie gone to any classmates' houses as well?"

"Yes, yes he has, on a few occasions. Each time, he was taken by Charles—that's Charles Bell, our chauffeur, who stayed there while he played and then brought him back home."

"And Mr. Bell drives him to and from the school every day also, correct?" Panzer asked.

"Yes. Tommie's school, MeadesGate Academy, is about six miles from here, a ten- or fifteen-minute drive," she said, studying her hands.

"What does the boy's nanny, Sylvia Moore, do while he's in school all day?" Panzer asked.

"She is very useful here in so many ways," Lillian Williamson said. "She acts as my unofficial social secretary. I am involved in numerous charities and fund-raising events, both here and in the city, and that entails a great deal of correspondence. Sylvia is not only wonderful with Tommie, helping him with his schoolwork and such, but she also takes shorthand and is an excellent typist. She has done as many as forty letters a day for me."

"You are very fortunate to have such a versatile individual in your employ," Panzer said.

"Yes, I am, and she also is a valued companion. As you may be aware, I ride a great deal, both competitively and simply for enjoyment. We have a bridle path on the property. Often Sylvia rides with me. She is wonderful company, and an excellent sounding board for ideas I have involving the various charities it is my privilege to work with."

"Where were you when your son disappeared?" I asked.

She looked down again, as if studying her lap. "I was up in my room on the second floor, talking on the telephone to my cochairman of a benefit ball we are planning at the Plaza Hotel. Burke had already left for his office, and Sylvia called up to me loudly from downstairs that Tommie had ... was ... gone." She put her head in her hands and began sobbing.

We sat in silence for close to a minute. Lillian Williamson looked up and took a deep breath, then another, sniffling. "Please forgive me, gentlemen," she said, composing herself.

"Nothing whatever to forgive," Panzer said. "We appreciate your taking time to see us. Is it correct to assume that you have no suspicions involving anyone in your employ?"

"That is absolutely correct, Mr. Panzer. I trust them all, completely and without reservation. And I simply cannot understand who could have telephoned Sylvia and then not been on the wire when she came inside. It is all so horrible."

We both agreed, and Panzer then asked Mrs. Williamson if we could talk to Sylvia Moore.

"I will get her for you," she answered, standing and leaving with the grace of one who gave the appearance of being fully in control of her emotions, although we knew otherwise.

About five minutes later, a slim and attractive blond woman with a heart-shaped face tiptoed into the room. She looked younger than her twenty-six years.

I flashed what I hoped was a winning smile. "Miss Moore?"

That drew a nod but no smile in return.

"Please sit down," Panzer said. "You will recall meeting me briefly yesterday."

"Yes, sir, I do," she said, backing cautiously up to a chair, perching on its front few inches, and looking as if she was ready to bolt out through the doorway at the first opportunity.

"This is my colleague, Mr. Goodwin. We are here at the request of Mr. Williamson, and we have a few questions we'd like to ask you."

"Are you policemen?"

"Private investigators. And I assure you that we want exactly what you want: the safe return home of Tommie Williamson."

"Oh yes, oh yes!" She blinked her red-rimmed baby blues and looked like she hadn't slept well.

Panzer leaned forward, elbows on knees and expression earnest. "First, it would be helpful to know something of the routine in this house. Yesterday morning, Tommie disappeared from the backyard before he was to leave for school. Is it common for him to be outside in the morning?"

She cleared her throat before speaking and kneaded a handkerchief in both hands. "Yes, very common. His mother likes him to get some exercise and fresh air after breakfast, assuming the weather is good. He doesn't get another chance to be outside until his noon break at school, when the students get some recess time after lunch."

"And you are usually outside with Tommie?" I put in.

"Always, at least until ... until yesterday." More twisting of the hankie.

"What does he normally do during that time?"

"Yesterday, he was gathering different kinds of leaves for a school project," she said. "Sometimes, we fly a kite or hit tennis balls around on the court or take a short swim in the pool or he has a brief ride on one of his mother's horses, the tamest one. When that happens, which is once or twice a week, I ride along with him on another horse."

"Is everyone on the household staff familiar with these routines?" Panzer asked.

"Oh yes. Our schedule varies somewhat in the summer, when Tommie is not in school, but even then, we usually are outside in the back at some point during the morning. The property is so large and so well equipped, there is always something to do."

"Were you surprised to get summoned to the telephone yesterday?"

"Yes—that has never happened before."

"Please describe the situation."

"I was … in the backyard, about, oh, only about ten or fifteen yards from the house, helping Tommie identify leaves, when Mary—that's Mary Trent, the housemaid—came to the door of the terrace and called out to me that I had a telephone call, and that it sounded urgent. My mother in Virginia has been very ill, heart problems, and I was afraid that's what the call was about. I ran inside without … well, without thinking about Tommie."

"Were the Williamsons and the others on the staff aware of your mother's health problems?" Panzer posed.

"Oh yes. We are a fairly close-knit group most of the time, particularly the women, which is comforting."

"So you ran into the house. What next?"

"Mary was waiting at the French doors and told me that the call came to the instrument in the hallway just off the dining room. When I got there and picked up the receiver, there was no one on the other end. I clicked the cradle several times, but got no answer, nothing at all. I'm afraid that I started shouting 'Who is there?' or something similar to that. Then, I got the operator on the wire, but she couldn't help me at all. I wasted all that time, while Tommie was …" She lifted her shoulders and let them drop.

"What did Mary Trent tell you about the voice of the caller and what this individual said to her?"

"She told me it was a man, and he said to her in a frantic voice, a hoarse voice, 'I must talk to Sylvia Moore right away. It is terribly important, a matter of life and death! Get her—and please hurry!'"

Panzer ran a hand through his hair. "How long would you estimate you were in the house?"

"Umm, maybe three or four minutes; I don't think any longer than that. It is really hard to tell exactly, though, because I was so upset about my mother. Also, it took time to reach the operator."

"And you went back out into the yard then?"

"Yes. When I didn't see Tommie where I had left him, I thought he must have come inside while I was on the telephone. But we—me, Mary, Emily Stratton, the housekeeper—all looked around the house and couldn't find him anywhere. That's when we told Mrs. Williamson what had happened, and we all moved out to the grounds. Everybody on the staff became part of the search."

"Did the rest of them, the staff that is, know that you would be outside with Tommie collecting leaves in the morning?" I asked.

"Why … yes, they did. I mentioned it when we were at dinner in our kitchen the night before, but that's not at all uncommon. I often talk about what projects Tommie and I are working on. The others, particularly the women, like to hear what he's up to. They're all very fond of him," she said, her upper lip quivering.

Panzer gave her an understanding look. "Miss Moore, has it occurred to you that the purpose of that call was to get you into the house and away from Tommie?"

She struggled to maintain her composure. "Not until some time later, after I had called my mother and learned she was all right, and found that no one back home had placed a long-distance telephone call to me. What I cannot understand is how the caller knew I would be outside with Tommie at that very moment, and how he got word to whoever took Tommie."

"That is what we intend to discover," Panzer said, "and very quickly. Can you show us the exact spot in the yard where Tommie was when you got called into the house?"

We left the house, walked across a terrace with its tables and umbrellas, and down four steps into a yard that seemed to go on forever, past the pool and tennis courts. Off to the left were both a greenhouse and what I later learned were the stables.

We crossed a gravel driveway that curved around the house from the front and led to the garage. A few yards beyond the driveway, Sylvia Moore bent down and pointed to a small stack of leaves. "These were what Tommie was collecting when I left him right here," she sniffled, picking up the leaves and handling them as though they were precious objects. We had not had rain for days, so any kind of tracks on the grass were out of the question, and the gravel on the driveway appeared to have recently been raked.

"Anything else that we should know?" Panzer asked the young woman.

Sylvia shook her head and studied her shoes. "Only that this is all my fault," she murmured, "all my fault."

"I don't believe the Williamsons are blaming you," I told her, placing a hand on her shoulder.

"Well, they should!" she said as she walked back toward the mansion.

# CHAPTER 8

As we piled into the Heron sedan for the trip back to Manhattan, Fred Durkin beat Orrie Cather to the spot next to the driver, drawing a frown from Cather. "Oh, can it, Orrie, you're slimmer than I am," Fred snapped, looking over his shoulder. "You can stand to be back there better than me."

"I can't help it if you're overweight. Besides, I'm the one who found out today just how the kid got hustled off the estate."

"What?" barked Del Bascom. "When did you—?"

"That's enough," Panzer interrupted as he started the car. "We're not going to discuss anything about this case till we're with Mr. Wolfe. He needs to hear everything fresh, not after we've hashed it over among ourselves."

"Oh yeah? Just who put you in charge?" Cather said, practically hissing.

"As a matter of fact, Mr. Wolfe did. Go ahead and ask him if you don't believe me."

That shut Cather up, and for the rest of the drive into Manhattan, the conversation centered on the pennant races, and whether both the Giants and the Yankees would make it into the World Series. The verdict: Yankees, yes; Giants, no. It turned out that neither team made it. As we neared West Thirty-Fifth Street, Panzer checked his wristwatch. "Mr. Wolfe should be coming down right now."

"Coming down from where?" I asked.

"The plant rooms, Archie," Durkin said. "He spends four hours a day in a greenhouse up on the top floor of his place, where he grows thousands of orchids, all different colors. I've only been up there once, but I will never forget the sight. I can't believe there's a nursery anyplace with more orchids than he's got."

"I'll be damned. Four hours a day?"

"That's right," Panzer said. "Nine to eleven and four to six. He is very rigid about it, almost never misses a day, even when he's knee-deep in a case."

"And he's got a crabby gardener up there to help tend them orchids," Cather put in. "Grouchy old coot named Horstmann."

"Anybody would figure to be crabby with you coming into the house, Orrie," Durkin shot back. "He's probably only grouchy when you're hanging around."

"Children, children," Panzer said as he pulled the Heron up to the curb in front of Wolfe's brownstone. "Remember, we are on the job, which does not include bickering like a bunch of grammar-school kids."

Fritz, whose last name I now knew to be Brenner, opened the front door and ushered us in. We trooped down the hall to the office, taking the same seats we had earlier in the day. Wolfe was settled in at his desk, two bottles of beer and a pilsner glass in front of him. "Gentleman," he said with a barely perceptible nod. "Can I offer you some refreshments?"

This time, everyone accepted. Saul asked for a scotch on the rocks, Orrie a bourbon highball, and Fred and Del, beer. Figuring it was time for me to learn how to drink, I ordered scotch and water.

After Fritz had efficiently filled our requests, Wolfe swallowed beer, dabbed his lips with a handkerchief, and fastened his gaze on Saul Panzer. "Well?"

"We each talked to the people we were assigned to," he said.

"And you have not discussed your discoveries with one another?" Saul shook his head.

"Satisfactory. Please proceed."

Saul gave what seemed to me to be a verbatim report of our meetings with both of the Williamsons and Sylvia Moore. On several occasions, he looked at me questioningly, as if seeking confirmation for his accuracy. Each time I nodded, awed by his recall and vowing to ensure that I could do as well—or better.

After the report, Wolfe asked Saul for his impressions of all three. "They are each pretty shaken right now, which is hardly surprising under the circumstances. Williamson is trying to put on a brave front, stiff upper lip and all, but the waiting for a call from the kidnapper is getting to him, wouldn't you agree, Archie?"

"Absolutely. The guy is trying to hold his emotions in, but he looks like he's about to snap. It's painful to watch."

"As for the wife," Panzer continued, "the strain shows on her a lot more, and like her husband, she resolutely rejects any suggestion that a member of the household staff has any connection with the kidnapping—and that includes that gardener and the stable master." He looked at me and I nodded my agreement.

"Then we have the, uh ... nanny," Panzer said as Wolfe made a face. "If anything, Sylvia Moore seems even more upset than the boy's parents, partly because she blames herself for what happened. She told us she has no idea who might have telephoned her and then hung up when she came on the line. Her mother in Virginia has been quite ill, and when the maid called to her out in the yard and said someone urgently wanted to speak to her, she immediately imagined the worst and dashed inside, although you probably know all that yourself from talking to Williamson."

"He recounted the occurrence essentially the same way, having also heard Miss Moore's description of it," Wolfe said.

Panzer went on. "I asked her if she had seen anyone suspicious on the grounds, and she said no. Have I missed anything, Archie?"

"No, it's all there."

Wolfe looked around the room, passing over Orrie Cather, who was squirming in his chair like a high school sophomore wanting to be called on by the teacher because he knew the answer. "Fred, your report?"

Durkin pulled out his notebook and knit his brow as he flipped the pages. "First, I talked to the gardener, Lloyd Carstens, who's worked for the Williamsons for about eleven years. And you sure were right about him, Saul. He's a crusty, crabby character, who obviously didn't want to waste any time with me. We met in the greenhouse, a huge place, and he kept telling me how busy he was. I didn't think he acted very concerned at all about the kidnapping. He seemed more interested about all his flowers and bushes and kept going on about what a big job it is to maintain the grounds and how hard he has to work."

"Does he have help in his work?"

"Yeah, he does, Mr. Wolfe," Durkin said. "Says he brings in outside crews to mow and plant flower beds in season. But he said none of these part-timers had been on the grounds in the last week or two. I asked if he had seen anyone around recently who didn't belong, and he said definitely not.

"Carstens has an apartment in Lynbrook, which he said is about an eight-mile drive from the Williamsons'. He's married, has no children."

Wolfe drained the beer from his glass and opened a second bottle. "Saul mentioned that there was animus between Mr. Carstens and Mark Simons, who runs the stable. Did you find that to be the case?"

Durkin nodded. "It came up, all right. Carstens griped about how Simons always acts like he's the most important person on the estate and that he's always complaining about how the mowing crew messes up the bridle path, which he then has to spend time raking smooth again."

"Is there a telephone in the greenhouse?" Wolfe asked.

"There is," Durkin said. "I made a point of locating it. Carstens has a small office nook in one corner, with the instrument sitting on a desk. And it's an outside line, all right."

"You also talked to Mr. Simons?"

"Yes, sir, I did. He has worked for the Williamsons for just over nine years. He's every bit as grouchy as Carstens, and even more arrogant. The main difference I could detect between them is that Simons seems much more concerned about the kidnapped boy. He also seems very devoted to Mrs. Williamson and talks about her almost like she's a saint. He said he used to ride around the estate's bridle path with her until Sylvia Moore got hired. Now the Moore girl usually rides with the missus, and I got the impression that Simons doesn't much care for that young woman."

"Did he comment on other members of the staff?"

Durkin said no. "And when I asked, he said he hadn't seen anyone out of the ordinary hanging around the house or the grounds. His stables are very clean and neat, at least for a barn. There's three horses in all, and he went on about what magnificent animals they are, almost as if he was talking like they were his children. And oh, yeah, he's got a phone with an outside line in his own little office, just like Carstens does. On the wall above his desk there's a photo of a horse. He says it's Man o' War, which he calls 'the finest piece of horseflesh that's ever lived and ever will live.'"

Consulting his notebook, the thickset detective continued: "Simons drives in every day from Hempstead, just a few miles from the estate. Says he's got what he describes as 'a small cottage' where he lives with his wife. A married son who's got a couple kids has a house close by theirs."

Wolfe gave Durkin a nod and turned toward Del Bascom, once again ignoring an anxious Orrie Cather, who clearly was dying to speak. "You talked to the chauffeur and the housekeeper?"

"Yes, I saw the housekeeper first, Mr. Wolfe," Bascom said. "As Saul has described, Emily Stratton is thin, almost painfully so, although she carries herself ramrod straight, and her demeanor matches her posture. It's like pulling teeth to get answers to even the most harmless questions from her. She seems to think anything she says will somehow reflect badly on her employers—and herself.

"I hammered away at her, though, and the more we talked, the more it seemed like she doesn't like any of the others on the staff. Oh, she didn't come right out and attack them in so many words; it was more in what she didn't say. I'd ask about one or another of them, and she would make a face or shrug. The closest she came to outright criticism was when I asked about Sylvia Moore. She said, 'Well, I have never felt little Tommie was looked after carefully enough. So now we are seeing the results of that carelessness.'"

"Did Miss Stratton indicate there had been other occasions when the boy had been left without supervision?" Wolfe asked.

"No, but I did press her on that point," Bascom replied, "and she just brushed it off. She added that there had never been another kidnapping attempt on the boy, at least as far as she knows."

"Tell us about the chauffeur."

"Charles Bell is very pleased with himself, to say the least. He's been driving for the Williamsons for three years, and he acts like he's the best thing that's ever happened to the family. He loves to talk about the cars he drives and says Williamson always takes his advice when getting ready to purchase a new automobile."

Bascom consulted his notes and continued. "Bell's single, never been married, he says. He lives in a nicely furnished four-room apartment above the garages—with an outside phone line. He showed me around and is very proud of the setup. I would be, too. He insists he has never seen anybody suspicious hanging around the house and grounds and says he was up in his rooms shaving and getting ready to drive Tommie to school when the boy disappeared. Never heard a thing," he said.

Wolfe shifted his bulk and frowned. "On his trips to and from the school with the boy, did Mr. Bell ever sense he was being followed?"

"No, sir," Bascom said. "I posed that question to him, and he told me he's always been on his guard when taking Tommie anywhere, whether to school or to a playmate's house. He may be a snobbish fellow, but I was left with the strong impression that he is very protective of the boy. At one point, he said, 'If I ever find the bastard that did this, I'll ...' His words trailed off, but he had a fierce expression and he pounded a fist into an open palm."

"Did you sense he was overacting?"

Bascom paused before responding. "No, not really, sir. In fact, it was the only time during our talk that he stopped behaving like a pompous, puffed-up jackass. It seemed like I was seeing the real Charles Bell just then, without any of those airs he likes to put on."

"Orrie," Wolfe said, "your report, please."

Cather tensed, leaning forward on the sofa as if he was about to leap to his feet. "I know how they took the kid away!" he blurted.

"Really?" Wolfe's eyebrows went up, and he took his beer glass away from his lips without taking a swallow.

"Yeah, here's how I figure—"

"Enough, Orrie," Wolfe snapped, holding up a palm. "You should know by now that I like to receive my reports in a methodical fashion, and in the order in which the information has been learned."

Cather looked chagrined, but only for a moment. "Well, I first talked to the cook, Mrs. Price, given name Hazel, and Saul is correct: the woman has never been married, despite the label. From the looks of her, she enjoys her own cooking a lot, and she rules like a queen over a kitchen that's got to be more than twice the size of my flat. Even though it's down in the basement, it's got a high ceiling, and—"

"That's enough description, Orrie."

"Yes, sir. The first thing I asked her was whether anything unusual had happened yesterday, and that's when I hit pay dirt." He glanced around at the rest of us with a grin, as if savoring his moment in the spotlight. A look from Nero Wolfe got him back on track.

"She says it was pretty much like most days, although one thing puzzled her a little bit. Around 8:45 or so, she said there was a knocking at the outside door of the kitchen, the one that opens to a few steps that lead up to the driveway and the backyard. It's the door where all the deliveries are received. Anyway, she opens the door and there's a guy she's never seen before carrying two crates of vegetables. He was tall and quite thin, she said, with dark hair parted in the center. 'Your order from Mitchell & Sons Purveyors, Mrs. Price,' he told her.

"'I have never heard of this Mitchell & Sons company of yours,' she said to him. 'I always get my produce from Baxter & Hart, and have for years.' At this point, the man pulled out a typewritten sheet with an order for vegetables—carrots, spinach, broccoli, and the like. She said it had her name on it and the Williamson address at the top.

"She told this guy—she never got his name—that there had been a mistake and asked him to take the food away. He argued, trying to get her to accept the vegetables, and she told me she finally had to practically push him out the door."

"How much time did all this foofaraw take?" Wolfe asked.

"She said she didn't know for sure, maybe two or three minutes, five at the most. I asked why she hadn't mentioned anything about this before, and she told me she didn't think it was important. Simply a mistake, or else one company trying to cut in on the business of another, she said."

"So she had told no one before?" Wolfe asked, eyebrows still raised.

"Only me," Cather said proudly.

"Did she get a look at the man's vehicle?" I cut in, receiving a glare from Wolfe for my trouble.

"Yeah, she did," Cather answered, looking at me as if he had forgotten I was in the room. "She followed him up the steps from the basement and watched as he got into a small enclosed white truck, the type food purveyors use. They're as common as street-corner hot dog vendors. But, of course, she didn't get his plate number, and she doesn't know enough about automobiles and trucks to know what make it was."

"And the truck had no lettering of any kind on it, right?" I put in.

"That's exactly it!" Cather said. "What do you want to bet the Williamson kid was inside it?"

"Anything else from the cook, Orrie?" Wolfe asked.

"No, sir, not really, although she seemed puzzled that I was so interested in this mysterious purveyor. 'That silly business can't have had anything to do with Tommie's … with what has happened,' she said. When I asked if she had any other ideas on who might have kidnapped him, she just shook her head and started muttering about all the evil in the world today. I thought she was going to launch into a sermon on sin."

"And the others you interviewed?"

"Next I jawed with the butler, Waverly, in a small parlor just off the living room, and I did ninety percent of the talking. The guy's a clam, I'll tell ya. If I was to ask him if the sun came up today, he'd mull over his answer. He told me he was up in his room on the top floor of the house going over the household accounts at the time the boy disappeared. He says the first he knew about it was when the Stratton woman, the housekeeper, knocked on his door, yelling 'something terrible has happened!'" Orrie took a sip of his highball and continued.

"I asked him if the family had been concerned over the years about the possibility of Tommie being kidnapped, and he said they always made sure there was an adult with him when he was out in the yard. But he added that most of the families of other kids in Tommie's school also were very protective of their children, given how wealthy the area is."

"Have there been other incidences of kidnapping in those environs?" Wolfe asked.

"I asked him that," Cather said proudly, "and he said that to his knowledge, there had been none, at least in the twenty years he has worked for the Williamsons. Before that, he says he was in England. I also pumped him on what he thought of the other members of the staff, and here he got very tight-lipped. If he has bad feelings about any of them, he sure as hell wasn't going to let on to me about them."

Wolfe drained his second beer. "Anything further to add on Mr. Waverly?"

"No, that's it. Next, I talked to the young housemaid, Mary Trent. Saul described her very accurately to you—she's small and dark haired, looks even younger than her nineteen years, and is very shy, I would even say timid. Maybe that's understandable, given that she is by far the youngest person on the staff and this is her first job.

"It was almost as hard to get her to talk as it was the butler. She did tell me how fond she is of Tommie and how she would spend time playing games with him when Sylvia Moore was out riding with Mrs. Williamson or otherwise occupied. I asked her if she recognized the voice of the person who telephoned for Miss Moore, and I thought she hesitated for just a second or so too long before saying no, as if maybe it really was someone she knew ... like perhaps somebody else in the house who had maybe disguised their voice."

"That is speculation on your part, Orrie," Wolfe said with a sniff, "although it very well may have some merit. Now if we can—" Wolfe got interrupted by the ringing of his telephone, and he scowled as he reached for the instrument.

"Yes? I see …" He picked up a pen and wrote on a pad for more than a minute. "Yes, yes, I have it. I understand, sir. Yes. I will be back to you shortly, and we will firm up the plan we discussed earlier," he said, cradling the receiver and looking at each of us in turn.

"Gentlemen, that was Mr. Williamson. He has received instructions by telephone from the purported kidnapper."

# CHAPTER 9

Here is the content of the message Mr. Williamson received over the telephone line at his home a few minutes ago," Wolfe said, reading from his notepad. "'Your son is safe. We mean him no harm whatever. But he will be returned to you only after we receive the money mentioned in the note, in unmarked, nonsequential bills. Tonight, you are to take the money in a briefcase or satchel to a telephone booth at the corner of the Grand Concourse and Bedford Park Boulevard in the Bronx. At precisely nine o'clock, the instrument in that booth will ring and you will receive further instructions. You are to be alone. No police. You will be watched.'"

"Where is Williamson going to get that kind of dough that fast?" Durkin asked.

"He already has it," Wolfe replied. "Immediately after he received the threatening note, he withdrew a hundred thousand dollars in used currency, fifty- and one-hundred-dollar bills. This money now fills a suitcase."

"Must be nice to have that kind of mazuma," Cather said.

"It would be a damn sight nicer to have your child back home with you," Bascom observed.

Wolfe drew in air and exhaled. "Mr. Williamson naturally is prepared to part with this money, and even more, if necessary, as recompense for the return of his son. My sole commission is to reunite the boy with his parents. The eventual retrieval of the money is of secondary importance, if indeed it is of any importance whatever to the Williamson family. Saul, you know every corner and byway of New York City and its environs. Describe the locale where the money is to be delivered. The Grand Concourse, it is called?"

"Yes, sir," Panzer replied. "The Concourse is a broad boulevard, with a grassy, tree-lined median strip separating the opposing lanes. During the building boom leading up to the crash, modernistic, streamlined-style apartment buildings with glass-block windows and curved corners, some of them fifteen stories or more, got put up all along the thoroughfare, which some people like to call the 'Main Street of the Bronx.'"

"Meaning that activities occurring at street level could easily be monitored from windows in any one of numerous tall buildings that line this boulevard," Wolfe remarked with a scowl, "which undoubtedly is why the location was selected. But to cite a comment I have heard Mr. Panzer make on more than one occasion, 'sometimes we have no choice but to play the hand that we are dealt.' This appears to be one of those times."

"You mentioned to Williamson on the telephone just now a plan that you and he had discussed," Panzer prompted.

"Yes. We decided jointly that when he received instructions as to the delivery of the ransom money, he would drive his automobile to the stipulated site, but that one of my operatives—one of you—would secrete himself in the vehicle in the event there was some unforeseen development. I would be willing to assume that role, but as you can readily see, I am hardly suited to such an operation. Nor are you Fred, nor you, Mr. Bascom, for similar although not as extreme reasons. That leaves you, Saul, and you, Orrie."

"Don't forget me!" I barked. "I may not be quite as skinny as Panzer, but I don't have the beginnings of a gut on me like Cather. And I'm younger than both of them. I'm your man."

Wolfe turned toward me, eyes wide, and started to speak, but Cather cut him off. "This is the trigger-happy hotspur talking, the guy who plugged two apes over on the North River docks a while back. Do you really want him involved in a delicate situation like we've got ourselves here?"

Wolfe threw a questioning look at Panzer. "Goodwin seems pretty solid to me," the big-beaked operative said. "Based on what little I've seen, he asks smart questions, and he knows when to keep his mouth shut. Having said that, I am perfectly willing myself to be the one hiding in the car with Williamson."

"From everything I've seen, Archie's jake," added Del Bascom. "He's done some good jobs for me, and I like his judgment. Besides, those two he knocked off on the docks were nothing but slime. It was a case of him or them. And this old burg's a damn sight better off with them dead and gone."

Now it became Durkin's turn. "I agree with Del. We were on that warehouse job in Long Island City that made the papers, and Archie held his fire when he could have started shooting. I'd trust him in a pinch any day."

"Mr. Goodwin, you appear to have acquired a cadre of admirers in a very short time," Wolfe observed.

"Just because I happen to be the youngest guy here don't mean I haven't got moxie," I told him.

"Hah! You're just barely younger'n me," Cather fired back. "And you don't have anywhere near the street smarts that I got. Hell, I was born in this town, and I'll probably die here, peacefully or otherwise."

"Gentleman, we are not gathered to quibble over qualifications," Wolfe said. "While I admire experience, I also appreciate resourcefulness. Mr. Goodwin, if you accompany Mr. Williamson, albeit out of sight, do you feel you can perform in his best interests, and—more important—in the best interests of the kidnapped child?"

"Yes, sir, I do."

"So do I," Nero Wolfe said in a tone that brooked no disagreement. "Saul, get one of the guns from the safe for Mr. Goodwin. I assume the rest of you are armed." Everyone nodded. "I see no reason for there to be gunplay, but we must be prepared for any contingency.

"Saul—you, Orrie, Fred, and Mr. Bascom will this evening drive out to a prearranged location near the Williamson estate along with Mr. Goodwin, arriving there no later than eight o'clock. Mr. Goodwin, you will ride back into the city with Burke Williamson for his rendezvous in the Bronx, although you will be out of sight, probably hunkered down on the floor of the backseat. You will doubtless be most uncomfortable," he said, making a face, "but sadly that cannot be avoided.

"Mr. Goodwin gets into the Williamson automobile and they drive off. You four will follow that machine at a discreet distance to ensure that no one is tailing it. And you also will keep watch on them, again from a distance, when they reach the telephone booth on the Grand Concourse. Saul, you and Mr. Williamson are to agree on a meeting place after all this activity has transpired—including, it is to be hoped, the return of the Williamson boy. Questions?"

"Yeah," said Panzer, scratching his chin and leaning forward in the red leather chair at one end of Wolfe's desk. "Am I correct in assuming that we are meeting Williamson at a location away from his house so that none of his employees will know what's happening?"

"You are indeed correct. Mr. Williamson stubbornly persists in his belief that every member of his household staff remains above suspicion. I do not share in that admirable but naive belief. When he leaves his home tonight, the only person to know his destination will be his wife. I have insisted upon this, suggesting he develop a plausible reason for his absence if asked by anyone in his employ. Any other questions, gentlemen?"

We all looked at one another, then back at our host. No one spoke.

"I reiterate that the sole purpose of this undertaking is to return an eight-year-old boy safely to his parents. While we, of course, also would like to apprehend the kidnappers and retrieve Mr. Williamson's money, those goals, albeit commendable ones, are not what I have been hired to do." Wolfe looked at each of us again, as if to detect some sign of disagreement.

"Very well. Each of you who does not have the telephone number of this office needs to record it now," he said, reading off the digits as

64

I scribbled them down. "I will call Mr. Williamson and establish the meeting place."

A half hour later, the five of us piled back into the Heron sedan, with Saul Panzer again behind the wheel, destination: an intersection near the Williamson estate on Long Island.

"What's with Wolfe not knowing anything about this Grand Concourse place?" I asked. "Sounds like it should be pretty well known, given that you called it 'The Main Street of the Bronx.'"

That drew a chuckle from the others, but Panzer remained serious. "Mr. Wolfe is brilliant, like nobody I have ever seen or ever will see. He has broken open cases I would have said were unsolvable, and how he has done it, I can't begin to tell you. But he also has his, shall we say ... *eccentricities*. He almost never leaves his home; why should he? He has got everything he needs right there: his ten thousand splashy orchids in that greenhouse up on the roof, complete with his own gardener, old Horstmann; his gourmet meals prepared by Fritz Brenner; his endless supply of beer; and enough books to stock a small public library.

"He reads three or four newspapers every day, so he knows what's going on in that outside world where he rarely sets foot," Panzer went on. "But for reasons known only to him, Mr. Wolfe has little or no interest in geography, local or otherwise, even though he's got that big globe in his office. For instance, if I handed him a map of Manhattan, I very much doubt he could locate Greenwich Village or Columbia University or Madison Avenue without poring over that map. And the fact is, he really doesn't care. That's part of the reason he has guys like us working for him. Among us we know pretty much all the neighborhoods and streets and byways in the five boroughs, and you'll get to know them, too, Archie, if you stay around this town long enough."

"I'll give you an idea of what Saul's talking about," Cather said with a sour laugh. "A year or so, Fred and I were on a case for Wolfe where we had to talk to a big-shot corporate lawyer who had an office in the brand-new Chrysler Building, and Wolfe asked us where it was. Here you've got the tallest, most-famous skyscraper in town—although that Empire State Building they're building is going to top it—and Wolfe had no idea whatever of its location, other than it was somewhere on Manhattan Island. Saul is absolutely right. Wolfe doesn't need to know where things are as long as he's got us around."

"All in all, I'd say the system works pretty well," Durkin volunteered. "We all go out and collect pieces in information, much of which doesn't mean a damn thing to us, and we drop it all in Wolfe's lap. Then he—don't ask me how—takes these pieces and puts them together to solve a puzzle."

"And on numerous occasions, that puzzle has been a murder," Saul said. "In the years I've known him, Mr. Wolfe has done the Police Department's work for them more times than I can count."

"How do the cops feel about that?" I asked.

"Hah!" Del Bascom snorted. "Just ask that question to Wolfe's old buddy Inspector Cramer."

"Oh yeah, I've heard his name before."

"And you'll doubtless hear it again, Archie, if you do more jobs for Wolfe," Bascom said. "They go back quite a ways."

"Well, Cramer may not enter into this case," Saul Panzer observed, "given that it's a kidnapping and not a homicide."

How wrong that prediction proved to be.

# CHAPTER 10

Saul Panzer steered the Heron along a dark country lane in the general vicinity of the Williamson mansion and pulled off the pavement near an intersection with another two-lane road, letting the engine idle. We sat there no more than two minutes when another car, a swell Packard sedan with side-mounted tires, pulled up beside us and a grim-faced Burke Williamson climbed out.

We all stepped from the Heron as Panzer and Williamson went over the plan. "Archie Goodwin will be in the car with you, out of sight, as Mr. Wolfe has told you," Panzer said. "We will be behind as you drive into the city to ensure that you're not being followed. You won't see us. Do you have the money?"

"It's in the car," the hotelier said. "Understand, I want no gunplay."

"Nor do we," Panzer said. "Let's go."

I got into the backseat of the big Packard. "I'll crouch down on the floor when we get closer to the Bronx," I said.

Williamson nodded curtly as we pulled away. "You seem awfully young," he remarked. "Have you ever done anything like this before?"

"Not exactly, although I've been in the game longer than you might think," I answered, exaggerating my experience. We drove the rest of the way in silence, and even in the dim glow supplied by passing streetlamps, I could see the veins standing out on the back of

Williamson's hands as he gripped the steering wheel. Periodically, I looked out the back window but saw no headlights behind us. Either the foursome was farther back than I would have thought or Panzer was driving with his lights off.

I hadn't looked at a map and had no idea what direction we were going in, but I was aware that we had entered the Queens section of New York City. "Are we close to the Bronx?" I asked Williamson.

"Yes, and you'll know we're there when we cross a bridge over water," he said in a hoarse voice. "It's coming up soon, and that's when you will need to get down."

The bridge came and I dropped to the floor behind the front seat, feeling the cold bulk in my jacket pocket of the automatic pistol Panzer had gotten for me from Wolfe's office safe. It was a Webley, so he said, and fully loaded.

"We're at the Grand Concourse," Williamson announced. "It should only be another two or three blocks.... Yes, there's the telephone booth, I see it. I have five to nine, Goodwin; what does your watch read?"

"The same," I told him, barely making out the dial on my wristwatch in the near darkness of the automobile's well-carpeted floor. He pulled the auto to the curb, got out, and walked to the booth as I rose to my knees and peered out the window. At precisely nine o'clock, the instrument jangled and Williamson answered it on the first ring. I could see his lips move and his head nod twice. He then cradled the receiver and walked back to the car.

"The voice told me to go to a second booth, three blocks from here at East 201st Street and Briggs Avenue. I was told I would get another call there. And, of course, I am to bring the money along."

"All this figures. They're trying to see if you've got reinforcements. Wait a couple of minutes, just in case we've lost our other car."

"I don't want to keep them waiting," Williams said, panic edging into his voice.

"You know how to get there from here?"

"It's simple; the voice gave me directions."

"A man?"

"Yes, a deep voice, very precise, with no accent that I could make out," Williamson said.

"Okay, I think it's safe to go now. Panzer seems like the sort who knows how to hold a tail."

"Back down on the floor, Goodwin."

After less than five minutes, the Packard stopped again. This was a far quieter intersection, although as I got partway up from the floor again and looked out, I saw apartment buildings several stories high on all four corners. The night could have many eyes. Then I saw something else as Williamson walked toward the phone booth with the suitcase full of ransom money. It was a figure, seemed to be a man, lying up against the apartment building nearest the phone booth and writhing.

I got out of the car. "Look out—it may be a trap!" I whisper-yelled to Williamson, who by now had noticed the figure, a guy in a gray jacket and flat cap, moaning and clutching his stomach. I pulled out my Webley and edged toward him, expecting trouble. But he made no move, other than to continue groaning and wrapping both arms around his midsection.

I knelt next to him. "What happened?" I asked, leaning down toward his anguished face.

"Shot … silencer … gut." Blood began to ooze out between his fingers and he slumped further down, mouth agape and eyes sightless. I did a fast pat-down of his jacket and felt a flat lump in one pocket.

"What is he saying!" Williamson hissed.

"He's not going to be saying anything more," I told him. "He's gone. Let's get out of here."

"But the phone call!"

"There isn't going to be any phone call coming now, believe me," I barked. "We've gotta go." I grabbed Williamson by the shoulder and pulled him toward the Packard. He tried to dig in his heels, but I pulled harder and got him and his suitcase full of dough up to the car. "But my son, I've got to—"

"You've got to get in, but you're in no condition to drive. I'll take the wheel. Give me your keys. We can't stay here."

He thrust the keys at me, and we both got into the Packard. I pulled from the curb and peeled away just as the Heron came into sight in the rearview mirror. "Where are we supposed to rendezvous with the others?"

"The same intersection as before," he said, holding his head in his hands as I began retracing the route back to Long Island. "Oh God, what do we do now, what do we do next?"

"First a call to Wolfe," I said, stopping at yet another Bronx telephone booth. I took out my wallet and got the sheet of paper with the brownstone's number, dialing it.

"Yes?" Wolfe answered on the first ring.

"Archie Goodwin, Mr. Wolfe." I began telling him where we were and what had happened. "The bozo was armed, had an automatic in his pocket. I got Williamson out of there fast. If the cops had showed up while we were around, we'd have been hauled in and had plenty of explaining to do. Then who knows—the kidnappers might have panicked, and, well ..."

He made a sound I would describe as a growl. "Confound it, I did not anticipate such an outcome."

"If you want my opinion, there was a falling-out between this bunch, whoever they are, and one of them, the guy lying croaked on the sidewalk, was moving to cut his colleagues out right there on the corner and grab the kale from Williamson."

"I did not ask your opinion, Mr. Goodwin, but I happen to concur with it. Where are the others?"

"Presumably heading back to our prearranged meeting place. That's where I'm going now with Williamson, who's not in very good shape."

"Understandable," Wolfe said. "Very well, have Saul telephone me as soon as possible."

We drove back to Long Island in silence, and I only had to ask directions of Williamson once. We waited for ten minutes at the now-familiar intersection before the Heron joined us.

"What the hell went on back there?" Panzer asked as we all climbed out of the autos and stood in a circle in the grass beside the country lane.

"I ran over and checked on the guy lying on the sidewalk, who said he'd been shot with a gun that had a silencer," I said, "and those were his last words." I finished my rundown and told Saul that Wolfe wanted to talk to him.

"But what's going to happen next?" asked a frantic Williamson.

"Do you want to bring the police into this now?" Panzer said.

"No! No, I don't. Those kidnappers said no police, and I don't want to do anything to jeopardize Tommie. Oh Lord, I can't bear to go back and face Lillian. She's been praying that I would bring him home with me."

"Mr. Williamson," Panzer said, "I continue to be convinced that your son has come to no harm, despite all that happened tonight. We believe"—he looked around to include the rest of us—"that the dead man was one of the kidnappers, or at least someone known to them, and that he planned to intercept the ransom money before it reached the others. You surely will get another call, perhaps as soon as tonight, with another set of instructions."

"I don't know how much more of this I can take," the millionaire said, "but I don't suppose I have a choice if I want to get my son back." It took an effort, but he squared his shoulders. "Now, Mr. Goodwin, if you will kindly give me my keys, I am going home."

After we drove off and headed back toward the city, Panzer found yet another telephone booth and called Wolfe, who said he wanted all of us in his office at eleven o'clock in the morning. "At this stage of the game, I got no idea what he wants to do, so I suggest that once we get back to the city, everybody get themselves a good night's sleep—and that's you, too, Orrie."

"What do you mean?" Cather said. "I always get me a good night's sleep."

"I'm suggesting that tonight, though, you might want to do your sleeping alone," Panzer shot back, getting a chorus of laughs from the rest of us.

# CHAPTER 11

I slept late and grabbed breakfast at the counter of a beanery I had come to like just down the block from my room in the Melbourne Hotel. As I gave my teeth a workout on the link sausage and fried eggs, I went over last night's activities, trying to dope out where we now stood and what Nero Wolfe would propose next. I didn't like our chances, what with one corpse and the boy still being held. But I wasn't calling the shots.

"Thanks, Mort," I told the counterman, sliding a dime under my plate as I rose to leave. "If this ain't the best damned coffee in town, then I sure don't know where you would find it."

"Just keep tellin' me that, Archie, and pretty soon I will nail a sign up on the wall that reads 'This is the best doggone java in New York' and sign it 'A. Goodwin, noted gourmet.'"

"Go right ahead. My only fee for that testimonial will be free refills of your fine brew."

"Which you already get anyway," he laughed as I pushed out into the sunny and pleasant morning.

By now, I was getting to feel like a New Yorker, and I liked the feeling. Wolfe's brownstone was thirty blocks south, which made for an unhurried stroll down Eighth Avenue, during which I smiled at seven well-constructed young blonds, brunettes, and redheads walking in the opposite direction. Five returned my smile, which seemed to me a good percentage. We were to meet at eleven o'clock, which I now knew would be when Wolfe came downstairs from his morning session with all those posies in his rooftop greenhouse.

I reached the Thirty-Fifth Street address at five until eleven and rang the doorbell, answered by Fritz. "Mr. Goodwin," he said with a bow, indicating I should hang my hat on the rack in the hall. I did and walked to the office, which already had a crowd, all of them with coffee. Panzer was in the red leather chair at the end of the desk, with Durkin planted in one of the matching yellow chairs and Cather and Bascom sharing the sofa. I dropped into the other yellow chair and accepted a cup of java from Fritz. It was at least as good as Mort's, and maybe even better.

"Good morning, gentlemen, did you sleep well?" Wolfe asked as he moved around behind his desk and placed an arrangement of vivid purple orchids in his desk vase. He got nods all around to his question, whether or not we really did have adequate rest. Cather, for one, looked like he could use a nap.

Fritz Brenner placed the usual frosted stein and two bottles of Canadian beer in front of Wolfe, who opened one and poured, watching the foam subside. He drank, then looked at each of us in turn.

"I confess to you all that I had not foreseen last night's occurrence. In my experience, kidnappers are not killers, of one another or of their captives. The commission of murder greatly decreases their chances of receiving a ransom."

"So where does that leave us?" Cather posed.

"I'm getting to that, Orrie," Wolfe said sharply. "I have been in conversation with Mr. Williamson. He called when I was up in the plant rooms to report that he has gotten another telephone message from the kidnappers. They even put his son on the line briefly. Tommie was crying, but based on his words to his father, the boy had not been physically harmed, although one is left to ponder the damage to his psyche.

"Enough speculation. Mr. Williamson has been ordered to repeat last night's exercise, albeit at a different location in the Bronx."

Panzer cleared his throat. "He still does not want to bring in the police, even though now it would be the supposedly high-powered New York City cops, given where the murder took place?"

"No, Saul, he does not. Now here is our—yes, Fritz, what is it?"

"Inspector Cramer is ringing the bell," Brenner said from the doorway to the hall. "Shall I let him in?"

Wolfe scowled, then nodded grimly. Seconds later, a stocky, angry man in a rumpled suit burst into the room, putting on the brakes as he saw all of us. "Well, I will be damned," he said. "You've got your whole crew here, and then some, Wolfe. Bascom, you don't care about the class of company that you're seen with, huh?" he barked at Del, then turned to me. "And you're one I don't recognize."

"Name's Archie Goodwin," I said.

"Huh! Now the name I do recognize," Cramer muttered, taking his hat off. "You plugged a couple lowlifes on the North River piers a while back. Rowcliff told me about you, said you are something of a smart aleck. I suppose you think that you should be thanked for ridding the community of those two punks. Son, let me give you a piece of advice: go back to wherever you came from, and fast. Consorting with this group will bring you absolutely nothing but grief."

"Mr. Cramer!" Wolfe did not raise his voice, but the words cut like a just-honed knife. "You burst in here unannounced, you rudely interrupt a meeting we are having, and you force me to look up at you when you know very well that I prefer to speak to others at eye level. Now please sit down."

"Move, Panzer," Cramer growled as Saul quietly surrendered the red leather chair and retreated to a seat in the back of the room. The inspector sat, pulled out a cigar, jammed it into his mouth unlit, and leaned forward, glaring at Wolfe. "I want to know what you're up to."

"Sir, I am a private investigator duly licensed by the State of New York, as are all of these men—including Mr. Goodwin. I am not aware that I have done anything that would imperil my right to keep that license."

"I will be the one to decide that," Cramer shot back. "You have a gray Heron sedan, I believe."

"That is correct."

"Interesting. A grifter named Barney Haskell who's got a record as long as his arm got himself shot dead on the Concourse in the Bronx last night, and an eyewitness said he saw a Heron at the scene."

"Mr. Cramer, do you happen to know how many Herons are licensed in the City of New York?" Wolfe asked.

"As a matter of fact, I do, because we got three men in the motor vehicle department to spend the early hours of this morning going over the records, page by page. There are one hundred nineteen. As you must know, they don't make a lot of 'em. It's a rich man's car," he added with a sneer.

"And did your eyewitness say the automobile at the scene was gray?"

Cramer frowned. "He thought so."

"He thought so. And how many of New York's Herons are gray?"

"Thirty-seven."

"Did the eyewitness note the license number?"

"No, he didn't. It was too damned dark," Cramer muttered as he kept gnawing on the cigar.

"So, to review, mine is one of thirty-seven gray Heron sedans licensed in the city, which means it has a ... two point seven percent chance of being that particular automobile, if indeed the Heron at the scene was gray, which seems uncertain."

Cramer's ruddy face became even redder. "Except that when there's trouble in this town, there's a much higher percentage that you are somehow involved in it."

"Twaddle. You have come here to bedevil me, sir, which I resent. A man has been killed, and you understandably seek his murderer. But you insist upon undertaking what is clearly a fishing expedition with no evidence whatever to link me or the men in this room to the crime."

"All right," Cramer said looking around at us, "just how does it happen that on the morning after this Bronx murder, you just happen to have your whole army gathered here?"

"Why they are present here and what we are discussing happen to be none of your affair," Wolfe said evenly. "I could have barred your entrance to this house, assuming you have no search warrant, but I chose to allow you in because you are a high-ranking officer of the law whom I have known for a number of years. Now that you have been here and stated your case, I ask that you leave."

"Nuts! Something stinks around this joint," Cramer spat, throwing his chewed-over cigar at the wastebasket and missing it by a foot. "By God, Wolfe," he said as he stood, "if I find out you're playing fast and loose here, I'll lift that precious license of yours faster than you can blink." He stormed out, hat in hand, and I noticed that Fritz Brenner followed him toward the front door.

Wolfe picked up the vase on his desk and squinted at the orchid, frowning. "All of you except Mr. Goodwin know my ambivalent feelings about Inspector Cramer," he said. "He is unimpeachably honest and unquestionably brave, two traits sadly not always present in members of this city's constabulary. However, he also is impetuous, imperious, and quick to anger when a more measured response would better serve him. So be it.

"Now, let us move on to the business at hand. One or more of you may well think ours is an unwise and ill-conceived foray, but I believe that tonight Tommie Williamson will be returned safely to his family. The kidnappers likely have committed murder, although it is barely possible the killing of Barney Haskell was done by someone not connected with this affair.

"In either case, the people holding Tommie will be eager to grab their money and flee, gladly releasing the boy. They—and I use the plural pronoun advisedly—are in enough trouble already, and they simply have too much to lose by harming an eight-year-old."

"What's the deal tonight?" Panzer asked.

"The deal is this: First, Saul, you are to rent an automobile, a sedan of some common make—you know them far better than I. We cannot risk having the Heron spotted again. As it is, we had the good fortune that the witness last night was unable to read the license plate.

"So much for that," Wolfe went on, glancing at a sheet of notepaper. "The caller ordered Burke Williamson to be at the Southern Boulevard gate to the Bronx Zoo at nine o'clock tonight with the money. He told Mr. Williamson to answer the phone in the booth near the zoo entrance, which will ring precisely at nine, and he then will receive further instructions."

"Geez, these characters sure love their phone booths, don't they?" Durkin said.

"This approach lets them remain anonymous and unseen for as long as possible," Bascom offered.

"Mr. Bascom is correct," Wolfe said, "and unfortunately, we must play by their rules, at least until the boy is released. As was the case last night, Mr. Williamson will drive from home to the specified meeting place with Mr. Goodwin hidden in the automobile. He specifically requested Mr. Goodwin again because he liked the way he handled himself when they happened upon the dying man.

"Saul, you will drive the second automobile again, and with the same passengers, unless any of you would prefer to avoid what may be a potentially perilous situation."

"Hell, I wouldn't miss this shindig for the world!" Orrie Cather said, clapping his hands.

"Me neither," chimed Fred Durkin.

"Count me in," added Del Bascom. "I haven't had this much action in weeks. I'm starting to feel almost young again."

"Here is where tonight's operation will differ," Wolfe said. "The machine driven by Saul will precede Mr. Williamson's automobile to the area by fifteen minutes, parking about a block away to the … Saul?"

"Southern Boulevard runs north and south, with the zoo bordering its east side, and we will be to the south of the gate."

"But you will be within view of the zoo entrance and the telephone booth in question, correct?"

"Yes, sir."

"All four of you will be armed again and are to stay inside the automobile. Mr. Williamson will know you are there, and he knows to signal you if the need arises."

"What about me?" I asked.

"You will remain out of sight but be prepared to rush to Mr. Williamson's aid, if necessary, or to rescue the boy. But resist playing the role of hero by trying to prevent transfer of the money to the kidnappers. As Mr. Williamson has told me twice now, 'They can have the blasted cash, every cent of it. It means nothing to me.' Any other questions?"

"It seems funny they would pick a busy street like Southern Boulevard," Saul said, "where they run the risk of being spotted by a passing police cruiser or a passerby who ends up calling the cops. The Concourse location made sense, because their initial telephone call took Williamson to a quieter street."

"They likely will follow the same pattern here and you may eventually find yourselves on some little-traveled byway once again," Wolfe said. "Any further concerns or questions?"

No one spoke as we got to our feet. Wolfe rose and came around the desk, looking at each of us in turn. "I fully realize that this assignment is not without some peril, as I am sure all of you do. But if each of you uses your intelligence guided by experience, I feel confident of the outcome."

Leaving the brownstone, I wished that I felt as confident as Nero Wolfe.

# CHAPTER 12

I could describe the events leading up to what happened just outside the Bronx Zoo, but it would basically be a rehash of the previous night's activities. One difference was that when the five of us, with Panzer at the wheel of a rented Model A Ford, drove out to the Williamson rendezvous on Long Island, nobody had much to say, unlike our trip twenty-four hours earlier when we all laughed and joked about Nero Wolfe's eccentricities, including his lack of geographical knowledge. Tonight, nobody seemed to be in a joking mood.

A second difference was that on this second trip into the Bronx, I lay on the floor of another of Burke Williamson's autos, his slick red Pierce-Arrow phaeton. "Just like Wolfe's men, I'm changing cars tonight," Williamson said tightly. He was on edge, of course, but then so were the rest of us.

"Okay, Goodwin, I'm turning onto Southern Boulevard now, less than a mile from the zoo. Isn't this something, though? Almost exactly a year ago, Lillian and I took Tommie here for his seventh birthday, and now ..." Williamson could not finish the sentence, which made me begin to worry that he would not hold up under the strain for much longer.

"Wait a minute," he snapped. "There's construction here, dammit!"

I popped up from the floor and saw the barricade and the ROAD

CLOSED sign. "The sawhorse doesn't go all the way across the street," I said to him. "Just swing on around it."

"It's like a washboard," Williamson complained as we bounced north along the rough pavement at about ten miles an hour, passing cement mixers and trucks that awaited the arrival of paving crews in the morning. We also passed Panzer's darkened Model A, which was parked at the curb and was pointed north.

"Could be that's why they picked this stretch," I said. "It's one way to ensure privacy, assuming you don't attract the cops' attention by ignoring the sign."

We had gone about a block, with the darkened zoo and its trees looming on our right behind an iron fence. "There's the phone booth," he whispered, "and it's now 8:57. Here goes."

He climbed out of the car, taking the suitcase with him, and slipped into the phone booth, closing its door. I watched from the lower edge of the backseat window, my hand gripping the Webley and my mouth as dry as a saltine cracker. I could hear the faint ring and watched Williamson pick up the receiver and speak a word or two, nodding grimly as if the voice on the other end could see him agreeing.

"Okay," he said, getting back into the car. "I'm to kill the headlights and keep driving until I see another auto parked up ahead, next to another phone booth. He—the voice—said this would be about two blocks farther along, just around a slight curve. When I get there, I'm to get out with the suitcase and walk toward the booth. My God, I hope that I never see another phone booth for the rest of my life."

"Before you start moving, hit your brake pedal three times fast, three times slowly, then three times fast again," I told him.

"What! Why?"

"Your brake lights will flash the Morse code for S.O.S., which will bring our other auto up closer."

"I've never heard of such a thing!"

"Standard procedure," I said without telling him that I got the idea from a story I read in one of the dime detective magazines.

"But I thought the plan was for them to stay in the background," Williamson said. "We don't want trouble, remember?"

"You don't have to worry; Panzer will turn off his headlights, too. You won't even know he'll be easing along behind us, at a distance. It's just a good idea to have a backup, in case something unexpected happens."

"I don't like it one bit," Williamson huffed, but he pumped the brakes as I had instructed, then shut off his headlights and eased forward along the bumpy road, which seemed nothing like a boulevard in its current state.

"There's the other car, Goodwin!" he rasped. Ahead of us, parked next to the phone booth where the call surely had come from, was a nondescript coupe that looked like a Chevrolet. It was difficult to tell if anyone was inside the car because of the dim glow thrown off by the streetlights.

Williamson exhaled loudly. "Well, here goes," he said, climbing out of the car with his suitcase. Slipping the Webley from my pocket and making sure the safety was off, I poised to jump out of the Pierce-Arrow.

Williamson walked stiffly toward the booth and as he did, a yell of "Daddy, Daddy!" came from behind the bushes along the cast-iron fence that separated the zoo from the sidewalk and boulevard.

"Tommie!" his father screamed, moving in the direction of the voice. But he was intercepted by a tall man coming from the direction of the Chevrolet. He wore a fedora, and some sort of mask covered his face, maybe a woman's silk stocking. "Stop right there, Mr. Williamson. You will see your son soon enough," he said, gesturing with a nickel-plated automatic that glistened even in the faint light. "Now the satchel, please. Give it to me."

The millionaire held out the suitcase and the tall man grabbed it, backing toward the Chevrolet and keeping his gun leveled. He then stopped and knelt down, snapped the latches on the suitcase, and opened it, peering inside. Apparently satisfied with what he saw, he shut the case and rose, backing toward the car with his gun still drawn.

"Daddy!" the anguished cry came again, and Williamson moved in the direction of the panicked little voice. I slipped out of the auto, and as I did a gunshot cracked. The man with the suitcase staggered once, recovered his balance, and fired, apparently at his attacker. I went into a prone position on the pavement and saw Orrie Cather fire and shout, "You child-snatching bastard, let's see how you like this!"

Cather and the tall man exchanged more shots, at least two or three each, and I heard a groan from somewhere behind me. It sounded like Fred Durkin's voice. The tall man clutched his side and climbed into the front passenger seat of the Chevy as the car squealed off, bouncing along the rough pavement. I fired twice from a crouch, trying for one of its tires, but all I hit was the car's trunk.

"Durkin's down!" Del Bascom yelled as he and Saul Panzer came running up to join Cather, who stood in the roadway cursing and watching the kidnappers' car disappear onto the night. "Geez, Orrie, you know you weren't supposed to start shooting," Panzer growled as he knelt next to Fred.

"I'm okay, Saul," the big man said, struggling to get to his feet. "Just nicked me in the shoulder and spun me around. My pride got hurt the most."

"We're over here," Williamson cried. "Give us a hand."

We all went to a spot along the cast-iron zoo fence where Tommie Williamson was sobbing, and with good reason. The boy was handcuffed to the fence, although apparently otherwise unharmed. "Any way we can get these things off him?" his father pleaded as he knelt in the grass next to his son.

"You got a tool kit in your trunk?" Panzer asked him.

"Not with anything that would work here," Williamson said as we began to hear the damnedest collection of noises from the darkness of the zoo—roaring and bleating and howling and cawing and other strange sounds coming from strange creatures. We had awakened the populace.

We also had drawn the attention of some of a particular two-legged species. A patrol car, siren wailing, had drawn up and played a spotlight on us. "What's all this and what about the gunfire?" a beefy patrolman demanded as he climbed out, revolver drawn and playing his flashlight on the strange tableau of a crying boy handcuffed to a fence and six men gathered around him.

"It's a long story," I told him when no one else chose to respond.

"I'll just bet it is, son," he said, "but my partner and me, we got us all kinds of time to listen."

# CHAPTER 13

First things first. The patrolman and his partner pulled metal cutters from their trunk, which they used to free a tearful Tommie Williamson from the fence. All of us, the two cops included, were anxious to learn details of the boy's ordeal, but his father refused to let anybody talk to him.

"I am Burke Williamson, you may have heard of me," he said to the badges, "and my boy here was kidnapped the day before yesterday. Thanks to these men, I have him back, and I am now taking him home, whether you like it or not. I will be happy to discuss the matter with you or your superiors, but not tonight."

It was clear from their expressions that the coppers indeed knew who Williamson was, and they made no attempt to stop him as he picked up his still-sobbing son and carried him to the Pierce-Arrow. "All right, boys," the patrolman, named Finnegan, said as Williamson drove away, "just stay right where you are while I call the precinct. Then we are all going down there so you can have a little chat with the lieutenant. He's going to want to know just how this peaceful piece of the Bronx got turned into a Wild West shootout."

"Didn't you hear Williamson!" Saul Panzer barked as Finnegan slid into the phone booth. "His kid got kidnapped, and while we're standing here, they're getting away, headed up Southern Boulevard in a black Chevy coupe."

"And who might all of you be?" Finnegan said, sticking out a chin as if daring someone to take a swing at it.

"Like Williamson said, we found the boy," Panzer said. "He hired us. We're all private investigators."

"Police not good enough for the job, huh?" his partner put in as Finnegan used the instrument in the booth.

Panzer wisely did not respond.

"All right, all of you into your car, and we'll be right behind you. Do you know where Webster Avenue is?" Finnegan asked Panzer, who nodded.

"That's where we're headed, Fifty-Second Precinct. Not six blocks from here. We'll be right behind you, and I wouldn't try making a dash for it. This Black Maria of ours has a lot more horses under the hood than your rattletrap, and you fellas are in enough trouble as it is. When we get to the station, we'll flash our headlights in case you don't recognize it or maybe decide to drive right on by."

We all jammed into the Ford and lurched along the torn-up pavement of Southern Boulevard with the patrol car right behind us. "What the hell is Wolfe going to say?" Orrie Cather whined.

"Let's worry about that later," Panzer snapped. "Fred, how are you? You need a doctor?"

"Nah," Durkin said, holding his shoulder. "Bullet just grazed me. I checked and there's hardly a drop of blood. A bandage should do it, when we've got time."

"Have you all got your PI licenses with you?" Panzer asked. Each of us told him we did.

We pulled up in front of the old station house and got marched inside by the pair of uniforms. "Sarge, these here are the desperadoes who was shooting up Southern Boulevard," Finnegan proudly announced to the desk sergeant, a stocky specimen whose bushy gray mustache at least partly offset the total lack of hair on his shiny dome.

"Don't look much like desperadoes to me," the sergeant observed with a smirk. "A pretty motley bunch, I'd say. The lieutenant's wanting to see 'em."

We got herded down a long, dark hall with paint peeling on both the ceiling and the pictureless walls and ended up in a bleak room filled with straight-backed wooden chairs, bare wooden tables, and a couple of desks pushed up against the walls. Before we could sit down, a tall, lean guy in shirtsleeves, a necktie, and suspenders burst in and looked at each of us with a tight grin.

"Cowboys right here in the Bronx, eh? What next? Sit down, all of you. I am Lieutenant R. L. Knapp, and that's with a *K*, just in case anybody here wants to file a formal complaint about me. Now I want names, identification, and the whole story about what the hell was going on out there. I'm sure you won't be surprised to learn that you've got people in that part of town all riled up, to say nothing of the animals in the zoo."

We all pulled out our licenses and handed them over. "I will be damned, all private dicks," Knapp said as he riffled through the IDs. "Does one of you speak for the whole bunch?"

"I do," Saul said, putting up his hand.

"And you are ...?"

"Panzer."

"Well, Panzer," Knapp said, sitting on one corner of a table, "how about you telling me what all this is about. Don't leave anything out, or you will have to go through it all again."

Saul did lay the whole thing out, and each time he mentioned Burke Williamson, the lieutenant tensed up.

"Interesting, Mr. Williamson hiring you and this bunch to find the boy," Knapp said derisively. "Just what is it that makes you so special?"

"Most of us have been around awhile."

The cop lit a cigarette and scowled. "Let me put it another way: Who's your boss? There hasta be one."

Saul shrugged, clearly uncomfortable. "It's Nero Wolfe," he murmured after a long pause.

"That fat eccentric who never leaves home? Well, I'll be double damned. So somehow he found out about the kidnapping and went to Williamson looking to get himself an assignment?"

"Other way around. Williamson went to him."

"Huh! Okay, I'm going to call Mr. Nero Wolfe right now and get his story. You got his number handy, or do I have to look it up?"

Saul gave him the number and the lieutenant dialed it from a phone on one of the desks. "Nero Wolfe? This is Lieutenant Knapp, that's with a *K*, calling from the Fifty-Second Precinct in the Bronx. ... That's right, the Bronx. I've got five private operatives here with me now who say they work for you. They are"—Knapp shuffled through our licenses—"Orville Cather, Archie Goodwin, Delbert Bascom, Saul Panzer, and Frederick Durkin. ... So, they are in your employ? Uh-huh ... yeah ... And Burke Williamson hired you to find his kid?"

Knapp's face flushed as he listened to whatever Wolfe was saying. "Yeah, I hear that the kid is back home safe now, but cases like this are really for the police, not amateurs ... no, the kidnappers—I should say alleged kidnappers—got away. They exchanged fire with your boys, right out there on the public street.... Oh, you've heard from Williamson ... he said *what*? ... well, I hardly think that's being fair to the Police Department. We have caught countless kidnappers over the years."

The lieutenant ground out his cigarette on the table leg and passed a handkerchief over his forehead. "No, we don't plan to hold them, although this town doesn't need a bunch of vigilantes shooting up our neighborhoods ... We—What? He wants to speak to you," Knapp snarled at Saul Panzer, handing him the telephone.

"Yes, Mr. Wolfe, all right. We'll be there. Yes, sir." Saul cradled the receiver.

"I wasn't through talking to him!" Knapp bellowed.

"Sorry, he hung up."

Knapp glowered at each of us in turn, exhaling loudly. "You're a fine bunch, and a good reason why we need tougher standards for certifying private dicks in this burg and this state. Why don't you all get the hell back to Manhattan where you belong and stay out of the

Bronx? We don't need the likes of you up here." He tossed our licenses onto the table and stormed out, slamming the door behind him. For several seconds, we just looked at one another.

Orrie Cather broke the silence. "I sure woulda liked to hear Wolfe's end of that conversation," he said, grinning.

"I can guess at least some of what got said," Del Bascom put in.

"Instead of speculating, let's get out of here before the lieutenant changes his mind," Saul said. "Mr. Wolfe wants to see us at eleven a.m. tomorrow."

"These morning meetings at the brownstone are getting to be standard procedure," I observed. "The Williamson boy is back at home safe. What needs to be talked about now?"

Saul shot me a look. "Archie, you don't know Nero Wolfe very well yet. Even though he's earned his money from Williamson, he's not going to be happy as long as the kidnappers are on the loose. It's a matter of pride. As far as he's concerned, the job is only half done."

"Then there's that little matter of Inspector Cramer," Durkin pointed out as we filed out of the precinct. "He still thinks we had something to do with that murder last night, and he'd like nothing better than to nail Wolfe—and us—with it. He figures the killing ties in somehow to the kidnapping."

Cather cut loose with a horse laugh. "For my money, Cramer's got the last part figured out right. That wasn't no coincidence."

"I think we all agree, Orrie," Panzer said as he fired up the rented Model A and we rumbled away from Precinct Fifty-Two, happy to be saying our good-byes to the Bronx and Lieutenant Knapp with a *K*.

Little did we know that before long, we all would be back in that borough.

# CHAPTER 14

We five already were sipping coffee in Wolfe's office the next morning when he came down from the plant rooms and got settled in the custom-made chair behind his desk. He nodded to each of us and rang for beer.

"That cretin lieutenant in the Bronx tried to bedevil me, but, of course, you all know that. I trust you were able to leave the police station immediately after my telephone conversation with him," Wolfe said.

"Very quickly," Saul Panzer said. "Something you told him seemed to upset the officer."

"No doubt," Wolfe replied, the folds of his cheeks pulling away from the corners of his mouth in what I later learned was his version of a smile. "Mr. Williamson telephoned me minutes after his son had been freed. I told Lieutenant Knapp that the hotel executive contemplated writing a letter to one or more daily newspapers praising our efforts in getting his son released and questioning whether the New York Police Department could have done as well."

"Think Williamson really will go ahead with that letter?" I asked.

"I confess the suggestion for such an epistle was mine, although when I broached the possibility, Mr. Williamson said he would consider it, so I was not indulging in total fabrication with the lieutenant," Wolfe said. "Now to business. First, something for each of you." He picked up a stack of envelopes and passed them to Panzer, who distributed them. I opened mine and pulled out a check, drawn on Wolfe's account, for $500. Delighted, and figuring mine was rightly the smallest amount of the five, I was hardly surprised to see wide grins on the faces of the others.

"Mr. Williamson will be here later to dine with me, at which time I plan to press him to let us continue the investigation," Wolfe said, interlacing his hands over his middle mound. "As I had feared, he seems content to close the books on the matter, now that his son is safely home. I will not, of course, expect any further remuneration from him, as he already has been most generous. But I am going to request continued access to his household staff because I feel the solution both to the kidnapping and the Bronx murder lies close to the Williamson home. Here is my question to all of you: Considering the sums you just received, would you be willing to consider those amounts payment in advance for additional work on the case? If not, I fully understand."

"I can't speak for the others," Saul Panzer said, waving his envelope, "but this is more dough than I've made in the last eight months combined. Mark me down as still being on board."

"Me, too," Del Bascom seconded. "I hate to see a job left unfinished."

Fred Durkin nodded his agreement. "Count me in. Like with Saul, this check is a godsend. It's going to make me a hero to my wife, and that's hard to do."

"I'm game," Orrie Cather said. "What the hell, I got nothing else cooking."

"I'll make it unanimous," I chimed in. "Besides, I work for Del, and if he's all tied up here, there's nothing else for me back at the office. And on top of that, I want to see how all this plays out."

"Satisfactory," Wolfe said. "I will inform Saul as to our next step, and he will relay that information to each of you. Two more things: Point number one, I was mildly disturbed to learn from Mr. Williamson that gunfire had broken out last night. Did you initiate that, Orrie?"

Cather nodded, wearing a chagrined expression. "Yeah, I did, but by that time the kid was safe with his father over by the fence, and the kidnappers were about to take off. I just hated to see those bastards get away clean. I think I clipped one of 'em, although he didn't go down and climbed into the car. Archie got off a couple of shots, too. They fired back, and Fred got nicked."

"It was nothin', barely a scratch," Durkin muttered.

"The shots disturbed Mr. Williamson, although they were of little importance to him compared to his getting Tommie back. By the way, the boy appears to be unharmed and in good health," Wolfe said. "Point number two, because none of you mentioned it, am I correct in assuming that the one kidnapper you saw, however briefly, bore no resemblance to anyone in the Williamsons' employ?"

"Correct by me," Panzer said. "This guy was taller—and thinner— than any of the men: the butler; Bell, the chauffeur; Carstens, the gardener; and Simons, the stableman. Anybody else see it differently?"

"Not me," Durkin said. "The guy was skinny as a rail, seemed like he was underfed."

"Unlike you," Cather gibed as we all broke into laughter.

"Gentlemen, we will gather again soon," Wolfe said, rising. That was our clue to leave, and we did.

Bascom and I took a taxi back to his office, talking about the case the whole way. "It's the damnedest business I've ever been involved in, Archie," he said, firing up a cigar and rolling down the cab's back window. "Williamson's got his boy back, which is the most important thing by far. But he doesn't seem the least bit bothered by losing all that money."

"Well, he is said to be one of the richest men in New York, right?" I posed. "The ransom probably just put a small dent in his fat wallet."

"Maybe, but still, I think he'd want to get all that cabbage back. Pride and all. Plus, it's possible that whoever took Tommie also plugged that grifter two nights ago on the street, which means that our Mr. Burke Williamson just might have a killer on his payroll."

"Be interesting to find out what the kid knows."

"That is, if Williamson will ever allow him to talk to anybody," Bascom huffed.

"Or if Williamson will even let us talk to his staff again," I said. "Loyalty is a fine thing, but it can be carried too far."

Bascom took out a fin and slapped it down on his knee with a flourish. "Five says one of his employees is behind all this."

"No bet," I laughed, "unless you give me odds—very long odds."

There was no reason for me to hang around the Bascom Detective Agency office, given that we had no business at present other than the Williamson case, so I left Del there with his paperwork and his cheap stogies and ambled down to my local bank to deposit the bulk of Wolfe's check, taking out enough to make me feel really flush for the first time since arriving in New York.

My next move, naturally enough, was to celebrate my new prosperity with a real dinner. For weeks, I had been walking by a restaurant in the East Sixties that seemed beyond my reach: starched linens, flowers on every table, polished silverware, crystal glasses, and elegant-looking customers who did not seem to be aware that we were in the midst of a depression.

I pushed in through a glass-and-chromium revolving door and got greeted by a mustachioed swell at a podium wearing a tuxedo, a carnation, and a smirk. "Yes, sir, may I help you?" He cleared his throat, giving me a once-over that suggested I should consider finding a new tailor.

When I told him I was there for dinner and didn't have a reservation, he cleared his throat again, studied his seating chart, and snapped his fingers, which brought a white-aproned waiter running over. "Show this gentleman to table nineteen," the maître d' said, turning away to warmly greet a well-dressed couple, obviously regular patrons, who had just entered.

Table nineteen was tucked into a corner at the back of the mahogany-paneled dining room not far from the swinging doors to the kitchen. The waiter handed me a menu and said he would return shortly for my order. He did, and he was clearly surprised when I ordered the most expensive steak on the menu, along with all the trimmings.

Alone but not lonely at a table for two, I had what was probably the best meal of my life, topped off by apple pie à la mode. The coffee, however, did not rank with the brew served at Mort's diner a few blocks away, or by Fritz at Wolfe's house.

"Nice to meet you," I told the mustache at the front desk on my way out. "Grub's not bad here. I might even consider coming back again one of these days for another steak." I didn't wait to see his expression.

The next morning, I got to Bascom's office a few minutes after nine to find him at his desk, hunched over the *Gazette* crossword puzzle. "These damned things," he muttered. "They drive me crazy, but I keep coming back to them. Guess I'm just a glutton for punishment—Oh, Nero Wolfe called a few minutes ago. He wants to see us at eleven."

"Another meeting of the whole crew, eh?"

"Not this time. Just the two of us."

"Huh! What's it all about?"

"Beats me, but after the payday we got yesterday, when Wolfe calls, I jump. I hope he treated you okay, too," Bascom said.

"No complaints here. I spent a small chunk of it on my stomach last night."

"And why not? Me, I took the wife to dinner myself, at her favorite Italian joint just down the block from where we live. They even slipped us some red wine, called it grape juice. First time we been out to eat in months. It was a treat."

"Well, since we've already been paid for this job, I hope we don't have to spend too much time working it off."

"Wolfe has always been a square shooter with me," Bascom said, taking a puff of his cigar. "He's not looking to chisel us. If we end up doing a lot more, he'll make it worth our while, I can tell you that."

In what now seemed to be a daily routine, we sat in Wolfe's office at eleven with coffee.

He walked in, placed orchids in a vase on the desk, and sat, dipping his chin to each of us. "Thank you for coming," he said. "As you know, Mr. Williamson dined with me last night. He shared two items of interest. First, he received a telephone call from Inspector Cramer of Homicide, who pressed him on a possible connection between his son's kidnapping and the death of that man, Barney Haskell, on a Bronx street.

"According to Mr. Williamson, the inspector seemed most anxious to implicate me, and by extension my agents, in the killing. To his credit, Mr. Williamson dismissed the idea and told the inspector that he and he alone went to the Bronx that night, only to find Haskell lying dead on the sidewalk. He apologized for not calling the police, but said he was distraught at failing to get his son back."

"Didn't Cramer chew him out for not going to the police in the first place?" Bascom asked.

"Of course," Wolfe said, "but Mr. Williamson insisted that he had done the right thing by coming to us. And when Cramer pointed out that he should not have paid a ransom, his response was 'I have my son back safely, don't I? End of discussion.'"

"You mentioned two items of interest," I prompted.

Wolfe dipped his head slightly. "Yes. The family chauffeur, Charles Bell, abruptly quit, leaving only a brief note."

"Pretty suspicious, I'd say," Bascom observed.

"Mr. Williamson told me Bell had complained that others on the staff suspected him of being involved in the kidnapping."

"Did somebody come right out and make an accusation?"

"Apparently, it was considerably more subtle than that," Wolfe said. "Furtive looks, conversations suddenly ceasing when Mr. Bell walked into a room. So the Williamsons are in need of a chauffeur, which is why I asked you here."

We both must have looked puzzled, because Wolfe quickly went on. "Mr. Bascom, would it be an imposition to spare Mr. Goodwin for a few days, possibly longer?"

Del lifted his shoulders and let them drop. "Archie's been a breath of fresh air in our little office, a real bulldog, Mr. Wolfe, but I gotta be honest. There's not a lot of business floating around town these days, so if you've got an assignment for him, I'm not about to stand in the way. A dollar's a dollar."

Wolfe readjusted his bulk and drank beer. "When Mr. Williamson was here and told me of the unexpected departure of his chauffeur, I suggested he hire Mr. Goodwin, on a temporary basis, of course—as a combination chauffeur and bodyguard for the boy. He had been impressed with Mr. Goodwin's resourcefulness under pressure that first night in the Bronx, and he was amenable to my suggestion."

"But nobody thought to ask Mr. Goodwin whether he wanted to take the job," I growled.

"A salient point," Wolfe conceded. "However, you appear to relish a challenge, so it seemed natural to suggest you."

"Don't patronize me, Mr. Wolfe," I said. "I may not be able to vote yet, but I am able to detect appeals to my vanity, such as it is."

"Well said!" Wolfe responded with raised eyebrows. "This is the first time I have been accused of patronizing anyone, and I assure you such was not my intent. If the job does not appeal to you, so be it."

"I didn't say that. I might be open to the idea, but I would like to know what you think would be accomplished by my being there as chauffeur and bodyguard."

"A fair question. I remain convinced that the key to the kidnapping of the boy and the murder of Barney Haskell lies at the Williamson estate."

"What about the chauffeur, Charles Bell?" I asked. "As Del says, his disappearance is suspicious, damned suspicious. Seems to me there's your man."

"Possibly," Wolfe said, leaning back and placing his hands palms down on the desk. "Mr. Bascom and the others will be pursuing that avenue."

"There's one other thing, of course," I said. "Several of these people on the household staff already have met me, and they sure as hell will tell the others who I am. I'll be seen as a spy in their midst."

"Not necessarily," Wolfe responded. "Mr. Williamson will present you to the staff as the young man who has the necessary attributes to protect young Tommie.'

"Sounds a little on the flimsy side," I said.

Wolfe considered me. "Would I be guilty of patronizing you if I said I believe you can pull it off?" he asked.

"I guess not. But as far as the chauffeur part of the job goes, you should know that I am no expert on automobiles. The closest I ever came to being a mechanic was when I used to change the sparkplugs on my father's old truck."

"It is my understanding that Mr. Bell is not an auto mechanic, either," Wolfe said. "All the work on the Williamson machines is done at a garage in the town near the estate."

"Okay, let's say for the sake of argument that I take the job. What is it that you expect me to learn? Chances are nobody's going to open up to me."

"Not right away," Wolfe conceded, "but you may be able to integrate yourself into the life of the estate faster than you think. One of your responsibilities will be to drive Tommie to and from school, and assuming that you and he develop a rapport, that friendship likely will find favor with other members of the staff who are devoted to the boy. Bear in mind also that Mr. Bell was not universally admired by his coworkers, so you may be seen as a great improvement."

"Speaking of Tommie, do you expect me to pump him about the details of his abduction?" I asked.

"Not overtly. But specifics of the ordeal may come out little by little during your trips to and from the school. Have you had any experience talking to small boys?"

"Some. I've got two nephews, ages six and ten, back in Ohio, and I've always gotten along pretty well with them. They seem to think that I'm funny—as in ha-ha, not peculiar."

"Perhaps young Master Williamson will find you amusing as well," Wolfe said. "While you are piloting the Williamson automobiles and getting to know the staff, an effort will be made at this end to locate Mr. Bell, who apparently took all his clothing and personal effects when he made his hurried departure."

"Am I expected to live in the chauffeur's quarters on the estate?"

"Yes, to help establish the illusion of semipermanence for you in this role."

"Swell. Being in an apartment tucked away above a garage on Long Island is a far cry from the bright lights and excitement of Manhattan," I complained.

"Excitement comes in many guises," Wolfe said. "And who knows, you just may develop an affinity for the country life."

"Not likely. I had enough of the country growing up in southern Ohio to last a lifetime."

# CHAPTER 15

The next morning, Saul Panzer drove me out to the Williamson mansion in Wolfe's Heron. "As I said before, you've got yourself an interesting task here, Archie," he remarked as we entered the grounds in a blowing rainstorm and wheeled around the big house to the rear.

"I'm not sure how you define 'interesting,' but I hope it doesn't equal 'boring,'" I said. "I'd rather be with you guys hunting for Charles Bell. For my money, he's the key to this whole business."

"Maybe, although Mr. Wolfe seems to feel it's important to have you out here, which makes me think that at least part of the puzzle lies with one or more of the Williamson staff—other than Mr. Bell."

"I will keep an eagle eye on all of 'em. Who knows, I may become smitten with one of the female members of this crew and we run away together to build a new life on an island in the South Seas."

"Have you been reading those dime detective magazines of yours again?" Panzer asked.

"No, it's just the romantic in me, bursting to find expression."

"Geez, I hope it isn't catching. Me, all I want out of life is my quiet little flat on East Thirty-Eighth Street with its piano, shelves of good books, Cuban cigars, champagne chilling in the icebox, and the occasional poker game to keep my mind sharp and my wallet full of Lincolns and Hamiltons and, if I'm especially lucky, Jacksons."

"Seems like little enough to ask," I said.

"Precisely my sentiments, Archie. Oh, I almost forgot—you will need this in your new role," he said, handing me a card that turned out to be a New York State chauffeur's license.

"Where did this come from? Don't I need to take some sort of test? And who got my address?"

"Isn't the address correct?" Panzer asked.

"Yeah, but ..."

"Archie, don't ask questions. You have just seen the power of Burke Williamson in action. He took care of everything."

"Sure seems like it," I replied, sliding the license into my billfold.

"Well, good luck with your assignment," Panzer said as I hauled my suitcase out of the backseat and headed for the house. "Have fun in the world of the very rich."

A few minutes later, I sat with Burke Williamson in his study. "I will introduce you to the staff just before lunch," he said. "Of course, you already have met several of them, and almost everyone will no doubt be somewhat suspicious of you. I will explain that you are here in the combination role of chauffeur and bodyguard for my son, and that your work as a private detective has trained you well for the latter role."

"How are members of your household reacting to Mr. Bell's disappearance?"

"I think it is fair to say they all are shocked in various degrees. Coming so quickly after Tommie's kidnapping, this has further unnerved everyone here, as you can imagine."

"Do you have any explanation for his disappearance?"

"As I told Mr. Wolfe, Charles believed that others on the staff—he would not say who—felt he had something to do with what happened to Tommie. I told him that was total rot, but he was not consoled by my support. He apparently left Monday afternoon after driving Tommie back here from school. He took everything of his and left a brief note saying he would inform us of his new address, where we could forward any mail he received here."

"How did he leave?"

"He had an auto of his own, a Plymouth coupe, which he kept in the garage here. We have room for five machines, and I have three of them myself, so there was plenty of space."

Williamson leaned back at his desk. "Young Mr. Goodwin, I must be honest with you. Having you come here was not my idea, it was Nero Wolfe's. He insists—and I continue to strongly disagree—that someone in my employ helped engineer the kidnapping. I yielded to him for two reasons: first, I am in his incalculable debt for bringing my son back; second, I was impressed with how you handled yourself under pressure in the Bronx both nights. You appear to be mature well beyond your years. If Wolfe had suggested anyone other than you for this role, I very well might have said no."

"Thank you for the vote of confidence, sir."

"Do not be too quick to thank me. I remain concerned about your presence here, which has the potential to cause further unrest among an already unnerved staff. Doubtless, they—or at least some of them—are going to view you as a Caleb in their midst."

"A Caleb?"

"A biblical reference. He was a spy in the Old Testament."

"Guess I must have stayed home from Sunday school that day. Mr. Williamson, I will go out of my way to avoid seeming like a detective."

"I appreciate that. Now let's go over to the garage. I will show you the vehicles you'll be driving and also your living quarters. You look to be about Charles Bell's build, so his uniforms should fit you. If not, you can wear a business suit until we get them altered."

As it turned out, Bell's uniforms were a near-perfect fit, although looking in a mirror in what was about to become my new home, I felt more than a little foolish in a black monkey suit and black beaked cap. I would have been right at home driving a hearse for a mortuary.

"That will do just fine," Williamson said, nodding his approval. "Now we will go down to the kitchen and I'll introduce you. They should be gathering for lunch."

As we entered the kitchen, conversations stopped in midsentence and all eyes bore in on me. "Excuse my barging in," Williamson said, "but I would like you to meet Mr. Archie Goodwin, who will be taking over the chauffeur's duties for the time being and also serving as Tommie's bodyguard. I believe one or more of you may have met him when he was here earlier this week with the other detectives."

Williamson then proceeded to introduce each member of the staff. Mostly, I just got expressionless nods from them, although the portly cook, Mrs. Price, stepped forward, grinning. "You've picked a good day to start, lad," she said. "Given it is so blustery and rainy outside, I have decided to prepare my lamb stew for lunch. Everybody here loves it."

"I'm sure I will, too. It has always been a favorite of mine," I said, causing her grin to widen and her face to flush.

We went to a long, sturdy wooden table at one end of the large basement kitchen. I waited until the others were seated, figuring they each had their reserved spot. I then parked myself in the last open chair, which put me between the housekeeper, Emily Stratton, and the gardener, Lloyd Carstens, and directly across from Sylvia Moore, the only member of the staff I had previously met. She nodded to me, showing the hint of a smile. I gave her a full-fledged grin in return, then turned to Carstens, as the housekeeper already was talking with the butler, Waverly, on her right.

"The grounds here are really beautiful," I told Carstens. "They seem more like a park than a yard."

He nodded, poker-faced. "Bigger'n any so-called yard you'd be likely to find. Eight acres in all, which takes a powerful lot of tending to."

"I'm sure it does. Do you enjoy your work?"

Another nod. "Yep, and we got us a mite longer growing season than up Maine way, where I hail from."

Just then, Emily Stratton made a noise in her throat to get my attention and passed me a steaming platter of lamb stew. I thanked her and received a thin-lipped nod for my trouble. She didn't seem like one who smiled much.

It was becoming clear that there would be very little animated chatting, at least in my immediate area. In fact, there wasn't much talk at all during that lunch. Whether or not it had to do with my presence, I couldn't say, but I was somewhat disappointed, because I had expected to be questioned on my knowledge of automobiles and was ready with all kinds of answers.

One thing that did not disappoint me, however, was Mrs. Price's lamb stew, of which I had two helpings. During the meal, I made a couple of halfhearted attempts at conversation with both Carstens and Miss Stratton, both of which died for lack of participation on their behalf.

After lunch, I reported to Williamson's study, as he had requested. He would ride with me to pick up Tommie from school, as I did not know the way. "How did lunch go?" he asked.

"All in all, they seem like a pretty quiet bunch."

"I couldn't say, as I have never intruded on the staff's meals," he said, "but perhaps they are simply getting used to your presence. However, I warned you they would be suspicious of you."

"That may well be, and I'll try my best to allay that suspicion," I told him as we went to the garage and climbed into the Pierce-Arrow, with me behind the wheel. "When you get out to the road, take a left," Williamson said. The auto handled beautifully, nothing like my father's rickety old truck.

"I have told Tommie that he would be getting a new driver this afternoon," his father said.

"How did he take the news?"

"Oh, he seemed fine with it. He's a pretty stoic boy on the whole, and I don't think he ever felt strongly one way or the other about Charles Bell."

"More important, how has he been since … well, since he's been back?"

"Surprisingly good. His mother and I were terribly worried about the emotional damage that might have been done, but so far we've seen no signs whatever of any, shall we say … scarring?"

"Has he talked much about what happened?"

"A little. He was blindfolded and bundled into that food purveyor's truck—that phony food purveyor, I should say—and got taken someplace in New York City, he couldn't tell for sure, probably the Bronx, given that's where we were told to go with the money both nights. It was an upstairs flat, he said, second or third floor. He was carried up, so he couldn't be sure. And all the window shades in the place were pulled down, so he was never able to see out."

"What about the kidnappers?"

"There were two men," Williamson said as he gave me directions to turn right onto a street that ran along some railroad tracks. "They both wore dark glasses the whole time that Tommie was without a blindfold. And to answer your next question, neither of them resembled anyone in my employ—and that includes the man you are replacing."

"Was Tommie treated well?" I asked.

"Absolutely. He was well fed and never harmed in any way. He was given fresh pajamas, and his clothes were laundered. Turn left here, it's just another block."

The MeadesGate Academy stood well back from the road, a respectable-looking two-story brick building with white shutters and a slate roof. Williamson directed me along a curving, finely graveled lane that wrapped around the structure to a parking lot in the back, where several other automobiles idled, all apparently waiting for students. Two of the vehicles, I noted, were Rolls-Royces, another an exotic-looking vehicle that I guessed had been made on the European continent. Among the other machines, I also spotted a Duesenberg, a Cadillac, two Packards, a Lincoln, and a Graham Paige phaeton.

"You could hold a chauffeurs' convention here every afternoon," I observed.

"Yes, and I would bet that several of them are armed."

"Count me as one," I said, patting my left shoulder.

Williamson shot me a look. "Is that really necessary?"

"You don't want a second surprise where your son is concerned, do you? After all, I am acting as a bodyguard as well as operating this fine machine."

He started to reply and then waved from the open window as the students, all boys and identically dressed in dark blazers, ties, shorts, and kneesocks, poured out of the school building. A blondish lad waved back, donning his cap and running toward the automobile.

"Hi, Dad!" he said, hugging his father, who had climbed out of the vehicle.

"Tommie, meet Mr. Goodwin. He will be driving you to and from the school for a while. Why don't you ride up front with him?" Williamson said, sliding into the backseat.

"Nice to meet you, Mr. Goodwin," the boy said, holding out a hand. I pumped it.

"Good to meet you, too, Tommie. Did your day go well?"

"I guess so," he said. "We had a fire drill, and everybody had to march outside in single file."

"I used to have those once in a while when I was in school."

"That must have been a long time ago."

"Tommie!" his father put in. "Mr. Goodwin isn't all that old, you know."

I laughed. "Everything is relative. I was surprised when I learned that my own father wasn't alive when Lincoln was president."

That drew a laugh from the boy, so we seemed to be off to a good start. Back at the mansion, Williamson hustled his son off to see Sylvia Moore, who as I learned went over his homework with him for at least an hour every afternoon.

"Tommie likes you," his father said. "But hear me, Goodwin, and hear me well: I do not want you questioning my son about what he has been through. I am sure one of the reasons Nero Wolfe wanted you here was to pry information out of him, but I will not have it, which I also told Wolfe. Do I make myself clear?"

"Absolutely," I said, putting the car on the garage and going upstairs to unpack and get settled in.

The chauffeur's second-floor quarters were plenty spacious—a large bedroom with windows overlooking the expansive grounds in the back, and two watercolor paintings of snowcapped mountains; a sitting room even bigger than the bedroom with windows, a sofa, two chairs, more watercolors—these of waterfalls—and a slick mahogany floor-model radio that looked new; and a yellow-tiled bathroom with both a tub and a shower. I guessed there probably was more space here than any of the others on the staff had in their quarters upstairs in the mansion proper, which may have contributed to the hostility some members of the household felt toward the recently and suddenly departed Charles Bell. And to top it off, he had *two* telephones, one upstairs and the other in the garage, although in this case, both were on the same outside line.

I gave the place the once-over, and not lightly. It seemed clean and dust-free, with nothing left that I could find to indicate that Bell had spent three years on the premises. Other than his uniforms, the closets and bureau drawers were cleaner than a surgeon's scalpel just before an operation, and the bookcases in the sitting room likewise contained nothing except an empty ceramic vase and a tin ashtray that had been filched from a Chinese restaurant in Trenton, New Jersey. I hung up my suit, sport coat, and slacks, and filled three drawers with the rest of my clothes, including a stack of dress shirts.

If I had to spend time out here in the distant provinces, at least I had nothing to complain about regarding the quality of the room and board. I contemplated taking an exploratory stroll around the property but quickly scotched the plan, which would have been interpreted—quite correctly—as detective-style snooping by a staff already suspicious of the reason for my presence in their midst.

I lay on the bed and looked at the ceiling, considering the situation. I was expected to be alert but not overly inquisitive when in the presence of other members of the staff, friendly with Tommie but not openly curious about his recent ordeal, and respectful toward the Williamsons without being a toady.

Okay, I could handle these challenges. But whether my stay in this palatial retreat would result in any concrete accomplishments in the eyes of Nero Wolfe was quite another matter.

# CHAPTER 16

At dinner that evening, conversation once again was at a minimum. The butler, Waverly, led us in a prayer of thanks that Tommie had been returned safely to his parents. Sylvia Moore volunteered that the boy seemed to be his old cheerful self during their late afternoon homework session. Emily Stratton added that Mrs. Williamson "has the color back in her cheeks and has regained her strength. I feared for our lady's health. That dear one is none too strong to begin with, as all of you know," she pronounced gravely. I wanted to question that last statement, given that Mrs. Williamson was an accomplished rider who seemed to be very fit, but I held my tongue.

The dinner contingent was smaller than at lunch, what with Carstens and Simons having gone to their homes. Mary Trent, the young maid, said nothing during the meal, mostly nodding at the brief pronouncements of the others. And Mrs. Price, whose pot roast was excellent, seemed reserved, perhaps because no one complimented her cooking, although they all cleaned their plates. I got no questions about my first day on the job and I volunteered nothing.

Back in my comfortable quarters, I telephoned Nero Wolfe at nine o'clock, our prearranged time. "There is not a great deal to report," I told him, "although I am slowly, make that very slowly, getting to know the closemouthed staff of this stately establishment. You will not be surprised to learn that I am viewed with a healthy dose of suspicion. I also met Tommie today. I think we are going to hit it off, although I'll take it slowly. Williamson has warned me not to quiz the boy about the details of his captivity."

"Nonetheless, I suspect that in the days ahead, you may very well learn some specifics of that event from him."

"Such is my plan. Do you have any further instructions?"

"Continue to proceed with restraint. Haste is the tool of the fool."

"That's very good. Who said it?"

"I did."

"Oh. Well, I will by all means avoid haste, and will telephone you at the same time tomorrow. Don't be surprised if my report is short again. Is anything going on with the investigation at that end?"

"No, unless Saul and the others have made a discovery this evening that I am not yet aware of. Good night."

Thursday morning, I got down to the kitchen before any of the others and had coffee with Mrs. Price. "My, but you are the early bird," she said. "We usually eat around eight. If you'd like, I can fix you some eggs. I'm always here by six thirty myself."

"I don't want to upset your routine. I'm just glad to have this excellent coffee."

"You are not upsetting my routine the least bit, laddie. I'm happy to have someone here who appreciates my efforts. I noticed how much you put away at lunch and dinner yesterday."

"I guess I'm just a growing boy."

"Well, I'll get the bacon and scrambled eggs started for the others, and you'll have the first serving, before the rest of them even arrive, if you'd like."

"Thanks. Did my predecessor have a good appetite?"

"Mr. Bell? Oh, it was all right, I suppose," she said without enthusiasm.

"Do I take it that you weren't fond of him?"

Mrs. Price shrugged. "I don't mean to speak harshly now that he's left, but he was a strange fellow who seemed to look down on the rest of us as though he didn't really belong in service. To me, service is a fine calling, something that one should always be proud of."

"Any thoughts on where he's gone?"

"No, although I don't like the thoughts I'm thinking."

"Oh?"

She seemed to be struggling with herself over whether to say more. She turned her back to me and leaned over the stove, working.

"I'm sorry, I didn't mean to be nosy. It's a bad habit of mine."

"Don't you worry any, laddie," she said, turning back and putting a chubby hand on my shoulder. "You weren't being nosy, just curious, which is perfectly natural, given that you've taken the man's place. It's just hard for me to say what has been on my mind."

"I won't ask."

"But maybe it will help me to get it off my chest," she said, putting a plate of bacon and eggs down at my place and sitting down at the table across from me. "I cannot help but think that somehow, Charles was … was involved with what happened to dear little Tommie." She put her head down and looked at her hands in her lap. "I know that sounds like a terrible thing to say, but why would he run away like that, Mr. …"

"Archie, just Archie."

"Why would he run away, Archie? He was not what I would call an overly friendly individual, but it seemed to me that the man was more or less satisfied with his position here."

"Do you think that perhaps he felt that others on the staff had the same suspicion you do?"

She wrung her hands. "All I can say is that when that poor boy was missing, everyone was on edge, nervous and cranky and snapping at one another, and it's possible some of them might have looked at Charles funny. I hope I didn't. I do remember that the second day Tommie was gone, he—Charles, that is—got very angry at Mr. Simons, saying something like 'I know exactly what you're thinking, damn it. I can read your mind!'"

"Had Simons said something to Bell?"

"I don't think so, but I'm not sure about that, and—" She stopped in midsentence as Waverly stepped into the kitchen.

"Good morning, Mrs. Price; good morning, Mr. Goodwin," the butler said. "Am I interrupting anything?"

"Not at all," I replied with a grin. "In fact, I was just complimenting Mrs. Price on her scrambled eggs. Best I've ever had."

"I always use extra butter and freshly ground pepper," she said. "That's really what sets them apart."

"Well, I look forward to having them again many times," I told her, rising. "Now I'm off to get the Pierce-Arrow ready for Tommie's trip to school." I could feel Waverly's eyes on me as I went out.

I had the automobile ready just outside the garage when Tommie came running over with his schoolbooks. I held the front passenger open for him, but he said, "I always sit in the backseat."

"But wouldn't you rather be up here?"

He bit his lip and looked uncertain. "I'm supposed to sit in the back."

"When we picked you up from school yesterday, your father had you sit up front with me."

"I guess that was special," he said.

"Maybe it was, although I have an idea. What if you climb into the backseat now in case anyone's watching, then we'll drive a block down the road and stop so you can move up front."

"I'd like that!"

So it was that Tommie rode beside me as we headed for the school. "Do any of your classmates ride in the front seat?" I asked him.

"Only Billy Reynolds. They've got a swell Duesenberg."

"If you want, I can stop down the road from the school and you can get into the back again."

"No, I want to stay up here. They don't care at the school. Where do you come from, Mr. Goodwin?"

"Call me Archie, everybody else does. I grew up in Ohio. Do you know where that is?"

"We study the different states in our geography class. I remember that in Ohio, Toledo makes glass, Cleveland makes steel, Akron makes tires, and Cincinnati makes soap."

"You know a lot more about my state than I do. I come from way down in the southern end near the Ohio River, a small town. The only one of those cities I've ever been in is Cleveland, and the only reason I went up there was to get the train when I came to New York."

"I'd like to ride a train sometime."

"I'm sure you will."

"Did you ever play football … Archie?"

"Yeah, in high school. I was a halfback, and I even scored a touchdown once, against Portsmouth, our big rivals. Closest I ever came to being a hero. Do you play football at MeadesGate, Tommie?"

"No, only the older boys do. The school has a team that plays against some other schools. But I did get a football for my birthday."

"Do you play catch with it?"

"Sometimes with my dad, but not very often. He's at work an awful lot of the time, or traveling around to his hotels. He's been everywhere in the world."

"I'll tell you what. Day after tomorrow is Saturday. If you don't have a lot of homework to do, we could toss the football around in the yard."

"That would be fun. I'm all caught up on my homework, and besides, I think Miss Moore is going away for the weekend."

"It's a deal then. We'll throw the pigskin to each other."

Tommie wrinkled his nose. "The football is a pig's skin?"

"Not anymore. At one time, so the story goes, that's what the balls were made of, though."

"I am really glad they quit doing that," he said as we drove into the schoolyard and he hopped out of the car, running to join his classmates as they filed into the building under the watchful eyes of several teachers.

Saturday at nine, Tommie and I were out on the expansive back lawn of the Williamson estate throwing the football back and forth in the warm morning sunshine. He was better than I would have thought, given his slight frame. He caught almost all my wobbly passes and threw with surprising strength.

"Hey, you're really good at this," I told him. "Are you sure you haven't been practicing more than you told me?"

"Uh-uh. Like I said, my dad's pretty busy, and Mr. Bell never seemed like he was interested in sports. I even asked him once if he wanted to play catch with a baseball, and he said no, he didn't do things like that."

"Too bad for him, poor fellow. He's missed a lot of fun. What we're doing is good exercise, although my arm is going to feel it tomorrow. It's been a long time since I've flung a football around."

"But we can do it again, can't we?"

"Of course we can," I said. "And we can practice punting the ball, too. There's plenty of space here."

Just then, Lillian Williamson and Mark Simons came into sight, riding horses at a leisurely pace along the bridle path. "Hi, boys!" she said with a wave.

"Hi, Mom. Watch this pass," Tommie said, sending a perfect spiral in my direction, which I managed to catch on my fingertips.

"Nice," his mother said, grinning. "Don't wear Mr. Goodwin out now. We need him to drive your dad and me into the city tomorrow."

"Let's take a little breather," I said. We went up onto the terrace, and as we were sitting down, Mrs. Price came up from the kitchen with a pitcher and two glasses. "I saw the two of you playing ball, and I thought you could use some cold lemonade," she said. "It's very warm for October today."

"Thank you!" we said in unison as I pulled out a handkerchief and took a swipe at my damp brow. "This is living," I told Tommie, stretching my legs out and pouring lemonade into our glasses.

"Yeah! So next time, we can do kicking, okay? I'm not very good at that."

"You will get better with practice. It just takes time."

He smiled as he drank his lemonade, then his expression turned serious. "Did you know that I got kidnapped?"

"Yes, I did hear something about it," I said, realizing with relief but not surprise that he hadn't recognized me that night outside the Bronx Zoo.

"My mom and dad don't want me to talk about it. It was sort of scary."

"I'm sure that it must have been."

"I was out on the grass—right over there," he said, pointing at a spot near the gravel driveway that wrapped around the house and led to the garage. "I was collecting different kinds of leaves for school, and Miss Moore was helping me. She got a telephone call and went inside, and right then a truck drove up. A man got out and said he wanted to ask me something, so I went over to him, and he grabbed me and threw me in the back of the truck. Then he blindfolded me and tied me up and he and another man I hadn't seen drove off. I started to yell and one of them stuffed something in my mouth like a handkerchief."

"Did you get a good look at them?"

"Uh-uh. They both wore dark glasses all the time, even at night when I was in that bedroom at wherever it was that they took me. But I'm not supposed to be talking about it."

"I understand."

"They really weren't mean to me. They never hit me, and they fed me stuff like hot dogs and chili and Rice Krispies for breakfast."

"Did they say anything that would help you identify them?"

"My dad asked me that, too. I don't think so. They looked alike, so maybe they were brothers."

"Or did they look alike because they both wore dark glasses?"

"Maybe so. I tried to hear what they were saying at night when they thought I was asleep, but they talked very softly. I thought I heard a word that sounded like 'Barney' once." He looked down. "I shouldn't be talking about this."

"Whatever you think is best," I answered.

"I know they were on the telephone lots of times, but I couldn't hear much of what they said. I was in a bedroom, and the door was almost always closed."

"But they did let you go."

"My dad said that was because some detectives from New York helped out. The men in dark glasses drove me in a car at night and handcuffed me to a fence. My dad came with a suitcase that he says was filled with money and he gave it to them. Then some of these detectives and the kidnappers started shooting at each other, which was really scary. It was dark, so I don't know who all the people shooting were or if any of them got hurt."

"But the good news is that you were free."

"Yes, but I was really scared."

"That's nothing to be ashamed of. When they drove you in the car that night, how long did the ride take?"

"Mmm, not very long, maybe ten minutes, maybe a little longer."

"So you must have been kept somewhere close to the place where they handcuffed you to that fence?"

Tommie nodded soberly and went on to tell me how the police came and cut him loose. "That's when I found out we were next to the zoo that I've been at before," he said. "After the shooting, the animals all started roaring and growling."

"That's quite a story."

"Yeah. Don't tell my parents that I told you about it, all right?"

"It will be our secret. And we'll throw—and kick—the football around again, maybe one day next week, okay?"

"Sure," he said, grinning.

That night, I called Wolfe and reported my conversation with Tommie. "Now there is something you should know," he said.

"I'm all ears."

"A man answering to the description of your predecessor, Mr. Bell, has been found dead, shot."

"I'll be damned."

"No doubt. Do not share this information with anyone there, including the family. It may be instructive to observe their behavior until the news becomes public knowledge. And even then, be alert to everyone's reactions."

"My ears are open and my mouth is closed," I told him and was rewarded with a grunt just before the line went dead.

# CHAPTER 17

Our lunch gathering that Sunday was sparse, given that both Lloyd Carstens and Mark Simons had gone home for the rest of the weekend, as was their routine, and Sylvia Moore was staying with a maiden aunt in Philadelphia for the next few days. Per Mrs. Williamson's orders, I had driven Sylvia to the nearby railroad depot that morning so she could take a commuter local into Manhattan and change at Penn Station for a train to Philly.

"Are you very close to your aunt?" I asked Sylvia when we drove to the suburban station.

"Yes, I am. She is my mother's sister, and we are going to be talking a lot about whether my mother should move up from Virginia and live with her in Philadelphia. As I told you, Mom, who's a widow, has a serious heart condition, and it worries me that she's all alone in that big old house in Richmond where I grew up. But I know it's going to be hard to persuade her to leave the home she has lived in for almost forty years."

"Well, it sounds like a good solution. I hope that you and your aunt can talk her into it."

"Thanks. How are you getting along here?" Sylvia had then asked me. As with Tommie, I had strongly suggested she sit up front with me, and she liked the idea.

"Okay, although all in all, the household crew seems to be a pretty closemouthed bunch."

"Oh, they were exactly like that when I started, too," she said. "They're very suspicious of newcomers."

"Are you, too?"

She wrinkled her pretty nose. "I wouldn't say so. I tend to be on the quiet side, and some people take that to be standoffish. I hope you don't."

"No, I don't. I just assumed you're shy. You have to be relieved now that Tommie is back."

"Oh dear, yes, yes I am. This has been quite an ordeal for everyone. Well, you know that. Of course, you were one of the detectives who came and talked to all of us after the kidnapping."

"Yes, I was, but as you know, I'm here in a different capacity now—as chauffeur and, more important, as a bodyguard for Tommie."

"You seem very young to be a detective—and a bodyguard," she said.

"I've had more experience than you might expect, although when I was here before, I definitely was the junior member of the team."

"Well, from what little I know, you and those other investigators must have done your work well, getting Tommie back for us. But how does it happen that you're working here now? Were you looking for a job as a chauffeur or a bodyguard?"

"Not really. I was also with Saul Panzer when he interviewed Mr. Williamson, and I guess for some reason he liked the way I presented myself. I wasn't going out of my way to impress him. Anyway, when Charles Bell left the employ here, Mr. Williamson called one of the other detectives and asked if I would be interested in this job. I've been looking for work—you know how tough things have been since the crash—and I thought, 'Why not?' I have always been interested in automobiles, and here was a chance to drive some really swell ones, as well as look after Tommie. I'm not really sure he's in any danger now, but I think my presence makes his parents feel better."

"Do you think Tommie has been traumatized by what happened?" she asked. "I haven't sensed it."

"Neither have I. We seem to have gotten along very well."

"I would agree," Sylvia said with feeling. "I know he's delighted that you play football with him. I am awfully glad you're here."

"I'm glad that you're glad," I said as we pulled up at the little depot where she was to catch her train into the city. She squeezed my arm and thanked me warmly for the ride as she climbed out of the car. And if she knew anything about what had happened to Bell, it wasn't apparent to me in her behavior.

Back to Sunday's lunch. The five of us sat at our usual places, leaving empty the seats of those absent. Heaven forbid anyone should change chairs. Waverly led us in a brief prayer, and we started in on Mrs. Price's ham and cheese sandwiches and German potato salad.

"A reminder, Mr. Goodwin, that no meal will be served here tonight," the cook said. "Sunday evenings, anyone is welcome to come down and fix something for themselves, as long as they put everything back and clean up after they are finished. I like my kitchen neat and tidy." Miss Stratton rolled her eyes, suggesting that she had heard those words before.

"Thank you, Mrs. Price, but I will be in the city at dinnertime," I said. "I'm driving Mr. and Mrs. Williamson into Manhattan for a concert at Carnegie Hall, and I will be bringing them back as well."

"That's right," the usually silent Mary Trent said, nodding earnestly. "Because Miss Moore is away, I'll be looking after Master Tommie tonight."

"And you are not under any circumstances to let him out of your sight," Waverly admonished. "I will be present all evening if there are any problems."

"I shouldn't think there would be any problems, Mr. Waverly," the girl said, biting her lower lip. "I would never let anything happen to Tommie myself."

The butler sniffed. "No? Well, we hardly thought there were going to be any problems the other morning, now, did we, my girl? And just look at what happened then."

On that sobering note, we all went back to eating. I had not forgotten Nero Wolfe's directive to look for signs of any awareness that Charles Bell had been killed, but if any of the people around the table knew about it, they gave no indication. I already had read all three Sunday newspapers delivered to the house, and none of them had any mention of the event.

As the others filed out of the kitchen after lunch, Mrs. Price put an arm on my shoulder. "Because you are going to be in New York until late tonight, laddie, I will be happy to pack a basket of food for you," she said. I thanked her for her kindness but said I had already made plans to have dinner with friends while the Williamsons were at the concert.

Burke Williamson had told me earlier that he and his wife wanted to ride into the city in the Packard, so I spent a half hour that afternoon running a soft cloth over its sleek burgundy surface. I was in full uniform, cap included, when they stepped out of the front entrance and down the stairs, he in a dinner jacket and his wife in a long beige evening dress.

"Ah, this old bus looks wonderful, Goodwin; did you wax it?"

"No, sir, I just took a cheesecloth to it and gave it a gentle once-over. The finish is so good, that was all that was needed," I said as I held the door for them to climb into the back.

"How are things downstairs now?" Williamson asked once we were under way. "Has everything returned to normal after the, well … the excitement we've had the last few days?"

"Yes, I would say so, sir, although I'm so new that I don't know definitely what constitutes normal among the staff."

"Of course, good point. On top of everything else, I was concerned that Bell's sudden departure might be upsetting to the others."

"Now, Burke, please try to forget all that for a while," Lillian Williamson said, putting her gloved hand on his arm. "We are out for a night in the city, and we should concentrate on enjoying ourselves. Let's clear our minds of everything but the music of Mr. Brahms and Mr. Tchaikovsky, which we will be hearing in a short while. Now just settle back."

I had planned the route into New York on one of the maps Bell had kept in the garage, and once I got to Manhattan, I had those streets down pat, too. I let the couple off in front of Carnegie Hall a half hour before their concert was to begin. "We'll see you back here at ten," Williamson said. I pulled away from the welter of taxis and ritzy autos that jammed Seventh Avenue around the concert hall and headed for the West Side.

Despite what I had told Mrs. Price, I did not have dinner plans, although I did intend to pay a visit to Nero Wolfe. I eased the Packard to the curb in front of the brownstone on West Thirty-Fifth Street and climbed the steps to the door.

Fritz answered my ring, giving me and my uniform a questioning look. "I know I didn't call ahead for an appointment, but I wonder if Mr. Wolfe could see me for a few minutes?"

"Let me ask," he said, easing the door closed. He returned in less than a minute. "Mr. Wolfe will see you. Please come in."

Wolfe was seated at his desk with beer and a book. "Sorry to barge in unannounced, but I happened to be in the city tonight, driving my employers to hear some music," I told him. "I would like to get caught up on what's been happening."

He put his book down and considered me. "You already know about the death of Charles Bell, of course."

"I know he was killed because you told me. What about the circumstances? What do we know?"

"Sit down, please. Would you like something to drink? Coffee? Beer?"

"Nothing, thanks."

"How about some dinner? Fritz made cassoulet de Castelnaudary, and there is enough remaining that he can prepare and heat a plate for you."

"I've already eaten," I lied, unsure as to what kind of grub this was.

He adjusted his bulk and scowled. "Very well. You asked about circumstances. Here they are: I received a telephone call yesterday afternoon from a very agitated Inspector Cramer informing me of a death. A man's body was found Friday night in a gangway between two buildings in the Bronx. He had been shot three times, and he had no identification on his person.

"The inspector, amid his sputtering, suggested I was somehow involved in this death, especially because it occurred not far from the shooting of Mr. Haskell, another event he suspects I was a party to."

"What makes you think the body was Bell's?"

"I surmised it but needed verification, which I have now received."

"How?"

Wolfe looked smug. "Saul Panzer asked an acquaintance of his, a man who is not known to the police, to go to the morgue and say a good friend from the Bronx was missing, never having appeared for an important meeting. He was shown the body."

"Which I suppose he then said was not his friend."

"Correct. But he made note of facial features including a cleft chin, a mole on his right cheek, and a short but visible scar above his left eye, all of which Saul had noted when he met Bell on his first visit to the Williamson home."

"So I assume Cramer still doesn't know the body is Bell."

"Correct again. And the inspector has kept the incident out of the press until the body can be identified and the next of kin informed."

"But he told you about the murder."

"Yes, futilely hoping to pry from me some sort of admission that I was involved. It was only a hunting expedition on his part. He knew he wouldn't get anywhere with it, which is why he telephoned rather than making the effort to come here and badger me. The latter tactic often ends with him storming out."

"Yes, I have now seen that myself. Do you have any idea how long Cramer's going to sit on the story?"

"No, although I strongly suspect he will release details of the shooting in the next day or two, hoping that someone comes forth to identify the body. He cannot wait indefinitely."

"This could have something to do with the kidnapping, but it also may have been a simple armed robbery gone wrong," I said. "After all, you say Bell's pockets were empty, no wallet, no money. He could have resisted a holdup man and gotten plugged for his efforts."

"I have never been a great believer in coincidence," Wolfe remarked. "More likely, Mr. Bell was killed because of some connection he had with the Williamson kidnapping. His wallet was then taken to make it appear to be a robbery—and perhaps also to hamper attempts at identification."

"That's a definite possibility," I conceded. "Do you plan to tell Inspector Cramer Bell's identity?"

"Not at present. Have you unearthed anything at the Williamson home since the last time we talked?"

I gave him a complete report on all my conversations since the last time we had spoken on the telephone.

"Did you embellish anything?" he asked after I finished.

"Embellish? I don't know that word."

"In this context, it means 'to enhance a narrative with fictitious additions.'"

"There was nothing fictitious about what I just told you. Every bit of it was, well, word for word."

Wolfe raised his eyebrows. "Oh, yes, Mr. Bascom did tell me you have the ability to recite long passages of dialogue verbatim. Do you concur?"

"Yes, sir. I have been able to do that for as long as I can remember."

"Would you indulge me by repeating all of it?"

I didn't see the sense in it, but I fed every word back to him again. He sat with his eyes closed and his hands interlaced over his middle mound. When I finished, he opened his eyes wide. "Most interesting."

"I'm glad you think so. I haven't found anything of particular value regarding the kidnapping in my time at that Williamson palace. And it really is a palace. Even the chauffeur's quarters are first-class, four rooms plus a bathroom. Do you have any specific instructions for me?"

"Just continue to be alert and observant, and continue to telephone me each evening at nine. Your stay there may not last a great deal longer, although from what you have said, the assignment hardly constitutes onerous duty."

"No, it doesn't, not at all. Oh, I admit that I miss being in the city, but don't get me wrong—I'm not crying. The food is decent, the autos I drive are top-notch, and the surroundings are fit for royalty, which I guess the Williamsons are, in a sense."

"You made no mention of remuneration."

"No, sir."

"I believe that will be resolved."

I figured "remuneration" meant something to do with payment, but I already had shown my ignorance about one word Wolfe used, and I was damned if I was going to give him the satisfaction a second time. Besides, I knew how to use a dictionary, and if I was going to be spending time around Wolfe, I would have to buy one.

# CHAPTER 18

Sunday morning, I was up and dressed even before the early-rising Mrs. Price. The newspapers got delivered at the front door of the house before daybreak, and I scooped them up at a few minutes after six. I sat on the brick steps and went through the *Times* first, page by page. There wasn't a word about Bell's death. Next I tackled the *Herald-Tribune* with the same result. That left the *Daily News*, which the Williamsons got for the household staff and which did a better job of covering crime news than the two silk-stocking newspapers. On page 22, down at the bottom, I spotted a brief piece with a one-column headline reading MAN SLAIN IN BRONX GANGWAY.

The details were sparse, describing "the body of an unidentified man who appeared to be in his thirties" having been found in the Bronx gangway by a passerby late Friday night. The article went on to say that he had been shot three times according to police and that "neighbors did not report hearing gunshots, suggesting that a silencer may have been used in the killing." The item ended, as so many of this sort did, with "police are conducting a thorough search for the perpetrator and also are seeking the identity of the dead man."

I placed the *Times* and the *Herald-Tribune* on the table in the entry hall and took the *Daily News* down to the kitchen, where Mrs. Price had now started breakfast. "My goodness, you're up early again today," she said, turning from the stove, where she was scrambling eggs.

"The early bird … you know."

"I know, 'gets the worm.' Well, instead of a worm, how about bacon and eggs? And the coffee's ready."

"My, but you are cheerful this morning," I told her.

"And why not? The sun is shining, the birds are singing, Master Tommie is back with us, and the meat purveyor is coming with a shipment of beef today, including filets, the kind of steaks that Mr. W. loves, medium rare. The Depression hasn't hit this house, at least not yet."

"Is any of that beef for us, or does it all get consumed upstairs?"

"Well, some of it is for us, Mr. Archie Goodwin," she said, shaking a finger at me in mock scolding. "The mister and missus have always wanted the staff to be well fed, and Lord knows, I try my humble best to make sure that happens."

"And based on these last few days, you certainly succeed, Mrs. Price."

"Well, I am so glad to hear you say that," she responded. "Not everyone is as gracious—or as grateful—as you are. Now you start eating, mind you, while the bacon and eggs are still hot."

"Oh, and before I begin, here's today's *Daily News*," I said, putting the tabloid newspaper on the table.

"Ah, doing my work now, are you?" she said with a chuckle. "I usually bring in the morning papers. What did you do with the other two?"

"Put them on the round table upstairs in the foyer."

She clapped her hands in approval. "That is exactly what I do. The mister, he likes to read his *Times* and his *Tribune* with breakfast in the dining room before he takes the train to work."

The others began filing into the kitchen. First Waverly, then Emily Stratton and Mary Trent, and finally, Carstens and Simons. The latter two, although they lived off the estate, took breakfast at the Williamsons' on weekdays because, as Mrs. Price had proudly confided in me, "they get better meals here than at home. They probably would prefer to have dinner here, too, but they would have to explain the reason why to their wives."

Lloyd Carstens sat down and picked up the *Daily News*, paging through it as he drank coffee. "Hmm, guy got shot in the Bronx, no identification on the body. Police guessed he was in his thirties. Maybe that's our vanishing Mr. Charles Bell," he said with a sour chuckle.

"There is nothing in any way humorous about that," Emily Stratton huffed, glaring at him.

"Aw, you wouldn't know humor if it hit you over the head," Carstens said, tossing the paper aside and beginning to eat.

"Sadly, neither would you," the housekeeper fired back.

"That's giving it to him, Emily!" Simons roared, clapping his hands. "He is just an old—"

"Nobody asked you to chime in, Mr. Horse Breath," Carstens jeered. "Stick to your manure-filled stables, that's where you belong—knee-deep in dung."

"Please, gentlemen, please! Let us all show a modicum of civility at this table," Waverly implored. "Everyone has been on edge ever since little Tommie got taken away from us, but he is home safe now. We should be giving thanks for that, not snapping at one another."

"That's not why we're on edge," Carstens whined. "It's him." The gardener pointed a gnarled index finger at me. "He is a spy in our midst. He doesn't know any more about being a chauffeur than I do. And I'd like to know what his credentials are as a bodyguard. He's just a second-rate private detective."

"Mr. Williamson selected him for the position. That should end any discussion whatever of the matter," the butler stated in clipped tones.

"Hah! He may be almost a kid, but remember that he came here with those other shamuses," Carstens persisted. "What does that tell you? He's here giving us all the once-over."

"Mr. Williamson hired me to be a bodyguard for Tommie, taking him to and from school, at least for the time being," I said. "And because Mr. Bell was gone, I combined that task with the job as chauffeur, also for the time being."

"Well, the chauffeuring part just might be permanent now, if that body in the *Daily News* story turns out to be Bell," Carstens said with a smirk.

"Really!" It was Emily Stratton again. "I find you most offensive."

"You are not alone in that opinion," Simons said. "Besides, people get bumped off in New York every day of the week. Why Carstens thinks this particular stiff happens to be Bell is beyond me."

"Maybe Mr. Carstens is right about one thing, though—that I'm the real reason for the tension here during meals," I said. "From now on, I will eat at different times from the rest of you."

"No, you will not!" Mrs. Price snapped, getting to her feet. "Don't forget that this is my kitchen, and I decide, along with Mr. Waverly, who eats here and who does not. Do you have any objection to Mr. Goodwin dining with the rest of us?" she asked the butler, hands on broad hips and chin jutting out as if daring contradiction.

"None whatever, Mrs. Price," he said stiffly. "The matter is settled."

"I think that Mr. Goodwin is very nice," Mary Trent said softly. Those few words, the only ones she spoke at breakfast, seemed to at least temporarily defuse the situation, and everyone spent the rest of the meal in silence, attacking their food but not each other—or me.

When we left for school that morning, Tommie Williamson immediately hopped in beside me, clearly not caring whether his parents saw him riding up front. "Can we kick the football around after school today?" he asked before we had even left the grounds of the estate.

"What about your homework?"

"I usually don't have much of it on Mondays," Tommie said quickly, expecting the question. "Besides, Miss Moore is still away until tomorrow."

"So you don't do homework when she is not here, is that it?"

"No, I always do it anyway, but when she's here, she helps me. I don't always need her help, but I let her think that I do. It makes her feel good."

"How much time do you spend on homework every day?"

"About an hour."

"I'll tell you what. When you get home this afternoon, do your homework for an hour, and we'll still have time for the football before dinner. It still will be light enough. But you have to get your mother's permission, because I don't want to get into trouble with her. Does that sound okay?"

"Yeah, it does, Archie," he said with a grin.

"Speaking of Miss Moore, are you looking forward to her coming back?"

"I guess so. She's pretty nice, except sometimes now she gets real sad, like she's going to start crying. I feel bad for her, but I don't know what to say."

"Do you have any idea what makes her sad?"

"I know her mother has been sick, maybe that's why."

"Yes, that could be the answer. Has she always been sad?"

"No, just maybe the last, I don't know, maybe a month or two."

"Well, I believe you are the type who can cheer her up," I said. "I'm sure she was terribly worried when you were gone."

"She really did cry when I came back, and she hugged me until I thought I couldn't breathe."

"That shows how much she cares about you. I'm sure the others on the staff feel just the same way."

He shrugged, looking out of the window. "I don't think Mr. Simons likes me very much. I like to go in and look at the horses in the stable sometimes, but he always looks angry when I'm there."

"It's possible that he's just trying to protect you. Horses can be pretty mean sometimes, I know. When I was about ten, I got kicked by a horse at my uncle's farm in Ohio, and all I was trying to do was pet him."

"Gee, did you get hurt?"

"My pride did, but I also ended up with a bruised shin that turned black and blue. I walked with a limp for two weeks. Anyway, perhaps Mr. Simons is worried about something of that sort happening to you."

"I still don't think he likes me."

"What about Mr. Carstens?"

"He doesn't talk much, but I can tell he's worried whenever I'm outside playing that I'll step on his flowers. I was flying a kite in the backyard in the spring, and he got angry because the kite fell into a bed of yellow tulips. And it didn't even hurt a single one of them."

"Do you and Miss Stratton get along well?"

"Uh-huh, she's okay I guess, but kinda bossy. She orders Mary around a lot, and I think she would try to order Mrs. Price around, too, if she thought she could get away with it," Tommie said with a chuckle.

"Do you like Mrs. Price?"

"I do. She's always making really good desserts, and for my last birthday, you should have seen the cake she baked. It was at least this high"—he held his hands about six inches apart—"and she made a picture of a train on top out of different-colored frosting. She knows that I like trains."

"And she also knows you like cake?"

"And pies, and cookies."

"How about Mary—is she nice?"

He nodded. "She plays games with me when Miss Moore is away, like now. Last night, we played a card game she taught me called 'old maid.' It was a lot of fun, except I think she let me win."

"It could be that you're just a good card player."

"Maybe, except I still think she could have beaten me last night. Funny thing, when we were playing up in my room, Mr. Waverly came up about four different times to see how we were doing."

"Perhaps he wanted to play the game with you, too."

"I don't think that Mr. Waverly plays games. He seems too serious. He doesn't smile very much."

"Does he get cross?"

"No, he has a very soft voice, and he talks different because he's English, but I think it sounds nice. He always calls me Master Tommie."

"I think English people tend to be very formal," I told him as we pulled into the well-manicured grounds of the MeadesGate Academy, and Tommie hopped out of the car to join his classmates who were filing into the building.

When I got back to the Williamson estate, I eased the Pierce-Arrow into the garage and had just started up the steps to my quarters when I heard my name being spoken in a voice just above a whisper. It was Mary Trent, who slipped in through the open overhead door and looked around as if she were being followed.

"Mr. Goodwin, I'm sorry to bother you, but I need to talk to you. Can we go up to your rooms?"

"I really don't think that's a very good idea, Miss Trent."

"I'm not a child, you know. I am probably just about your age."

"I was not suggesting you are a child. But we can talk down here, with the automobiles for company. I've got a small desk over in the corner, and a guest chair, too."

"I would rather be somewhere more private," she said as if afraid she would be overheard.

"Let's make this more private then," I told her, lowering the garage door. "Now, sit down and tell me what it is you want to talk about."

She parked herself uneasily on the edge of the straight-backed chair and fixed large brown eyes on me. She was not at all hard to look at. "I am sorry you were spoken to so rudely at the breakfast table, Mr. Goodwin."

"That didn't bother me. And please call me Archie."

"I will, if you call me Mary."

"It's a deal. Anything else you'd like to say?"

"Are you really a detective?"

"Yes, I am."

"There are things you and your colleagues should be aware of," she said, clasping her small hands in her lap.

"Go on."

"For one thing, Miss Stratton and Mr. Carstens are really very good friends."

"It certainly did not seem that way at breakfast."

"They were putting on an act, Mr.—Archie. I believe it has something to do with Tommie's kidnapping."

"Really?"

She nodded primly. "I try not to eavesdrop, but sometimes I hear things because I go about my work quietly. The day after Tommie came home, I heard part of a conversation between the two of them. I was dusting in the dining room, and Mr. Carstens had come into the parlor. He almost never enters the house, but it was clear to me that he was looking for Miss Stratton.

"'What are you doing here?' she said to him in a sharp voice, and he answered 'We have to be careful, really careful now. I'm worried about Charles having—' At that point, Archie, Mr. Carstens quit talking and came through the doorway into the dining room. I ducked behind a tall Chinese screen that shields the serving staff from the diners. I know he did not see me, and I heard him say to Miss Stratton, 'I just wanted to be sure that no one was around.' Then they went off to somewhere else, I suppose to finish their conversation."

"Uh-huh. And what do you think that conversation was about?"

"Well, I know this is a terrible thing to say about the people I work with, but I think they might have, well …"

"Might have what?"

"Might have … had something to do with the kidnapping," she murmured.

"Then what do you think Carstens was going to say about Charles Bell when he stopped talking in midsentence?"

"I believe he was starting to tell Miss Stratton that he was worried Charles found out about the plot to take Tommie."

"So you believe this whole business started inside the house?"

"Don't you?" she answered.

"Well, I seem to remember you telling one of the other detectives that you did not recognize the voice of the man who telephoned Miss Moore, bringing her indoors and away from Tommie."

"That is correct, I didn't."

"Well, if it was an inside job, the caller had to be one of four men— Waverly, Bell, Carstens, or Simons."

She shook her head. "It did not sound like any of them, Archie."

"Bear in mind the caller could have disguised his voice—in fact *would* have—if he were on the household staff. It also could have been a woman disguising her voice to sound like a man. Now think about it hard, Mary, and see if you can remember that voice."

"It's no good," she stated with conviction. "I don't believe it was any of them. I'm so sorry."

"There's nothing to be sorry about. All that proves is that one or more of the people here may have worked with someone on the outside, as seems likely."

"I wish I could have been more helpful," she said as she got up. "I'd better get back, or they—Miss Stratton, that is—will wonder where I am. Thank you for taking the time to listen to me … Archie." She went up on tiptoes and kissed me firmly on the lips. I started to push her away, but then kissed her back, quickly wishing I hadn't.

"I think we have both been wanting to do that for the last few days," she said in a husky tone, and before I could answer one way or the other, she turned and went out through the small door next to the big garage doors.

I cursed myself silently and ran a handkerchief across my face to get rid of the lipstick that I was sure she had left as her mark.

The rest of the day was uneventful until I picked up Burke Williamson early that evening at the little commuter rail station. When I took this job, one of the things that surprised me was that this man, one of New York's wealthiest, rode the old Long Island Railroad to and from work most days, alongside the great masses of salesmen, secretaries, stockbrokers, store clerks, and myriad others who toiled in Manhattan's concrete-and-steel canyons.

As if to answer my unspoken question, he had told me earlier that "thousands of ordinary folks of all types stay in my hotels every week, and I want to spend time around these people, feel their energy, observe them, and talk to them, get to know a little bit about them, at least twice a day on these trains. It makes me feel connected to my clientele."

Williamson did not seem connected to any of his fellow commuters that evening as he got off the train and stormed over to the waiting car, face frowning and red, with arms churning like pistons at his sides. This appeared to be one angry man.

"Goodwin, we are going to see Nero Wolfe tonight!" he growled as he dropped into the backseat and slammed his briefcase down next to him.

"Yes, sir?"

"After dinner. I would drive myself, but my night vision is not good. It was bad enough going into the Bronx those two nights when Tommie was missing, but then I had no choice. Now I do. I got a telephone call at the office today from Inspector Cramer of the Police Department, who informed me that Charles Bell was found shot to death last Friday night in the Bronx."

"Bell, dead … killed?" I said in a shocked tone, doing my best to feign both ignorance and surprise.

"His body was identified at the morgue by his sister, who got worried when he never showed up at her house over in New Jersey. He was supposed to move in with her and her husband temporarily after he bolted from our household. Anyway, this Cramer wants to see me tomorrow about Charles's death. I telephoned Wolfe to ask his advice, and it turns out that he got a call from the inspector, too, an angry one, he said."

"The upshot is, you feel that you need to see Wolfe?"

"He wants to see me, says that we've got a lot to discuss. I asked if we could meet in my office tomorrow, before Cramer comes to see me, but he said he never leaves home on business. What do you think of that?"

"Mr. Wolfe seems to be—what would you call it—eccentric?"

"Yes, I would call it eccentric, all right," Williamson snapped. "I told him that you would be driving me, and he said that was all right, and that you could sit in on the discussion."

"I guess I'm flattered."

"Huh! Myself, I don't find it the least bit flattering to be told— ordered is more like it—to show up somewhere. I find that damned high-handed."

"What time do we leave?"

"Can you get to Wolfe's place in forty-five minutes?"

"At night, yes. That's how long it took us to get to Carnegie Hall."

"Then we will set off at eight ten from home. He is expecting us at nine," Williamson growled.

I smiled inwardly. Here was one of New York's ten richest men dancing to Nero Wolfe's tune.

# CHAPTER 19

In fact, we made it door to door in thirty-six minutes according to my watch, which read 8:46 when we pulled up in front of Wolfe's brownstone on West Thirty-Fifth Street. Williamson had grumbled during the entire trip about having been "summoned by an ego-saturated private detective."

Clearly, Burke Williamson was not used to being summoned to any location by anyone. I wanted to point out to him that the ego-saturated private detective and his minions were responsible for having his eight-year-old son returned home safely, but I held my tongue in the interests of a good working relationship.

I got a mild surprise when Wolfe's front door was opened not by Fritz Brenner but by Saul Panzer. "Hi, Archie; hello, Mr. Williamson. Please come right in," Saul said, stepping aside smartly. Waverly could not have done it any better.

Williamson muttered something that sounded like "thank you," and we went down the hall to the office, where Wolfe sat reading a book. He set it down as we entered. "Good evening, sir. Thank you for coming. Can I get you something to drink? I am having beer."

"I did not come here to drink," Williamson snapped, dropping into the red leather chair.

"Just so. However, I do have an excellent selection of liquors, wines, and cordials. Also, if I may suggest it, a superb brandy, and I use that adjective sparingly."

"All right then," the hotelier said, still grumpy. "I'll have one of those."

"Mr. Goodwin?" Wolfe asked.

"A glass of milk for me. I'm driving."

Wolfe gave a slight nod to Panzer, who went to a serving cart against one wall and poured an amber liquid into what I later learned was a snifter. He then placed it on the small table next to Williamson and left the room, presumably to get my milk.

"Is Panzer filling in for Brenner?" I asked to be conversational.

"Even Fritz needs some time away from the kitchen," Wolfe said as Saul handed me a glass of milk and threw me a wink. "Now, we need to discuss the situation we find ourselves in, Mr. Williamson."

"All right, now that I have taken the trouble to come, why don't you lay it all out?"

"I shall, sir. The violent death of Mr. Bell would seem to suggest your son's kidnapping may well have been facilitated to some degree by one or more members of your household staff, a premise I know from an earlier conversation that you find abhorrent."

"I still cannot believe Charles had anything to do with what happened."

"Do you have an explanation for his death?"

"I do not, except that—my Lord, this cognac is beyond compare," Williamson said, holding the glass up to the light from a lamp. "What in the world do you call this nectar?"

One corner of Wolfe's mouth moved up slightly, which may have been a smile. "Remisier. There are no more than four-dozen bottles in this country, well over half of them in my cellar. You shall leave here with one of those bottles tonight. You started to say something about Mr. Bell's death."

"Yes. All I can surmise is that he somehow learned about the plot and the persons involved in it. He likely threatened to expose them and, well ..."

"A possible scenario," Wolfe conceded, drinking beer. "Do you remain adamant that others in your household employ had no involvement in the kidnapping?"

"Absolutely. All of them have been in service with us for quite some time—except, of course, for Miss Trent, who has been on the staff for a little over a year now."

"Speaking of Miss Trent," I cut in, "she confided something to me today that I believe you both will find interesting."

Williamson jerked his head toward me and started to speak when Wolfe said, "Proceed."

I fed it to them verbatim. Out of the corner of my eye, I could see Burke Williamson's expression go from shock to anger to disbelief. Wolfe's face betrayed no emotion.

"This is all rot!" Williamson snorted. "Mary Trent is barely more than a child. And no doubt her active imagination stems from seeing too many of those talking moving picture shows that seem to be on every corner these days."

"Perhaps," Wolfe said, "but we would be remiss indeed if we did not at least consider what the young woman reported to Mr. Goodwin."

"Bah! I dismiss her tale as nothing more than a flight of fancy. I simply refuse to believe that Miss Stratton and Carstens are involved in some sort of plot. The very idea is ludicrous."

"That may well be," Wolfe stated. "Although by all accounts, Miss Trent has been an exemplary employee, is that not so?"

"True, she has," Williamson nodded, drinking the last of his Remisier. Panzer, who occupied the yellow chair next to mine, quickly got the bottle and refilled his glass.

"Enough on the young woman for the moment," Wolfe said. "Let us turn our attention to Charles Bell. Mr. Panzer has some information of interest, and then we will discuss Inspector Cramer."

Panzer cleared his throat. "After we learned Mr. Bell's identity, I talked to someone I know who has connections at the morgue. Through that individual, I reached Mr. Bell's sister, Arlene Perkins, who had identified his body. Per Mr. Wolfe's instructions, I visited her at home in New Jersey, and—"

"I should have been the one to talk to her and give her our

condolences," Williamson interrupted, "but Charles left us no forwarding address. And I also should be paying for his—"

"Please, sir," Wolfe said, holding up a palm. "That can wait. Let Mr. Panzer continue."

"I learned from Mr. Bell's sister that he had planning for some time to give his notice to the Williamsons. She told me that he hinted to her that he had some 'big plans,' but that he was very secretive regarding details. When I suggested that those plans might have to do with Tommie's kidnapping and the subsequent ransom payment, Mrs. Perkins became very angry and—"

"As I would have, too," Williamson said, although without his earlier fervor. Maybe the Remisier had begun to mellow him.

"She got angry with me," Panzer continued, "so I backed off fast. I went on to ask about whom his friends were, and she said she didn't know, that she and her brother had not been close the last few years and rarely saw each other. She told me she was surprised that after all this time, he had asked to stay with her and her husband until he got himself resettled."

"Did Mrs. Perkins say anything about her brother's reason for leaving the Williamsons when he did?" I asked.

"Yeah, Archie, she sure did. Bell told her that the others on the staff acted like he was part of the kidnapping plot, and that he just couldn't take their suspicious attitudes anymore."

"That is outrageous," Williamson said, shaking his head. "If only I had known this sort of thing was happening right under my own roof. All of it was so unfair to poor Charles, rest his soul."

"There is something more," Panzer said after taking a sip of his scotch. "Mrs. Perkins told me that during the time she was waiting for Bell to move in with them, she got three telephone calls for her brother, all from the same man, deep voice, no discernible accent. Each time, she asked if she could take a message, and each time he told her he would call again."

"There you have what we know about Mr. Bell," Wolfe said. "It would be instructive to know his movements from the time he left your employ until his death, but determining them would no doubt be difficult."

I turned to Williamson. "You mentioned that Bell left your home in his own vehicle, a Plymouth coupe, I believe you said?"

"I wasn't there when he left, and yes, his machine was a Plymouth, which I allowed him to keep in an empty stall. I have to assume that he departed in that vehicle because it is no longer in our garage."

"Has the auto been located?" I asked.

Wolfe looked questioningly at Panzer and Williamson, both of whom shook their heads. "Saul, do you have any suggestions as to how we can locate this—what is it?—Plymouth?"

Panzer's expression was one of chagrin. "I'm sorry, sir. That should have been the first thing to come to mind. I will get on it first thing tomorrow."

"Only when you are able," Wolfe said with a flip of the hand. In his eyes, it seemed that Saul could do no wrong. "Now, Mr. Williamson, let us discuss your impending meeting with Inspector Cramer. From my brief and rancorous telephone conversation with him, it became clear that the Police Department finally has connected three events: the murder of Barney Haskell, your son's kidnapping, and the shooting of Mr. Bell. The inspector will no doubt try to bully you, and my advice is to answer all his questions fully and truthfully. That includes my involvement and that of operatives who are in my employ."

"I do not know this Cramer, other than as a testy voice at the other end of a telephone wire," Williamson said, "but he does not intimidate me. I happen to be a close friend of his boss, Police Commissioner Humbert, whom I have known for years. Further, I am probably the largest single donor to the Police Athletic League, which has sponsored so many good programs for the city's poorer children. I say this not to boast, but to establish my standing with the Police Department."

"I did not mean to infer, sir, that you might be intimidated by Inspector Cramer," Wolfe said. "Rather, my point is that the time has come to show him our cards. I am no more intimidated by the inspector than you are, overbearing though he can be. Having said that, I have found that on occasion it becomes advantageous to concede certain points to the man, particularly when he feels his authority has been usurped. Such a move on our part makes it more likely that he will then share at least some of what the police have learned, based on my past dealings with him."

"Meaning that we bow to his wishes?"

"By no means, sir. But bear in mind that Mr. Cramer commands an army of men, while we possess only a handful of foot soldiers, albeit intrepid and talented ones. I suggest that we meet with the inspector together, presenting a united front."

"So that our stories are consistent?" Williamson posed with a tight smile.

"That is part of it," Wolfe allowed. "But, in addition, together we present a formidable combination: you are a well-known and respected public figure and civic benefactor, and I have been known to solve criminal cases that have left the police baffled."

"You are not one to indulge in false modesty, are you?"

"No, sir. Nor, I suspect, are you. False humility is a transparent plea for praise and recognition, neither of which I find worth the price of the pretense."

"Well put!" Williamson said with a grin, clapping once. His mood had lightened measurably since partaking of the Remisier. "I assume we would meet with the inspector here."

"Correct."

"I would like to request that Mr. Goodwin be present. I have grown in the last days to appreciate his perspective and his opinions."

"Because he possesses the same qualities, Mr. Panzer also will be a party to the discussion," Wolfe said.

"When will we meet?" Williamson asked, rising.

"Tomorrow night, nine o'clock," Wolfe said, nodding to Panzer, who got up without a word and left the room.

As we reached the front door, Panzer moved up and thrust an

object into Williamson's hand. "For you, sir, with Mr. Wolfe's best regards," he said.

The tycoon took the sealed bottle of Remisier, cradled it, and smiled down as if it were his firstborn. "Thank Mr. Wolfe for me," he said softly. As we went to the car, the world's leading hotelier walked with a spring in his step that had been absent earlier in the evening.

# CHAPTER 20

On the drive back to Long Island, Williamson slumped down and dozed in the well-upholstered backseat while I mulled over our meeting with Cramer tomorrow and the case in general. It seemed inescapable that the late Charles Bell was involved in the kidnapping, but in what way? I had already scoured his quarters the way I thought a detective should, looking for anything that might provide a lead, but without success.

Bell had left his onetime home barer than Old Mother Hubbard's infamous cupboard. And he had done every bit of the clean-out himself, as I had learned from Emily Stratton, who told me he never wanted anyone else on the household staff to enter his rooms. "Not that any of us would want to set foot in the place anyway," she had said with a sniff. "Not with the kind of things that went on up there."

When I gave her a questioning look, she lowered her voice, nodded, and silently mouthed "women," pronouncing the word as if it were a disease.

I gave her my best imitation of a shocked look. "Oh no."

"Oh yes, many times, and many of them." She nodded again, turned on her heel, and walked off, head held high in judgment.

Even as I congratulated myself on how thoroughly I had combed those upstairs rooms, I finally came to the realization that there were other places where I should have been looking. The glove boxes of the three Williamson autos, for starters. And the garage itself, where no maid apparently ever went and which is larger than most homes, with more places to hide a possible clue than a magician's closet full of props.

It was after eleven when we returned to the estate. Williamson, still fuzzy from his nap, yawned, wished me a good night, and trudged into the house, clutching his precious bottle of Remisier to his bosom. I then began a search.

The glove boxes yielded nothing other than maps of the New York metropolitan area and New England, owners' manuals, and registration documents. Although the garage was generally well lit, there were some dark corners. After playing the beam of a flashlight along the walls and floor and opening every one of the automotive tool drawers, I started in on the wooden desk that served as what amounted to a chauffeur's office.

I found that Charles Bell either had done little office work during his years with the Williamsons or else had once again meticulously purged every object from the premises. Even the wastebasket between the desk and the back wall was as empty as a senator's campaign promises. As I turned away from that wire-mesh trash receptacle, I almost missed it. A crumpled scrap of paper intended for the wastebasket had gotten wedged into a crack between the wall and the baseboard. I pulled the sheet out and smoothed it on the desktop: a single word was scrawled in pencil, *Pollard*, presumably in Bell's handwriting.

On a chance, I pulled down the stack of telephone directories from the shelf above the desk and started paging them. For those of you who are fascinated by statistics, there were eighty-eight listings for the last name Pollard in the Manhattan directory, twenty-one in the Bronx book, and forty-three in Queens. Those numbers were more than I wanted to deal with, so I went to the Yellow Pages. Turning to the alphabetical listings, I found a Pollard Engraving Co., a Pollard Furniture Store, and—what do you know?—a Pollard Truck Leasing service. Even more interesting, that last establishment was located in the Bronx.

A glance at my watch told me it might be too late to call Del Bascom at home, but I dialed his number anyway. He answered on the second ring.

"Goodwin here. Did I wake you?"

"Nah, Archie, not me. The wife and I stay up till midnight, sometimes later. We both like to read. For her, it's romantic stuff, for me, good old Zane Grey and his western tales. How's things at the Williamson palace?"

"They're getting more interesting all the time. Have you ever by chance impersonated a cop?"

"On occasion, although I don't care to. It's a quick way to get your license lifted, likely for good. I've known that to happen to a few tecs over the years."

"But not guys as smart as us, right?"

"Uh-oh. I don't like the sound of that, Archie."

"Just listen, will you?"

Monday morning at breakfast, I told Waverly that after dropping Tommie off at school, I would be heading into New York on an errand for Burke Williamson and would be back by late morning or early afternoon. Because the butler was my nominal supervisor, I wanted to stay on the formal Englishman's good side. And as I had expected, he did not question the details of my errand. If the assignment was one requested by Mr. Williamson, it had to be all right as far as Waverly was concerned.

After watching Tommie jump out of the car and run to join his friends on the MeadesGate Academy playground, I pulled off the road in a quiet spot and peeled off my uniform jacket, replacing it with a sport coat and exchanging my chauffeur's cap for a snap-brim felt hat. Looking in the rearview mirror to straighten my tie, I then followed what was becoming a familiar route into New York, specifically to the borough of the Bronx.

The Pollard Truck Leasing Service occupied a dumpy-looking, single-story brick building along a commercial stretch of Jerome Avenue that had elevated train tracks running above it. Next to the building was a lot filled with trucks and vans of various shapes and sizes. I parked the car a block down the street and checked my watch. Bascom was due in five minutes.

He showed up right on time, marching down the sidewalk and spotting the Pierce-Arrow. This was a Del Bascom I had not seen before: wearing a fedora and a belted raincoat with the collar turned up, hands jammed into the pockets, and a belligerent expression pasted on his mug.

"The name's Lieutenant Danahey," he muttered out of the corner of his mouth as he slid into the front seat next to me, "and you are Sergeant Rourke. And by God, this better be worth it, Archie."

"Will they get suspicious if they don't see a patrol car?"

"I don't plan to give 'em time to think about that. The plan is to have these bozos back on their heels so fast they won't remember their own names, right? Let's go."

We got out of the auto and strode resolutely down the block toward our destination. I wondered if we looked like plainclothes cops to passersby. I hoped so, although I wasn't sure I looked old enough to be any kind of cop.

With Bascom leading the way, we entered the leasing outfit's cluttered and grimy office. "Help ya?" a fat specimen wearing an undershirt and three days of beard drawled from behind the counter as if he had no interest in helping us.

"Yes, I believe that you can," Bascom snapped. "We are looking for information about a truck that we believe got leased here." He gave the date of the kidnapping.

"And just who might you be to go around asking questions?" the fat man asked in a surly tone.

"Detective Lieutenant Danahey of Homicide, that's who, pal. And this is Sergeant Rourke. We are here investigating a murder." He whipped out a police badge that looked to me like the genuine article, quickly jamming it back into his pocket.

"That so?" fatty said, leaning porky elbows on the counter. "And just why should that concern me?"

"I will spell it out for you, mac," Bascom spat, leaning across the counter and sticking out his chin until it almost touched the slob. "A while back, we had a case where the owner of a restaurant didn't want to cooperate with us about the identity of a couple of his regular customers who were wanted for a killing. We closed that eatery down the next day, and it ain't been open since. I can give you the address if you'd like to go and see it, all boarded up. It was a nice place, too." Bascom looked around the room idly. "Be a real shame for that to happen here, this being a going concern and all. By the way, what's your name?" he asked, pulling out a notebook and pencil.

"Skelton, Ken Skelton. Okay, Officer, okay," he said, holding up his palms as beads of perspiration began popping out on his forehead. "What kind of truck was it supposed to be? We got all sizes and models here."

"Small enclosed truck, white. No printing of any kind on it. The kind that food purveyors would use."

"Lemme check my books. We do a lot of business here." He repeated the date Bascom had given him.

"Yeah, or maybe it got leased the day before," the would-be cop answered.

Skelton opened a hefty ledger book and flipped a few pages. "Let's see," he said, tracing down a page with a finger. "Okay, this has to be the one, and it was leased on the earlier date you mentioned, then returned less than twenty-hours later: one of our Ford Model A Deluxe Delivery Trucks. We got three in our fleet. Ford sells 'em to us black, of course, but we paint 'em white. Makes 'em look a lot classier, you know what I mean?"

"Name of the person who leased it," Bascom demanded, feigning impatience.

"Let's see … Lloyd Evanson, address 690 West Eighty-Seventh Street, Manhattan."

"We'd like a description," Bascom said. "And did this Lloyd Evanson come in here alone?"

"That I couldn't tell you, Lieutenant, sir," Skelton said, wiping his damp forehead with a dirty handkerchief. "I work the seven-to-three shift, and the truck got leased at, let's see … ten past four. That means Kirby would have been doing the paperwork on this one."

"I would like to talk to Mr. Kirby—right now!"

"Yes, sir, anything to help the police. He should be at home now. Would you like to call him from here? You can use this instrument. I'll dial the number for you," Skelton said.

Bascom nodded, maintaining his strong, silent cop pose. He put the receiver to his ear, and when he got Kirby on the wire, he gave him the same routine Skelton had been fed.

"So, Mr. Kirby, describe this Lloyd Evanson to me. "Uh-huh … I see," he said, scribbling in his notebook. "Did he come in alone? Really—and how about his description?" Bascom listened and then wrote some more.

"And did Evanson have a valid New York driver's license? Okay, yes … How did he and the other man behave? Did they pay in cash or with a check? I see … What about how they planned to use the truck? Oh, is that so? Well, is there anything else at all you can tell me that would be helpful? All right, thank you. You may be hearing from us again." Bascom cradled the receiver on its hook and pushed the telephone across the Skelton.

"Thanks, we appreciate your cooperation," Bascom told the fat man. "The Police Department relies on the cooperation of its citizenry."

"Yes, sir, glad to help. So … all this is about a murder?"

"It is indeed, Mr. Skelton. Unfortunately, regulations prevent me from commenting on the details, as I'm sure you can understand," Bascom said, touching the brim of his fedora and executing a smart about-face.

"Oh, I understand, yes, sir, I do," Skelton said, exhaling in relief. He was not sorry to see us leave.

Homicide squad, huh? Murder case, huh? Pretty nervy, I'd say."

"In for a penny, in for a pound," Bascom said, shrugging. "When you pump them full of fear, like I did with that guy, they'll believe damn near anything you tell them. Their main goal at that point is just to see the last of you."

"Well, his manners certainly showed a marked improvement after you explained the facts of life to him, Lieutenant Danahey," I said.

"I do what I can, Sergeant Rourke," he shot back with a lopsided grin.

"I got much of the telephone conversation with Kirby by hearing your end of it, but can you fill in the blanks?" I asked Bascom.

"Okay, here's the sum of it. Kirby described Evanson—if that's his name—as tall, an inch or two above six feet, very thin, and with deep-set dark eyes and black hair parted in the center. Long face, no facial hair. Another man came in with him who Kirby said could have been his brother, they looked so much alike. This second man said nothing. The one calling himself Evanson had an up-to-date New York driver's license. Oh, and he paid for the rental in cash. Kirby said they don't accept checks, only the coin of the realm.

"And when I asked Kirby if he knew what Evanson wanted to use the truck for, he sniffed and informed me that folks at Pollard never ask customers why they need a truck. 'That certainly is none of our business,' I was informed. Who'd of thought you would find a pompous ass working behind the counter of a truck rental joint in the Bronx."

"You keep suggesting that maybe Evanson isn't his real name. But he did have a driver's license to prove it, right?"

"Archie, I'm easily old enough to remember when you didn't even need a driver's license in this state to pilot an automobile on the public thoroughfares. Since we've had licenses, I'd be hard put to swear that drivers are any better than they were fifteen or more years ago. But one thing I do know: licenses are easy to forge, and they get forged for all sorts of reasons. I don't put much stock in them these days as a means of identification."

"So where does that leave us?"

"First off, it's at least worth looking Evanson up, just to see if he's real and he's listed," Bascom said, heading for a corner phone booth just as an elevated train rumbled overhead, rattling windows in the nearby storefronts. "We're in luck," he said over his shoulder as he edged into the booth. "There's a Manhattan directory in here." He flipped the pages, then scowled. "Now we are out of luck," he said with a snort, closing the book. "There is no Lloyd Evanson listed at 690 West Eighty-Seventh Street, or anyplace else on the island, for that matter."

"That's not what I wanted to hear."

"Me neither, although I'm really not surprised."

"As I said a minute ago, where does that leave us?"

"Seems we might want to pay a visit to that Eighty-Seventh Street address," Bascom said, "just to see what's going on."

"Are we still on duty, Lieutenant?" I asked as we climbed into the Pierce-Arrow.

"Oh, why not? We can only get hanged once. Think you can find your way to the Upper West Side from here?"

"Hey, just who do you think you're talking to? I'm an old hand around here now. Let's roll."

I proved that I really did know my way around the city. I didn't check my watch, but I think we made it to West Eighty-Seventh Street in fifteen minutes, although I did hit a lot of green lights. Over near the Hudson, we found the address—the Old Dutchman Hotel, a weary four-story building on a block lined with pawnshops, diners, a bakery, a Chinese laundry, and a couple of darkened storefronts that Del Bascom guessed morphed into speakeasies after dark.

"I might have known it," Bascom said when he saw the Old Dutchman. "A flophouse, more properly referred to as a transient hotel, Archie. Filled with winos, grifters, ex-cons, and poor saps who lost their jobs after the crash and might never find another one, unless you count panhandling on street corners. Chances are, nobody in this joint will have heard of Lloyd Evanson. But since we're here, let's you and me find out what we can."

We parked and crossed the street to the building, which had an ornate canopied entrance that, as Bascom said, "dates from when this probably was an honest-to-goodness hotel, before the neighborhood went to pot."

The lobby may have been a glamorous and welcoming area for

lodgers once, but those days were gone, probably forever. More than half the bulbs in the ornate brass overhead fixtures had burned out, and the paint on both the ceiling and the walls was peeling. The overstuffed chairs, once occupied by tuxedoed men smoking cigars while waiting for their primping wives to come down to join them for a night on the town, now were unoccupied except for one bearded and shabby specimen, who snored discreetly, his Adam's apple bobbing with each raspy breath.

A short, skinny guy with a thin mustache who wore a soiled necktie and a scowl eyed us suspiciously from his post at the registration counter. "Help you gents?" he said in a world-weary tone.

"I believe you can," Bascom said, again flashing his badge. "Lieutenant Moran, vice squad, and this is Sergeant Baker. We've got some questions for you."

"Vice? We got no vice around here," he said defensively.

"We will be the judge of that," Bascom snapped. "What's your name?"

"Peterson, Merle Peterson."

"Well, Merle, we are looking for a man named Lloyd Evanson."

"Nobody like that been around here," he muttered. "Don't remember ever having somebody by that name staying with us."

"Hmm. Maybe he was using a different tag. He's tall, a few inches over six feet and thin, with dark eyes that are deep set. And black hair parted in the middle. He's got a friend who looks a lot like him."

Merle's pockmarked face broke into a sly grin. "Shoot, that ain't no friend, that's his brother. You gotta be talking about them Jasper boys, a couple of surly, no-account bums if you ask me. I'm glad to say they're gone."

"Gone where?" I asked.

"No idea. They checked outta here two, three days ago. And happy as could be, they was."

"Jasper, huh?" Bascom said. "What are their first names?"

"Leon and Edgar was what they put down when they checked in here a month or so back."

"Did they fill out a registration card?"

"Nah, we ain't that formal. Just wrote their names in the ledger."

"Let's see it," Bascom demanded.

Merle rolled his eyes as if he was being asked to perform strenuous work. He turned pages until he nodded and smacked his cracked lips. "Here we are." He spun the big book around to Bascom, pointing a bony index finger at names.

"Both Leon and Edgar signed in, let's see … more than three weeks ago now, but they didn't put down a previous address," Del said.

"Most of 'em don't," Merle said. "They like to keep private."

"And they don't always use their right names, do they?" I asked.

"We don't ask a lot of questions here, Sergeant. If they got the money—always in advance, that is—they get a room."

"These Jasper brothers, are they twins?" Bascom asked.

"Nah. They do look sorta alike, but Leon, he must be the older one, because I heard him call Edgar 'little brother' a few times. And Leon's slightly taller, too."

"You didn't like them, did you?"

"They was mean ones, Lieutenant, it didn't take long to see that. A lot of rough customers have come through here these last four years since I've been working the front desk, but those two, they gave me the willies, I'll tell ya."

"Oh? In what way?"

"They'd come in from the outside and laugh about somebody they beat up just for the fun of it. One night I heard Edgar tell Leon that he had knocked some old man down over on Amsterdam and when the poor sap's glasses had fallen off, he stepped on 'em and smashed 'em, then took his money, all of two or three bucks. They both got a good laugh out of that. Made me sick to hear."

"I can understand that. You said they were happy when they left here."

Merle nodded. "Plenty happy. They came down from their room laughing, slapped the key on the counter, and one of 'em, I forget which, said to me, 'So long, sucker. You may die here, but not us, no siree. We just found us that big ol' pot of gold at the end of the rainbow.'"

"And, of course, they didn't tell you where they were going or what their new address would be, right?"

"Right. But that ain't surprising. Most of 'em who leave here don't give us a forwarding address. Lots of times, they probably don't know themselves where they're headed. Most likely to another hotel that's cheaper'n this one."

"One more thing, Merle," Del Bascom said, "does the name Barney Haskell mean anything to you?"

He scratched his head, nodding. "The old-time grifter? Didn't he just get himself shot dead?"

"That's the one. Did you know him?"

"No, just heard tell of him; he was pretty well known on the street. He never stayed here, though, at least not since I been on the job."

"Well, thank you for your time, Merle. We appreciate it," Bascom said as we left the seedy flophouse.

"Hard to imagine that there are places cheaper than this one," I said when we were outside.

"As far as flophouses go in this old town, you haven't seen anything yet, Archie. Some of the joints have more rats than people in them. This one's elegant by comparison, if you can believe it."

"I'll have to take your word for it. Well, seems like there's no doubt who those two guys were that had Tommie in the auto that night in the Bronx. Both of them tall, dark, and skinny. The Jasper boys, if—to use your words—that's their real name. And the one matches the description of the guy who went to the Williamson kitchen keeping the cook occupied with that phony story about delivering produce she had ordered. All the while the other guy, likely the brother, was snatching Tommie Williamson right out of his own backyard."

"Looks like it had to be them all right, although I never got a good look at either one in all the confusion and gunshots and darkness. Cather nicked one, though, didn't he?"

"Yeah, I think so. The guy let out with a yell. Well, I've got to head back to Long Island and pick Tommie up from school. Then it's off to Nero Wolfe's place tonight with Williamson to meet with Inspector Cramer. Figures to be a damned interesting session."

"No doubt. Drop me off at the nearest subway station. When I get back to the office, I'm going to telephone Saul Panzer and see if he knows of any pair of brothers who work cons. He's got all kinds of sources. And I'll give three-to-one odds that when we do find them, their names won't be Evanson or Jasper."

"I'm not touching that bet, Del. I value my dollars too much."

# CHAPTER 21

On the drive into Manhattan that night, Burke Williamson sat up front with me, and I was wearing a suit and tie, rather than my uniform. "Goodwin, you are going as my associate, not my chauffeur," he had said earlier. "And in that role, I'll want you to remember every bit of dialogue. You told me once that you have what is being called total recall."

"Yes, sir, I seem to."

"Good, because that will be the equivalent of having a stenographer present. I don't want to be misquoted later by Cramer or anybody else."

We arrived at Nero Wolfe's brownstone at five minutes before nine, pulling to the curb behind what was almost certainly a police sedan. Fritz Brenner ushered us to the office, where Cramer and Panzer already were seated. The inspector glowered from his spot in the red leather chair at the end of Wolfe's desk but said nothing when we entered.

Panzer nodded from a sofa in the rear, while Williamson and I dropped into the twin yellow chairs. There doubtless would have been an uneasy silence had Wolfe not entered the room moments after we had gotten seated.

"Gentlemen," he said, as he settled into his chair, "would you like something to drink? I am having beer." He looked directly at Cramer when he spoke, daring the inspector to challenge this flouting of the federal statutes.

"You know damned well that I did not come here in search of a drink, Wolfe," he snarled. "In fact—"

Wolfe cut him off. "Your presence is appreciated, sir, as is your indulgence in agreeing to meet here. Anyone else, drinks?"

Willing to defy the law in the presence of a high-ranking policeman, both Panzer and Williamson ordered scotch and water, while I chose milk. After the drinks had been served by Brenner and Wolfe had taken his first sip, Cramer leaned forward and slapped a palm down on the desk.

"Before we get started, I want it on record that I object to being maneuvered into this meeting. The only reason I agreed to come is out of respect for Mr. Williamson, who has for many years been a loyal friend to the Police Department and its charitable programs." Cramer punctuated his comment by pulling out a cigar and jamming it into his mouth unlit.

"Your objection is duly noted, Inspector," Wolfe said. "However, despite the location, this really is your meeting. You wanted to see us, so proceed."

"It was you and Mr. Williamson I wanted to see, but separately, not together. And not with an army present," he said, looking around the room.

"Two others hardly constitute an army, sir. It is possible Mr. Panzer and Mr. Goodwin may contribute to the discussion."

"Maybe. As for you, Goodwin, I see that you didn't take my advice, and you insist on hanging around with Wolfe's bunch," Cramer snarled, chewing on his cigar. "Suit yourself, but by heaven, you will live to regret it. All right, on to business, some of it monkey business. Unfortunately, it often takes news of police activity a while to find its way down to Manhattan from the far reaches of the Bronx, but that is the department's problem, not yours, and it will be dealt with.

"Here is what I now am faced with: one, the unreported kidnapping of an eight-year-old boy; two, the shooting death on a

Bronx street of an old-time hustler named Barney Haskell; three, a gun battle, also on a Bronx street, between a posse of shoot-'em-up private investigators and kidnappers in which the child is endangered but somehow is saved; four, the escape of the kidnappers, who remain at large; and five, the shooting death on—you guessed it—a Bronx street of the chauffeur to the family of the kidnapped child." Cramer leaned back and blew out air, shaking his head in disgust.

"Inspector, there is what I feel to be a valid reason that my son's kidnapping was not reported," Williamson said.

Cramer glowered at the hotelier. "It had better be a good one, sir."

"We were told by the kidnappers that if we called the police, it would endanger Tommie's life."

"Kidnappers always use that threat as leverage."

"That may well be, Inspector. But with my son in their hands, I was not about to call their bluff."

"Our force has had a lot of experience with kidnappings over the years."

"Bear in mind that this kidnapping did not occur within your jurisdiction, but in Nassau County, which, the last time I checked, is not within the boundaries of New York City."

"We do, however, work closely with neighboring counties where crimes such as murder and kidnapping have been committed," Cramer countered.

"Gentlemen," Wolfe said, addressing Williamson and Cramer, "in the interests of moving the discussion along, let us stipulate that there is a difference of opinion between you regarding the handling of the kidnapping."

"You're damn right there's a difference of opinion," Cramer groused. "This is not the sort of situation that should be left to a bunch of quick-draw amateurs like your band of vigilantes."

"You certainly are in Wild West mode today," Wolfe remarked, "using terms like posse and vigilantes. After all the bombast gets sifted out, however, the central fact remains: Tommie Williamson is back at home, no doubt shaken by the experience but nonetheless unharmed."

"All right," Cramer said, "enough about the kidnapping for now. We still are left with two dead bodies, one of them an employee of the Williamsons. What can any of you tell me about that?"

"Inspector, I was shocked beyond words by Charles Bell's death," Williamson said. "He had been a loyal and dedicated employee for several years, and I continue to find it hard to believe that he had anything to do with Tommie's kidnapping."

"And I find it hard to believe that he didn't have anything to do with it," Cramer fired back, waving his unlit stogie. "Given what I now know, this had to have been at least partially an inside job."

"The inspector is correct," Wolfe said. "How else can one explain the arrival of an unexpected truck on the grounds of the estate at the very moment when Tommie was outside—and suddenly alone?"

"Yeah, I would like to know more about that truck," Cramer said. "I'm just getting up to speed here."

Williamson took a sip of his scotch and set the glass down. "The truck is a mystery, all right. One of the men in it went to the kitchen with produce—produce the cook had not ordered. Further, he claimed to be from a purveyor other than the one she normally uses."

"Anybody get a look at the truck?" Cramer asked.

I wore my best poker face, and so did Panzer. "Mrs. Price—she's our cook—sent the guy packing, but she followed him out the kitchen door and up the steps that looked out onto the yard," Williamson said. "She said the truck was enclosed and white, no lettering on it."

"Of course no lettering," Cramer fumed. "It has all the indications of your classic inside-out job. Somebody on the inside, surely in this case the chauffeur, Bell, was in cahoots with somebody on the outside to work the snatch on the boy. After they got the ransom money, Bell understandably wanted his cut, and the outside man—or men— weren't having any of that. Things got rough, and ..." The inspector turned his palms up in explanation.

"Very possibly," Wolfe said. "Saul, do you have any thoughts?"

Panzer shrugged. "Seems like the inspector has it well pegged."

"Well, thanks one hell of a lot for your endorsement," Cramer said with a sneer. "Want to suggest who worked this from the outside? And by the way, how does that two-bit swindler, Barney Haskell, fit into the picture? From what we know about him, which is quite a bit given his record, he's not smart enough to be in on the planning of something as complex as this. He's no great loss to the community—that is off the record—but I am in charge of homicide in this town, dammit, and when somebody gets themselves murdered, my department is expected to find out who did it, no matter the social status of the victim. Wolfe, I do need a drink—rye on the rocks—and if you won't say anything about my having one, I won't say anything about you serving it."

"An equitable arrangement," Wolfe said, reaching under his desk to hit a buzzer I now knew about. Seconds later, Fritz Brenner appeared.

"Nobody has answered my question about Haskell," New York's top homicide cop complained moments later after sipping his illegal beverage. "Since everybody in this room apparently knows more about what's been going on than I do, I welcome any contributions."

I did not know Cramer, other than by reputation and having seen him in this room once previously, but it was clear that the man grudgingly sought help.

"Sir, unless anyone else here has information I am unaware of, I fear we cannot be of assistance," Wolfe said. "Do you have any evidence whatever to connect this Haskell to the Williamson kidnapping?"

"I do not. However, I do find it interesting that both Charles Bell and this Haskell were shot in the same general area of the Bronx within days of each other."

"Are shootings in the Bronx rare?" Wolfe asked.

"Unfortunately, no."

"Given the life Mr. Haskell chose to lead, it would seem his violent demise is hardly surprising," Wolfe observed.

"Maybe, although he was a small-time operator. It's hard to imagine his cheap con games causing anyone to want to kill him. You haven't talked much tonight, Mr. Williamson," Cramer said. "We already have strong circumstantial evidence linking Mr. Bell to the kidnapping. Is it possible one or more of the others in your household were involved?"

"Absolutely not! For that matter, I do not believe Charles had anything to do with it. I think he was killed because he was trying to solve the case himself and had closed in on the solution," Williamson declared, his face red and the veins standing out in his neck. "Instead of trying to implicate my employees, you should be trying to find those men who took Tommie, the ones we faced off against that night next to the Bronx Zoo. They are the real culprits, Inspector."

"Believe me, we've been looking for them, but so far, we don't have a lot to go on," Cramer said. "Has your son been able to give you any descriptions or other information?"

"Just that there were two of them, both tall and thin and dark, and every time he saw them, they were wearing dark glasses. Also, that he was being held in a second- or third-floor apartment—probably somewhere within the city, because there was a lot of street noise."

Cramer leaned forward, elbows on knees. "We would like to talk to Tommie. With you being present, of course."

"We don't want you to get him all upset," Williamson said, making me wonder just how well the man knew his son. Based on my observations these last few days, Tommie had quickly gotten over being upset about his ordeal. The kid had a backbone.

"I assure you we would not get him upset," Cramer said. "We've got people who are skilled at talking to children, specialists who have been trained to be sensitive."

"Let's talk about this later," Williamson said curtly.

"We also will make every effort to retrieve some or all of the ransom money," Cramer went on. "If we had been involved from the beginning, it's likely the cash never would have changed hands." He shot a look at Wolfe and then Panzer. Apparently, I didn't merit one of his glares.

"The money does not concern me," Williamson said. "Obviously it would be nice to have it back, but I am not about to lose any sleep if I never see a cent of it again."

Cramer turned his attention to Wolfe. "You know my feelings about your involvement in all of this," he said. "Enough is enough. This is police business—period."

"I, for one, owe Mr. Wolfe an immeasurable debt of gratitude," Williamson said, holding his glass high as if in a toast.

"Everything he does comes with a price," Cramer observed dryly. "Don't forget that. Although I suppose I should not be speaking that way about my host."

"My hospitality is not contingent upon my guests' attitudes toward me," Wolfe replied. "To me, the relationship of host and guest is sacred—regardless of that guest."

"Nicely put," Williamson said. "And, Inspector, just to set the record straight, I approached Mr. Wolfe on the recommendation of a friend, seeking his aid in getting Tommie rescued. I quoted him a fee, to which he readily agreed. He made no attempt whatever to counter my offer with a higher amount, and I certainly felt I got value received."

"Glad to hear you're happy," Cramer muttered, "but two murders remain unsolved and at least two kidnappers—who also may very well be killers—are at large. We need your help and your cooperation, Mr. Williamson."

"Call me at my office tomorrow, Inspector, and we can discuss this further."

Cramer rose. "I will. And Wolfe," he said, jabbing an index finger at his host, "stay out of this from now on. That goes for your hired guns, as well," he added, this time favoring me as well as Panzer with one of his glares. He stomped out of the office and down the hall.

"The man is irascible and permanently angry, isn't he?" Williamson observed.

"Do not be too hard on Mr. Cramer," Wolfe replied. "His job is a difficult and often thankless one. He constantly receives assaults from all sides. His superiors in the department demand arrests, the newspapers demand arrests, the public demands arrests. I agree that he is cantankerous, contentious, and often thickheaded. But he also is honest, hardworking, and fearless. The department would do well to have more men like him in their ranks."

"Well, I will take that into consideration when he and I talk tomorrow. Thank you for your hospitality," Williamson said, standing and motioning me to follow.

In the Pierce-Arrow on the way back to Long Island, Williamson spoke first. "How do you feel the evening went?" he asked.

"Not much got accomplished, other than Cramer blowing off some steam. It's obvious the police are nowhere on this, and the inspector is frustrated almost beyond words."

"Do you think I should let them question Tommie?"

"Why not? Maybe something he remembers can be of help to them. Besides, you will be present in case you think they get too rough on him."

"Has he talked to you about the kidnapping?"

"No," I lied. "We chat about other things, like sports."

"Tommie likes you a lot," Williamson said. "If he's told me once, he's told me ten times that you have taught him how to throw a spiral pass."

"And that's pretty impressive, given how small his hands are. He is a really nice kid, very enthusiastic. You should toss the football around with him yourself."

"Are you telling me how to be a father?" he snapped.

"No, sir. Sorry, I was out of line."

Williamson sighed. "Damn! No, you really were not out of line, Goodwin—I was. You are absolutely right. I need to spend more time with Tommie, and less time with my work. I really appreciate the attention you've given him. It won't be the same when you're gone."

"Well, the job was for the short term. We all knew that going in."

"True, and I need to bring you up to date on that subject. I have begun a search for a new chauffeur, both through newspaper advertisements and conversations with acquaintances. I realize Wolfe wanted you on the job to determine if one of my employees was part of the kidnapping plot. That seems unlikely, with the possible exception of poor Bell, who I still feel was not involved. Do you now have any suspicions as regards the household staff?"

"None that I can put my finger on."

"Then I believe the time has come to make a move. But Tommie is really going to miss you."

"For what it's worth, sir, I'll miss him, too. One thing that should make you feel good: I've noticed that at school, he seems to have a lot of friends. When I drop him off in the morning, four or five other boys always run over to greet him, and they all head off playing one game or another until they get herded inside. I always wait until he's in the building before I drive off."

"That's good to know, and I'll make sure that the next man in your job does the same thing. I may even arm the man with a gun, to be on the safe side. By the way, Tommie has also told his mother and me about how well he gets along with the other lads. I gather you don't think the kidnapping has been too traumatic on him."

"No, sir, I don't. Now I haven't been around eight-year-olds much, but he seems very well adjusted to me."

"Well, I believe you are at least partly responsible for that, Goodwin. Say, I have an idea. Since Tommie seems to like football so much, how about the three of us going to a Columbia University game in the next few weeks, maybe against Princeton? I've got a good friend who can get us seats on the fifty-yard line."

"I would like that."

"Good, I'll go ahead and make the arrangements. What are your plans after you leave us?"

"I haven't given it a lot of thought, but I'd like to see if I can really make it as a private investigator."

"Perhaps you could go to work for Nero Wolfe," Williamson said. "He seems to like you."

I laughed. "He's already got himself a good bunch of operatives—particularly that Saul Panzer, who could find a black cat in a coal bin without a flashlight."

"You may be right, but I still think Wolfe could use a resourceful young man like you."

"Well, you've given me something to think about," I said as I steered the big automobile through the Long Island darkness.

# CHAPTER 22

Less than a week later, my stint as the Williamson chauffeur came to an end. My replacement was a stocky, good-natured chap of about fifty named Gentry, who had been the longtime driver for a recently deceased dowager up in Scarsdale, which I learned was a prosperous suburb.

"I thought I would be in the breadlines after dear Mrs. Parnell passed, God rest her soul," Gentry said, "but then this opportunity blessedly came along. I sincerely hope it does not inconvenience you."

"Not in the least," I told him after I had gone over some of the particulars of the job. "It was only a temporary position for me."

Before Williamson and Waverly the butler introduced Gentry to the staff, I made it a point to go to each of them individually and bid them good-bye. Their reactions were varied, to say the least.

Waverly, not surprising, remained stiffly formal, shaking hands and wishing me well "in all your future endeavors." Emily Stratton coughed delicately and observed that I had turned out to be "more mature" than she had expected.

Lloyd Carstens stopped watering plants in the greenhouse long enough to peer at me over his half-glasses. "Huh! On your way, eh? Seems like you came aboard only yesterday. I always figured you was a snoop, and to be honest, I ain't changed my mind on that. I hope they get themselves a real chauffeur this time around, not like you or that nose-in-the-air Bell."

Simons, the stable master, was only slightly less hostile than Carstens. "Thought you were too young to be handling those pricey autos," he snorted. "I made a bet with myself that you'd run one of 'em off the road, and I still think you would have if you'd stayed around much longer."

Mary Trent seemed genuinely sorry to see me go, although she didn't try to kiss me again, maybe because there were people around. "You were the friendliest one here, along with Miss Moore," she said, offering her small hand. "I hope really that we meet again sometime … soon." I had no answer for that, other than to say that I hoped so as well.

Sylvia Moore told me she was sorry I had been at the Williamsons at such an unhappy time, and she hoped I would not judge the staff by their actions of the last weeks. "Everyone has been so upset over Tommie and then Charles Bell. They all are really nicer people than their recent behavior would indicate."

I thought Mrs. Price would squeeze the life out of me as she wrapped those pudgy arms around my middle and pulled my head down so she could nuzzle my neck. "I will truly miss you, laddie. No one has ever enjoyed my cooking as much as you," she said. "I do wish you were staying with us, but a young fellow like you, I can understand your wanting to get out and see more of the world than a big old estate stuck away on Long Island."

My hardest farewell was with Tommie. "I'm really sorry that you're leaving, Archie," he said, sniffling as I drove him home from school my last day on the job. "I really had fun with you."

"I believe you will like Mr. Gentry," I told him. "He seems to be very friendly."

"He won't want to play football with me though, or fly a kite like we did that one afternoon," he said, jaw set and arms folded across his chest.

"Speaking of football, you and I will be going to a game with your dad at Columbia University in a few weeks, so we will be seeing each other again. This is big-time football, in a stadium and everything." That quickly turned his face from a pout to a smile, and at that moment, I realized how much I would miss the boy.

That evening after dinner, Gentry drove me to the commuter station with my suitcase and I rode a Long Island line local into Penn Station, then took the subway north to the Melbourne Hotel. My room was far smaller than my quarters in the Williamson house, but I felt I was returning home, which was a good feeling. I was asleep seconds after my head hit the pillow.

The next morning, I resumed what had previously been my Manhattan routine: up at seven thirty, fifteen minutes of exercise, take a shower down the hall, get dressed, then amble along the block to Mort's little beanery for some breakfast.

"Archie Goodwin!" he boomed when I walked in. "Haven't seen you for what seems like ages. I figured you gave up on New York and went back home to Indiana."

"Ohio," I said, dropping onto one of the stools at the counter.

"Illinois, Indiana, Ohio, they're all the same to me," Mort said, gesturing in a westerly direction and sliding a cup of coffee along the counter from ten feet down. It came to a stop directly in front of me, with not a drop spilled.

"How do you always do that?" I asked, taking a sip of the delicious brew.

"Years of practice and great wrist action," he said, flexing an arm. "Where have you been lately? I thought that you liked this joint."

"Oh, I do, Mort, but I had to go out of town on a hard-driving job. When duty calls, I answer."

Half an hour later, having breakfasted on wheat cakes, bacon, and eggs, I hoofed it south to the office of the Bascom Detective Agency. Wilda looked up as I stepped off the elevator, her mouth twitching in what may have been a smile. "The man around?" I asked, and she tilted her head toward his office. "Go on in, he's expecting you."

"Ah, home from the land of the rich," Del said, looking up from the *Gazette* crossword puzzle and grinding out what was left of his nickel stogie. "Saul Panzer told me that you had got sprung from that rough duty out on the island."

"Save your sympathy," I told him, dropping into the guest chair and setting my hat on the corner of his desk.

"So, during your stay out in the country, did you figure out who in the Williamson household is not to be trusted?"

"I'm not sure I would trust several of them very far," I said, "but I'm not ready to send anybody to the chair yet. What's happening back here among the riffraff?"

"Well, for one thing, we're having yet another meeting in Wolfe's office today, and you, lucky chap, are invited."

"He doesn't want to let go of this business, is that it? How does he expect to get paid from here on out? Williamson already forked over a nice hunk of cash to get his son back."

"Archie, I don't claim to know Nero Wolfe and how he thinks as well as Panzer and others who work with him more often than me, but I believe his pride is at stake here," Bascom said. "Sure, his planning was responsible for getting the boy back, but Wolfe is still smarting from those two murders and the ransom money. For him, the job is unfinished."

"If I might ask then, who are we working for now?" I posed. "And who's going to pay us?"

Bascom leaned back and torched another cigar. "Truth is, I got no work right now, which means neither do you. I'm willing to take my chances that something comes out of this meeting with Wolfe."

"Okay, that's good enough for me. If you're in, I'm in," I told him. "When do we meet?"

"Eleven o'clock. From what Panzer said, it sounds like every operative Wolfe has ever used will be there."

"Gee, a regular detectives' convention. How exciting!"

"All right, Archie, cut the sarcasm. I don't think our host is going to be in the mood for that kind of humor."

"My distinct impression is that Nero Wolfe is never in the mood for any kind of humor, but I promise to be a good boy and keep my ears open and my mouth shut—more or less."

"Good idea. Wolfe seems to like you, and I leave it to you to figure out whether it's because of your smart-alecky comments or in spite of them."

At five before eleven, Fritz Brenner swung open the door of the brownstone on West Thirty-Fifth to admit Bascom and me. "Everyone else is here, please go on in," he said. The usual faces were seated in the office, plus one I did not recognize.

"Hi, Bill," Bascom said to a husky, balding guy seated on the sofa next to Cather. "Meet Archie Goodwin, who works with me. Archie, this is Bill Gore, a first-class operative I've had the honor to work with a few times."

"Thanks for the nice words, Del," Gore said, rising. He went at least six foot two and two hundred pounds, none of it fat. A good man to have on your side when things got rough. "Nice to meet you, Goodwin," he said, pumping my hand.

Wolfe walked in, greeted us with his usual dip of the head, and moved around behind his desk, ringing for beer. Everyone passed on his invitation for refreshments.

"Thank you all for coming," he said, adjusting his bulk. "Saul, I assume you have brought Mr. Gore up to date on the situation."

"Yes, sir, I have."

"Very well. As you all are aware, I no longer possess a client, Mr. Williamson having settled his account with me after his son was freed and the ransom paid. By the way, Mr. Goodwin, did you receive remuneration for your services in his employ?"

"I got a check from him," I said, again making a mental note to look up "remuneration" in the dictionary I had yet to buy.

"You merited payment," Wolfe replied, opening the first of the beers Fritz had placed on a tray in front of him. "Speaking of remuneration, I want each of you to know that you will be paid for your work on this endeavor, regardless of our success. You will not find me stinting on the amount. Saul, if you please, a review of the situation."

Panzer cleared his throat. "We know that the kidnappers—who presumably also killed both Barney Haskell and Charles Bell—are a pair of tall, thin brothers who have been involved for years in a variety of long and short cons and other grifting. Through sources, never mind who or how, I found three sets of brothers who could fit the bill," he said, consulting his notebook.

"By name, they are: the Harkers, James and Melvin; the McCalls, Reese and Ronald; and the Bagleys, Chester and Calvin. All of them, no surprise, have records, although none for murder or even for armed robbery."

"So, nobody on your list is named Edgar or Leon Jasper, eh?" I asked.

"No, why?" Panzer asked.

"They were the names given by a hotel desk clerk for two guys who Del and I think rented the truck used in the kidnapping."

"None of these characters ever use their real names in hotels," Orrie Cather muttered.

"True," Panzer said. "Did those Jaspers fit the description?"

Del Bascom nodded. "Yeah, both of them tall and dark and skinny."

"I know all of you except Mr. Gore got glimpses of at least one of the two kidnappers that night in the Bronx," Wolfe said. "Based on that brief skirmish, does anyone think they could make a definite identification?" We all shook our heads.

"I thought not. Gentlemen, here is my position: despite Mr. Williamson's approval and payment, I remain dissatisfied and irritated at what I view as an incomplete job on my part. I want those two men found and brought in. I also want the ransom money retrieved if possible."

"What about the police?" Durkin asked.

"What indeed, Fred? They are angry with me, a not unusual occurrence, nor one that disturbs me. More important, they seem to have no idea how to proceed, other than to question Tommie

Williamson. I suspect Mr. Goodwin here got more information from Tommie by being patient and conversational than the police will get with their heavy-handed approach."

Wolfe drank beer, dabbed his lips with a handkerchief, and continued. "Any one of you might accuse me of petulance, and I would be hard put to deny the charge. At this point, my self-esteem demands reparation. There are six of you here tonight. There are three sets of brothers at large, one brace of which is very likely guilty both of kidnapping and murder. You are to divide into groups of two, with each group assigned to find a pair of brothers. Saul?"

"Yes, sir. Here is how I have divided the assignments up: Fred and Del, you've got the Harker boys; Orrie and Bill, take the McCalls; and Archie and I will go after the Bagleys. I have some leads, albeit questionable, on where all these lovable lads might be found."

"So it has been decided that none of Williamson's employees were in on it, huh?" Cather asked.

"Not necessarily, Orrie," Wolfe said. "But if we locate the felonious brothers, we almost surely will discover the identities of anyone else involved in the Williamson case. I already have formed some assumptions in that direction."

Cather, arms folded, looked unconvinced. Panzer moved among the men with such information as he had on these sets of brothers. I waited my turn patiently.

# CHAPTER 23

"Okay, here is what we know about the Bagleys," Panzer told me after briefing the others. "These two have been running scams of all sorts, mostly two-man short cons, for at least fifteen years in New York, maybe longer. They could have written the book on three-card monte, the pigeon drop, the fiddle game, the Spanish prisoner, the pig in a poke, the badger game, and half a dozen others."

"You're speaking a language I never learned back in Ohio," I said. "Someday, you'll have to translate for me. Just out of curiosity, how do you come by all the information you've gotten?"

"It's a long story, Archie, with plenty of wrinkles. I know a lot of people, some of them cops, who know a lot of things about a lot of other people. Back to the brothers: their father, the late 'Beer Barrel' Bagley, was well known around town. The man took grifting to new levels. It was said that he once conned a famous old-time jewel thief out of five grand's worth of hot ice by claiming he could fence the diamonds for twice their value."

"So the supposedly clever thief gave the diamonds to Beer Barrel, who he never laid eyes on again, of course."

"Of course," Panzer said. "And his sons take after the old man. They've operated mostly out of the Bronx under a variety of last names, including Keller, Cunningham, and Schmidt. And like most grifters, they move around a lot, from one cheap hotel or flophouse to another."

"Aha, the good old Bronx again. That means they figure to be the ones we're looking for."

Panzer shook his head. "Not necessarily, Archie. It turns out that all three sets of brothers come from the Bronx."

"So it's a hotbed of con men up there?"

"I never thought of the borough that way, when I've even thought of it at all, but you may be right."

"I'm really puzzled by the murders, Saul," I said. "What I've heard about con men these last weeks is that they go out of their way to avoid violence. As I understand, they don't want the grief that comes with it."

"You're absolutely right in most cases, but every one of them has dreams of getting that one big strike that will put him on easy street, maybe for life. The Williamson kidnapping, with its hundred-grand ransom, sure as hell qualifies. Where that kind of dough is involved, the stakes go up and behaviors change. Case in point, Archie: most con men don't want anything to do with firearms, but at least one of those two was armed that night at the Bronx Zoo, and I will lay odds that the other one, the driver, also carried a gun."

"Do you figure that Haskell guy who got plugged was part of the team, and that they had a falling-out?" I asked.

"More likely he somehow learned about the plan and demanded to be dealt in. I located a half brother of Haskell's, a bookie who lives over in Brooklyn, and he said Barney had told him he was on to something 'really big' but that he couldn't talk about it."

"Okay, so where do we go from here?"

Where we went was to yet another transient hotel in the Bronx, a place Panzer had sniffed out as a possible lead to finding the Bagley boys. I had become spoiled, riding in Wolfe's automobile and driving the dandy Williamson machines, but all that was over now. Panzer didn't own an auto and, as I now knew, neither did any of the operatives Wolfe normally used. If I was going to stay in this town, I had better get to know the public transportation system, I thought as we came up out of the subway and onto a busy commercial street. Half a block down, we arrived at a shabby-looking establishment whose faded sign proclaimed it to be the HOTEL ELEGANT.

"Seems like all I'm doing lately is dropping in on flophouses," I complained.

"If you're going to be an operative in this vast and colorful metropolis, you'd better get used to it," Panzer said as we paused before entering. "This business of ours is not what one would term glamorous, despite what you might read in those pulp magazines of yours."

"When Bascom and I went into another fleabag not far from here, he passed himself off as a police lieutenant," I said. "What's the plan at this joint?"

"Archie, I can see Del Bascom filling that role, but do you honestly think that I could convince anyone that I was a cop?" he asked, gesturing to his thin, stooped frame. "Playing an officer of the law is not my métier and never has been. I take different approaches."

We walked into the dark, narrow lobby of the Hotel Elegant to find a heavy bleached blond of uncertain years sitting behind the counter and painting her fingernails a fire-engine red color. She looked up, eyeing us from under dark lashes that were thick enough to run a comb through.

"Can I help you fine gents?" the woman drawled in a South-of-the-Mason-Dixon-Line voice.

"I earnestly hope you can, Gloria," Saul Panzer said, taking off his flat cap and grinning.

Her brown eyes widened, lifting the mighty lashes. "Hey—how is it you know my name?"

"Who doesn't know the great Gloria McCracken? I remember you well from your days at the Spider Web Club over on West Eighty-Sixth. I recognized you the instant we walked in."

"Well, I've, um ... put on a few pounds since those days," she said, fluffing her hair self-consciously.

"Ah, but you look the same as ever to me," Panzer said, leaning his elbows on the counter. "And I will never forget the way you could warble 'Let Me Call You Sweetheart.' You always had the whole room in the palm of your hand with that one. I think it got requested every night, didn't it?"

Gloria got a dreamy look. "Ah, do I remember those days! That was just before the stinkin' Prohibition stuff came in and ruined everything. Say, you don't look old enough to have been goin' into the clubs back then."

"I'm a lot older'n I look, Gloria," Panzer said. "'Fraid to say I've been around the block a good many times."

"Tell me about it. These last few years, well ..." She lifted her shoulders and let them drop.

"I hear you. It's the same with everybody, which is why we're here."

"Tell me about it, soldier," she said, holding out an arm to study her newly lacquered nails.

Panzer ran a hand though his hair, feigning nervousness. "It's like this. There's a couple guys who owe me and my nephew here some money, and—"

"Stop right there, soldier," Gloria said. "You're not the first ones who have come into this place puttin' the touch on me. Now I know that I got a reputation for being softhearted, but —"

This time, Panzer did the interrupting. "No, no, Gloria, I am not trying to hit you up for a few bucks, although Lord only knows I could use them. What I'm trying to do is find these guys—brothers, or so they claim." He then described them, and Gloria nodded with a thin-lipped smile.

"Yeah, I happen to know just who you're talking about. What did you say your name is?"

"I didn't, but it's Berg, Norman Berg."

"Well, Norman, you gotta be talkin' about the Schmidt boys, or so they called themselves when they was bunking here. A couple of mean ones, those two, nastier than any other flimflam artists I've ever seen."

"That so? When did they stay here, Gloria?"

"It's been a few weeks back now, it was. I can check if you want," she said, opening the big guest book on the counter.

"Please do," Panzer replied. "I'd appreciate it, Gloria."

She flipped pages. "Let's see ... here we are. They checked in on the second of this month, stayed ... until the eleventh." She turned the book around so we could see it. One of them had signed his name, "Earl Schmidt and Brother, New York U.S.A."

"They didn't stay here long," I said.

"Huh—too long!" Gloria shot back. "A pair of surly so-and-sos, always complaining about their room, using foul language, spitting on the floor, even though we got spittoons all over the place. What the hell did they expect for what they were paying, a suite at the bloody Plaza? By the way," she said, turning to Panzer, "how did you happen to know they stayed here?"

"I've got a friend who has a friend, you know how it is. I suppose they didn't leave a place where any mail could be forwarded?"

"Nah, nobody ever does," she said, brushing the question away with a hand. "More than half the time, they don't even know where they're headed next. They—wait a minute. I did hear something that might help you track them down."

"I'm all ears—if you overlook my snout," Panzer said, grinning.

"Well, after they had checked out of here and the one brother had made a remark to me that I won't repeat, the other one, who called himself Carl, said to knock it off. 'We gotta get to Barney's place,' that's what he said. 'Barney's place.' I don't know if that helps you any."

"It might at that, Gloria. Well, thanks. It's been a pleasure seeing you. Do you still do any singing?" Panzer asked.

"Those days are gone and so are my pipes, Norman," she said, patting her throat. "Too many late nights, and way too many Lucky Strikes, if you get my drift."

"That is indeed our loss," he answered, turning back to bow before we headed out the door.

"That's really something, you remembering Gloria's singing from years ago," I told Panzer when we were out on the sidewalk.

"Archie, I never saw that woman before in my life."

"What! But you knew all about her, the club where she performed, and that song of hers."

He looked at me with a lopsided grin. "My source, the one who knew that the Bagley brothers had stayed at that flophouse, also knew a lot about Gloria and her past life. Besides, how ancient do you really think I am? She was right to say I didn't look old enough to be hanging out in clubs back before Prohibition kicked in."

"Well, I'll be damned. At least you made her feel good, Mr.—what is it?—Norman Berg."

"I just may have done more than that."

"True, Saul. The Bagley boys, if that's really their name as seems likely, would now appear to be definitely linked to Barney Haskell, assuming that's the Barney who they were going to see. It begins to look like they're the ones we're looking for. There's one other thing, Saul."

"Yes?'

"I told Wolfe this: when the kidnappers had Tommie Williamson, he heard them mention the name Barney."

"I know, Mr. Wolfe mentioned that to me. We'll want to hear from the others, though, to see if they've found out anything about the Harker and McCall brothers."

"I still think we're getting warm," I said.

"So do I, Archie."

# CHAPTER 24

By prearrangement, the six of us met the next morning in a coffee shop on West Sixty-Seventh Street to go over our findings and compare notes. Fred Durkin and Del Bascom went first.

"Here's the story on James and Melvin Harker," Del said, consulting his notebook. "We found the flat where they had been living up until August, in a walkup just off Third Avenue in the South Bronx. The building super said they moved out because they had what they called some 'important business' in St. Louis. They gave him a forwarding address, and he says he's sent a couple of pieces of mail to it."

"That doesn't mean they're really out there," Cather said.

"Of course not, Orrie," Del snapped, turning to Durkin. "Think we didn't check? Fred?"

Durkin took the cue. "I got a good friend named Alvin who's now in Saint Loo, an operative I worked with back when I was just starting out," he said. "I called him with the Harkers' address, and he went over to the flat, claiming that he was a termite inspector for the city. James Harker bought the story whole, even showed Alvin his identification to prove his residence. Alvin then did some checking around, and it turns out the Harkers have muscled in on the bootleg business in Missouri through a cousin there. Got themselves a real sweet deal."

"So we can cross off the Harkers," Panzer said. "Orrie, Bill, what about the McCall boys?"

"You can cross them off, too, Saul," Cather said. "One of the brothers, Ronald by name, has been residing in the Tombs for the last three months now."

"The Tombs? What the hell is that, a cemetery?" I asked.

"Formally known as the Manhattan House of Detention," Panzer said. "What's he in for?"

"Pulling the old three-card monte con," Bill Gore put in. "An undercover cop he tried to scam ran him in. Seems Ronald's not exactly an Einstein. That's his third or fourth trip to the cooler, according to my source."

"Well, that narrows it down to the Bagleys," Del Bascom observed. "What did you boys learn?"

Panzer went over our recent activities, and everybody nodded. "So now all we have to do is find them," he said.

"What about checking the hospitals?" Durkin asked. "After all, we think Orrie winged one of them."

"With all the hospitals we've got, that could take us forever," Panzer said. "Besides, the guy may have gone straight to some hard-up sawbones for treatment and paid him hush money to keep his mouth shut. Lots of docs treat gunshot wounds these days without reporting it."

Cather laughed. "Well, why not? Those boys sure weren't lacking for cash, were they?"

"Seems to me once the wounded brother got himself patched up, they'd get out of town," Gore said. "Make a new life someplace else."

"I don't think so, Bill," Panzer said. "They probably figure nobody's on to them. After all, both Haskell and Bell are dead, maybe the only two guys who could have fingered them. And they figure we didn't get all that good a gander at them during the gunfight. No, I believe that they've stayed in New York, where they know their way around."

"So what do we do now?" Durkin posed.

Nobody said anything for a half minute. Finally, I broke the silence.

"I know that I'm the new kid in this group, but I can't believe that the five of you, all veteran operatives, act like you're stumped. How tough can it really be to find these two?"

"Damned tough, Archie," Bascom argued. "It's easy to lose yourself in this town. Remember that camera salesman you nailed? He almost pulled it off."

"But he didn't," I retorted.

"Del's right, though," Panzer said. "There's any number of places the Bagleys can lie low, and for a long time."

"What about us offering a reward?" I asked. "All of you must know your share of grifters, and some of them gotta have some inkling of the Bagleys' whereabouts. Or do all these con men stick together in a code of silence?"

As I talked, Bill Gore's face grew red. "Okay," he said, "it's confession time. Years back, I did some grifting myself, petty stuff, before I went straight—if you call this business we're in straight. Anyway, Goodwin here has a point. Almost all these bunco boys would sell any other one of them out for the price of a decent meal or a bottle of bathtub gin. You know that old phrase, 'there's no honor among thieves'? It's really true."

"Yeah, but then where in the hell are we gonna get the money to dole out?" Cather growled.

"Wolfe should be rolling in it from what Williamson paid him for getting his kid back," Durkin said.

"Hold on," Panzer cut in. "I think Archie might be on to something. I'll talk to Wolfe today and see if he'll go along with the idea and fork over some dough that we can spread around. I agree with Bill that it won't take much to get someone to sing to us about the Bagley boys."

That afternoon, I was sitting with Bascom in his office chewing the fat when he got a telephone call from Panzer. "That's great, Saul!" Del said into the mouthpiece. "Yeah, Archie and I will see you then. Wolfe came up with some jack that we can use," he told me after hanging up. "We're to meet at Panzer's place on Thirty-Eighth Street between Lex and Third Avenue tonight and map out what comes next."

At seven thirty, the six of us sat in the big living room of Panzer's spacious quarters on the top floor of a remodeled house. He clearly had done well for himself as a freelance operative, as indicated by the grand piano in a far corner and floor-to-ceiling shelves filled with books and relics that included chunks of minerals and walrus tusks. I know absolutely nothing about art, but the landscape and portrait paintings on the walls looked to me like they belonged in a museum.

Like Wolfe, Panzer ignored the existence of Prohibition, offering drinks ranging from beer and wine to scotch, rye, and gin. We all took him up, me with scotch and water. "Okay, as I told you all on the telephone, Mr. Wolfe liked the idea of using cash to loosen lips. I thought we'd split up and all go solo, except Archie, who's so new that he can team with Del. I've got a stack of fins for each of you. Give them out sparingly."

"Whose gonna tell us anything for a measly five bucks?" Cather whined.

"Are you kidding, Orrie?" Durkin asked. "The con business ain't what it used to be in this town. Bill was right when he said that just about any one of these guys would sell a fellow bunco artist out for the price of a decent dinner or a bottle of damn near anything, let alone a whole finif."

"Hell, I may even break a few of those bills into singles," Bascom said. "Some of these boys will turn handstands for even a picture of Washington."

Panzer looked around at us in turn. "Everybody here, other than Archie, either knows plenty of grifters or at least knows where they hang out. You can't be in this business for long without practically tripping over them on every corner. So each of you take a small stack of these greenbacks and hit the streets. We'll meet back here tomorrow morning at eleven, maybe with some results."

"That's not very long to dig something up," Cather complained.

"Except that Archie's right when he says we've all been around awhile and shouldn't let this stump us. Let's all do some digging," Panzer urged.

"Do we start right now?" I asked Del when we were out on the street.

"Why not? It's just a little after nine, for Pete's sake. The night is young, particularly in the world of the lowlife. We're going to start out in a speakeasy over on Second Avenue and Twenty-First, where a lot of these blacklegs and sharps drop in for a quick nip or two during their breaks from running short cons out on the street."

We walked up to a dark, shuttered storefront. "Looks like it's closed up," I said.

"That's just what it's supposed to look like," Del responded, rapping hard on the windowless wooden door. It opened a crack. "Bascom, I'll be damned!" a voice rasped. The door swung open, revealing a figure who made Nero Wolfe look slender by comparison. "I haven't laid eyes on you since Hector was a pup," the fat man boomed. "C'mon in."

"Good to see you again, Tiny," Del said. "It's been a while all right. Meet my trusted sidekick, Archie."

"Pleased to meetcha, Archie. Any friend of Del's ... et cetera, et cetera."

The high-ceilinged room was dimly lit, crudely furnished, and noisy, but the joint must have had thick walls, because nothing could be heard from the street. We found two stools at the rough-hewn wooden bar, and a tall, angular, bearded guy with long gray hair ambled over to take our orders.

"Well, if it isn't ol' Del," he drawled. "Thought you must have found a better place to drink these days."

"I been busy lately," Bascom replied. "Archie, say hi to Whiskey Dick, who runs this so-called establishment."

"What do you mean, 'so-called'?" Whiskey fired back, trying without success to look offended. "We serve only the finest clientele."

"Right," Bascom said, "that is if you count winos, con men, card sharps, and bunco boys."

"All part of the warp and woof of life's grand tapestry," the owner observed, serving us two beers.

"Spoken like the true publican you are. What have you been hearing out on the street lately?"

"Aha, here to pump me now, are you? I might have known, you being a shamus and all. I hear all sorts of things, some of them maybe even true."

"Give me some samples," Bascom said, sliding a five-dollar bill across the bar. "This picture of Abe is over and above our drink tab."

"Not sure I have anything that will live up to that fin, Del. I can tell you this, though: poor Barney Haskell got gunned down in the Bronx a few days back," he said, smoothly pocketing the five-spot.

"Old news, Whiskey. But while we're on the subject, you have any idea why Barney got erased? I always saw him as a harmless old two-bit operator."

"That he was indeed, Del," the bartender said, nodding and leaning bony elbows on the bar. "I hear tell he got himself involved in something that goes way beyond simple cons."

"Is that so? Like what?"

Whiskey Dick leaned across the bar and lowered his voice, which was unnecessary given the din. "Kidnapping," he mouthed.

Bascom looked shocked. "Barney Haskell involved in a kidnapping? I find that hard to swallow."

"I know, me too. Apparently he got hooked up with a couple of brothers who planned the grab of some nabob's kid, at least that's the talk I been hearing. What's it to you, anyway?"

"Nothing, probably. Interesting story, though, and I always like a good story. Any idea who these brothers are?"

Whiskey Dick's bloodshot eyes narrowed to slits. "Del, you *are* interested, you old rascal, or you wouldn't be parting with lettuce. Does that fin happen to have a cousin by any chance?"

"It just might, depending on the answers I get. Now ... what can you tell me about those brothers?"

"They go by several names, or so I hear. Cunningham, Schmidt, Jasper, Bagley, maybe more. Far as I know, they've never been in here,

I'm glad to say. Story I get is that they work up north, mostly in the Bronx, and that they're a surly pair. Do I get that other fiver now? You know that I have cops that I've gotta be nice to if I expect to keep this operation going."

"Not so fast," Bascom said, slapping a palm on the bar. "Archie and I were hoping you could tell us where these brothers are holed up now."

"Are you kidding, Del? How would I know that? I don't keep tabs on every second-rate shark working the long cons or even the short ones for that matter."

"Maybe not, but you hear talk. For instance, you knew who the kidnappers were. Now I would just love to give you that second Lincoln, but I simply can't without some more help. Sorry, but that's how it is."

"What's your angle, Del?" Whiskey Dick asked. "And how does the kid fit in?" He jerked a thumb in my direction.

"I'll answer the second question first, you old rumrunner. Archie here is the smartest young operative I've seen come along in a dozen years, maybe more. As for my angle, I have a client who—"

"I thought so! And I'll bet it's that swell whose kid got snatched, isn't it?"

"I'm not at liberty to divulge any names, but I will say certain people are extremely interested in locating those brothers."

"I'll just bet they are, given that those boys probably have a trunk stuffed full of ransom money."

"Chances are you're right," Del said. "Now let's—"

"I think that maybe we can work out a deal," Whiskey Dick said, his ruddy, pockmarked face breaking into a snaggle-toothed grin. "Now if I can locate these Schmidt or Bagley or Cunningham brothers for you, or whatever their name is, I get a piece of the—"

"It's my turn to do the interrupting, you chattering chiseler," Del barked. "One minute you say you got no idea where to find these guys, and then, when you start to sniff out some big bucks, all of a sudden it seems like you just might be able to locate them. Why does it feel to me like you've got your hand on my wallet?"

"Now hold on a second," the barkeep said, holding up his palms as if surrendering. "I was just trying to help you guys with your problem."

"Yeah, right," Del scowled, leaning in toward Whiskey Dick. "It's just possible you still might be able to earn that second fiver, which I'm sure would nicely grease the palm of a beat cop. After all, we want you to stay in business. Now, how were you planning to find those brothers?"

"I ... uh, wasn't sure, but I had this idea. It's kind of a long shot, though," the barkeep said.

"We like long shots, don't we, Archie?" I nodded. "Let's hear it," Bascom said, pulling a five-dollar bill out of his pocket and smoothing it out on the bar.

"Well, there's this mouthpiece who seems to represent a lot of the grifters who've ever worked a con from Staten Island to Yonkers and everyplace in between. Talk is that in the courtroom, he has gotten a lot of these characters off with just a small fine or a slap on the wrist. It's just possible he might know of the two that you're looking for."

"What's his name?"

"Harding."

"Related to our late and unlamented president?"

Whiskey Dick shrugged. "No idea. His handle is Stanley, or maybe Steven. I've never met the mouthpiece, just heard his name a bunch of times from guys talking to each other in here."

"Get any idea where his office is?" I asked. He shook his head and looked longingly at the banknote lying on the bar.

"Go ahead," Del said, "Take it, it's yours. And here's for the beers." He dropped another dollar on the bar. "Let's go, Archie. Dick's got other thirsty customers to serve. We don't want to monopolize him."

Out on the sidewalk, I turned to Del. "You know, President Harding came from my home state of Ohio."

"Whatever you do, don't brag about it," he said. "The sooner people forget that crook, the better."

# CHAPTER 25

"Ever heard of this Harding character?" I asked Del as we walked away from the speakeasy.

"Nope, but then I haven't spent all that much time around con men," he said. "He sounds like one of your typical shysters, though, particularly given the caliber of his clientele."

After we walked a block, I reached into a phone booth, finding an alphabetical directory chained to the shelf. "Here it is, Stanley Harding, attorney, at an address on Catherine Street."

"Lower East Side. Not exactly a high-end location, although I would hardly expect him to have his office in some skyscraper in the Financial District or on Madison Avenue," Del said.

"Shall we drop in on him first thing tomorrow?"

"No, Archie, we've got time. Let's report in at Saul's at eleven and see what the others have come up with."

We were the first ones at Panzer's the next day. He was ready with a pot of steaming coffee and bagels. "Your joe is as good as I remember it," Del said, savoring his first sip.

"It's the chicory I put in that makes the difference," Panzer replied with a smile. "I can't drink the stuff without it now."

The others arrived in a cluster, Durkin first, followed quickly by

Cather and Gore. Panzer served everyone efficiently and we all sat. "Well, who wants to report?" our host asked.

"Archie and I had an interesting evening," Del said. "I'll let him tell you about it." I related our visit to the bar and the conversation with Whiskey Dick. When I brought up Stanley Harding's name, both Panzer and Orrie Cather started chuckling. "What's so funny?" I asked.

"You go first, Orrie," Saul said.

Cather sipped coffee and shook his head. "Last night, I looked up a short-con specialist I've known for years, a seedy little shrimp who usually goes by the name of Mercer, and he told me that the man who knows the most about grifters in the five boroughs is a somewhat shady mouthpiece named Harding. I figured on stopping by to see him later today."

"It is indeed a small world," Panzer said, shaking his head and grinning. "Like Orrie, I visited a man known for his ability to relieve suckers of their dimes and their dollars. He claims not to know anything about the Williamson kidnapping, and although he is hardly trustworthy, I tend to believe him in this instance. When I told him two brothers were said to be involved in the kidnapping, he also denied any knowledge of them or their whereabouts.

"What he did say, however, after receiving five dollars from me, is that any con runner who finds himself in some kind of trouble with the law probably will seek the aid of a lawyer named—you guessed it— Stanley Harding. He has availed himself of Mr. Harding's legal expertise on more than one occasion when he has run afoul of the gendarmes, and he said Harding got him off lightly. Fred and Bill, are you also going to report that your sources mentioned this same individual?"

Durkin and Gore both shook their heads and went on to describe their evenings, which were essentially uneventful. When they finished, Panzer rubbed his palms together and looked at each of us. "Gentlemen, I wonder whether all of you are thinking what I am thinking?"

"Let me take a wild stab here," Fred Durkin said. "We pay a visit to Stanley Harding?"

"Exactly!" Panzer said. "And we do it en masse. Let's see; it is eleven thirty. If we leave now, we may catch him in his office before he goes out for lunch."

We piled into two taxis and fifteen minutes later found ourselves on a street of warehouses and other nondescript buildings within a block of the East River, where two spans—which I later learned were the Brooklyn and Manhattan Bridges—arched across the gray water. Harding's address was a narrow, three-story brick building wedged between two other equally tired structures.

The six of us trudged up a narrow stairway to the second floor, choosing not to trust the ancient elevator and its equally ancient operator, who was dozing on his stool with a girlie magazine on his lap. Painted in black on the glass door at the top of the stairs were the words S. HARDING ESQ. ATTORNEY-AT-LAW. Panzer rapped once on the glass, then pushed on in as a man's voice asked, "Hello. Who's there?"

No one sat at the desk in the anteroom, presumably where a secretary would normally be stationed. The door to the inner office was ajar, and the voice called out again.

This time, Panzer spoke. "Mr. Harding? Several of us are here to see you, sir."

"Come in, come in, by all means. My door is open to all."

We took him up on his offer, and the fiftyish little man stood—he couldn't have been taller than five foot four—registered shock as we all squeezed our way into his small and unadorned office.

"My goodness, my goodness, so many of you," he said, adjusting his wire-rimmed glasses and running a hand over an almost-bald dome. "How can I help you, gentlemen? I'm afraid I can't offer seating to all of you." He gestured to his pair of guest chairs with a shrug of apology.

"That's quite all right, we will stand," Panzer said. "We understand that you frequently represent men who … well, who have operated certain games of chance and other questionable enterprises."

Harding nodded and ran an index finger along his little gray mustache. "I fervently believe that every American is entitled to adequate and able defense in a court of law. It is part of a citizen's birthright," he said in what sounded like a well-rehearsed speech. "Do all of you seek counsel?"

"Of a sort," Panzer said. "My friends here and I are looking for certain individuals and feel you may be able to help us."

"I'm sorry to say that missing persons are not my specialty, sir. For that, you would need to hire a private investigator," Harding said, his pinched face beginning to register unease.

"Oh, I believe in this situation, you may be exactly what we are looking for. We want to locate two men, brothers who go by various names, among them Jasper, Schmidt, Bagley, and—"

"Now see here, you have come to the wrong place!" Harding yapped, standing and pointing at the door. "I want you all to go—"

"Sit back down!" Fred Durkin barked. "I think we have come to the right place." Fred turned to Panzer.

"I agree with my colleague," Saul said. "How is your standing with the Bar Association, Mr. Harding?"

"What do you mean by that?"

"Just what I said. I am wondering whether there have been other complaints about you, because my friends and I may choose to file one."

Harding reached for his telephone, but before he could lift the receiver off its cradle, Bill Gore's beefy hand enveloped the lawyer's wrist. "No phone calls just now," he grunted.

"This is outrageous!" Harding squeaked. "Help! Help!" This time, Gore's hand went to the man's neck, gripping it. "Enough of that, or you'll have a good reason for needing help. Now sit down and shut up until we're through with you."

"Sorry, but my friend tends to have a quick temper," Panzer said to the lawyer. "Bill, that's quite enough. I am sure the gentleman will be calm now and, I hope, cooperative. Here is the situation, Mr. Harding," Panzer continued, sitting on the corner of the desk and chatting as if to an old friend. "It's one thing to defend and even harbor minor criminals, such as confidence men who use certain methods to separate greedy fools from their money. Well and good, but kidnapping is quite another matter, a felony to be precise. And in this particular case, it becomes even more newsworthy because it concerns the offspring of an extremely prominent New York figure whose name you would instantly recognize."

"I ... I have no idea what you are talking about," Harding said.

Panzer leaned in toward the little lawyer. "I believe that you do, sir. My friends want to know exactly where we can find the brothers who were mentioned earlier, and they will not leave this office until they learn where these men are." As Saul was speaking, Orrie Cather pulled out his revolver and began polishing it with a handkerchief.

"Let us go back to the Bar Association again," Panzer continued. "It seems likely they would be interested to learn that one of its members—you are a member, I assume—has knowledge of alleged kidnappers and their whereabouts."

"I didn't know anything at all about a kidnapping," Harding whined. "They told me that—" He stopped himself in midsentence, nervously looking at each of us.

"Just what did they tell you?" I snapped.

"Uh, what I mean is ... well ..." He slumped in his chair, head down.

"Mr. Harding, you could be in a whole lot of trouble, both with the lawyers' group and the police," Panzer said patiently. "You should also know that these men we are looking for may be involved in two murders."

"Murder? Oh my God!"

"You had better talk to us—and right now."

"Who are all of you, anyway?"

"It does not matter who we are, other than for you to know we won't hesitate to turn you in for concealing the location of men who certainly are felons."

Harding made a sound somewhere between a sigh and a moan. "They go by several names, but their real surname is Bagley. I happened to be a friend of their father," he said.

Panzer nodded. "The legendary Beer Barrel."

"You knew him, too?"

"Only by reputation. Please go on."

"I liked the old man," the lawyer said. "The boys, well, they always seemed to find trouble, although for the most part, they confined their shenanigans to petty cons. I can't see them involved in kidnapping and murder, although ..."

"Yeah?" Cather prompted. "Don't stop now."

"Although they had a nasty streak, even as kids, which surprised me, because their father, con artist that he was, did not have a mean bone in his body. Larcenous, yes, but mean, never in my memory."

"Interesting," Panzer said. "But this isn't helping us find the brothers. You know where they are."

"What do you want them for?"

"That is our concern, Mr. Harding."

"I must insist upon something."

"You are in no position to do any insisting, pal," Durkin growled.

The lawyer turned to Panzer. "Please, Mr. ...?"

"My name is unimportant, Counselor. What is it you want?"

"If I tell you where they—the Bagleys—are, you must promise not to say that I was the source."

"That much we can do," Panzer said. "I'm curious about one thing, though. How did they happen to get in touch with you recently?"

"One of them, Carl it was, telephoned me, yesterday, it was, and told me that he and his brother were in some trouble—he was not specific—and told me they might need my help. When I asked where they were in case I needed to get in touch with them, he told me."

"And now you are going to tell us."

Harding heaved another sigh. "They are in a hotel on Webster Avenue in the Bronx, the Farnham."

"What name are they registered under?"

"Cunningham."

"All right," Panzer said to us, "we're headed for the Bronx, except for you, Bill. Stay here and keep Mr. Harding company until you get our call. And we certainly do not want him using the telephone, do we?"

"We certainly don't," Gore agreed. "In fact, I'll take possession of the instrument right now. Any instructions if the brothers in question happen to ring this number?"

"Do not answer any calls for at least an hour. When we telephone, it will be twice: I will hang up after two rings and then phone again within seconds."

"Got it. What about food?"

"You just read my mind," Panzer said. "I noticed there's a deli down on the corner. Archie and I will go down there and get sandwiches for you and Mr. Harding. What's your poison, Bill?"

"Ham on rye," Gore said. "I'm awfully hungry. Can you make it two?"

"It's Wolfe's money, and you're a growing lad. Done! And what can we get for you, Mr. Harding?"

"I am not hungry," the lawyer said petulantly, folding his arms across his narrow chest and pouting.

"Come now, you need sustenance," Panzer urged. "I have great admiration for Mr. Gore, but you may not find him particularly good company. He tends toward the quiet side, so there is not likely to be much conversation. You will need something to help pass the time, and what better for that than food?"

"Oh, all right," Harding said, still pouting. "Corned beef on rye."

Out on the street as we walked toward the deli, Panzer turned to me. "I wanted to talk to you, just the two of us. We are about to enter a new phase in this operation, and I could use your advice."

"Me advising you? It seems to me that it should be the other away around."

"I don't think so. I've been observing you over these last days, and I like your instincts and judgment. We are going to need those qualities as we move ahead in this business."

"And just how do you see us tackling the Bagleys?"

"I'll answer a question with a question: What would you do, Archie?"

"I assume the plan is to take them alive?"

"Your assumption is correct."

"Okay, let's say that we pull that part off—more about the details in a minute. Then what?"

"We deliver them to Nero Wolfe," Panzer said.

"The police are going to love that," I said with a laugh. "Cramer will go straight through the roof."

"Without question. But this is what Mr. Wolfe has instructed."

"All right, if that's the deal," I said. "Now that Bill Gore will be staying here to keep watch on our lawyer friend, that makes five of us, all armed, against two Bagleys, also probably armed."

"Go on," Panzer said.

"They don't know that we're on to them, so we've got the element of surprise working for us, wouldn't you agree?"

Panzer nodded. "I would."

"I didn't get as much as I should have out of high school, but in one of the history courses I took, we learned about diversionary tactics during wars."

"And ...?"

"And that's what I think we need here. Do you have any idea what that hotel in the Bronx is like?"

"Oddly enough, I do." Panzer said. "I once caught up with an embezzler in a room at the Farnham, where he was holed up with a girlfriend, a henna-headed floozy whose best years were behind her. The place is either five or six stories high, and it's quite a few cuts above a flophouse, quite respectable."

"That figures," I said. "The Bagley boys are walking around with plenty of dough at the moment. They could even have afforded a suite at the Plaza or the Waldorf."

"No question about that." Panzer agreed. "So you were talking about diversionary tactics, Archie. Go on."

"We could try to take the brothers in their room at the hotel, but there are too many problems with that approach. For one, how would we get them to open the door? We could try to shoot our way in, of course, but they're armed, and that risks a gun battle in close quarters, where everybody could be hurt—or worse. We need to get them out of the building."

"I'm listening," Panzer said.

"What gets people out of a hotel—fast?"

His eyes narrowed. "Archie, you are not going to tell me that you're planning a fire, are you?"

"That's my idea."

"That's also arson."

"Not a real fire, Saul, but a phony one, which sends everybody rushing out into the street."

Panzer flashed a lopsided grin. "A false fire alarm is a crime, as I know you are aware."

"So are kidnapping and murder."

"Okay, tell me exactly how you see this working, and I'll tell you whether I think you've gone soft in the head."

As we got sandwiches at the deli, I laid out my plan in detail to Panzer, watching his long face go from disbelief to surprise to acceptance, then back to disbelief and, finally, to acceptance once again.

# CHAPTER 26

By using the jump seats, four of us squeezed into a taxi heading north, destination: the Bronx. Saul Panzer had left in another cab to brief Nero Wolfe on our plans and to take Wolfe's Heron sedan, which we hoped would be needed later. We had left Gore with Stanley Harding, and as we walked out, the terrified lawyer kept begging us not to tell the Bagley brothers how we found them. "If he keeps on like this, I'm going to gag the little bastard," Bill said.

The cabbie stopped a half block from the Farnham Hotel. "That's it," he said, pointing to an imposing five-story brick-and-stone building. Cather, Durkin, Bascom, and I climbed out and stood on the sidewalk, waiting for Panzer.

"I still say this is a cockeyed plan that will land us all in the soup," Cather carped, as he had been doing all the way up in the taxi. "We don't even know that these two are even in their room now."

"True," Bascom said, "but nobody else, you included, has come up with a better idea."

"I agree," Durkin added. "What've we got to lose?"

"Maybe our licenses," Cather shot back. "Anybody stop to think about that?"

"We'll be okay," Bascom assured. As the oldest among us by a generation, he tended to have a calming effect. We went into a coffee shop for a quick lunch at a table by the front window, keeping watch for the big Heron. We were just finishing when the sedan pulled up and Panzer climbed out, looking around.

I went to the front door of the café and waved him in. "Are we set?" he asked.

"Huh! As set as we're gonna be," Cather groused. "What did Wolfe think of this crazy scheme?"

"He raised his eyebrows when I started describing the operation," Panzer said, "but then, the farther I got into it, the more he seemed to feel it had a chance of working. Do all of you think you'll recognize the brothers?" We nodded.

"All right, everyone know his role?" Panzer asked. More nods all around, and after the bill was paid, we soberly trooped out, crossing the street to the hotel.

The high-ceilinged lobby still bore hints of a previous elegance, including elaborate chandeliers, fluted columns, and a ten-foot-high painted mural, albeit faded, of the Manhattan skyline in an earlier era. Three ancient characters sat in overstuffed chairs, two reading newspapers and the other one apparently asleep. The young, bespectacled desk clerk was seated, talking on the telephone, and he didn't notice us as we walked to the stairway, bypassing the lone elevator and its uniformed operator.

Panzer remained in the lobby fingering a police-style whistle while the rest of us climbed the stairs. I stopped at the second floor, and I knew that Durkin would go to three, Bascom to four, and Cather to five. We were set. The wait couldn't have been more than thirty seconds, but it seemed longer. Then, from the bottom of the stairwell came the screech of the whistle.

"Fire!" I yelled down the corridor, "fire from upstairs! Get out, get out, everyone!" Doors began opening as I ran down the stairs, hearing the others on the floors above me yelling the same words. "The fire's coming down from above!" I shouted as I raced through the lobby and headed for the front door.

I recognized Fred Durkin's booming voice, and I think I caught Bascom's as well. Out on the street, I met up with Panzer, and we watched as people began surging through the entrance, many of them disheveled and distraught. One man was frantically buttoning his pants, while a gray-haired woman in bedroom slippers clutched a bathrobe to her gaunt frame.

Durkin, Bascom, and Cather were among the first outside, and we gathered across the street, watching the faces of the panicked hotel guests as they burst into the sunlight, free from what they thought was an inferno.

"There they are!" Cather barked, pointing to a pair of lean, dark-haired men who muscled their way out of the building, elbowing one old pensioner to the ground in the process. The Bagleys, and it surely was them, walked across the street, cursing and laughing. They stood apart from the rest of the horde of hotel guests and onlookers, which was perfect for us. We eased over toward them without being noticed. They, like everyone else, had focused their attention on the building, looking up for smoke or flames.

They never realized we were behind them until each one felt something jab him in the small of the back. "Just take it real easy," Orrie Cather said, pressing his revolver against the taller of the brothers. "One peep or one movement out of you, and you are as dead as yesterday's newspaper. In case you haven't figured it out, this roscoe has a silencer on it, so the only noise if I plug you will be the sound of your skinny carcass hitting the concrete."

Fred Durkin didn't say as much as Cather when he talked to the second brother from behind, but apparently the words, which I couldn't hear, were effective, because the guy appeared to be terrified. All of us then closed in around the Bagleys, who were frisked. They each had an automatic, both of which Bascom pocketed. We then began moving them toward the Heron sedan when two fire engines, sirens wailing, careened around a corner and pulled up in front of the hotel.

The timing could not have been better for us. The arrival of the engines and their crew of firefighters distracted the crowd, none of whom paid us the least bit of attention as we moved the brothers down the block, surrounding them as we pushed and pulled them toward the auto.

"You guys don't look like cops," the taller one snarled, "and this sure don't look like no police cruiser to me."

"Don't worry about it. As far as you're concerned, we might as well be cops," Panzer shot back. "Orrie, get the bracelets." Cather pulled two sets of handcuffs from his pocket and started to put them on one of the brothers, who jerked back and cocked a fist as if to take a swing. I hit him in the temple with the butt of my Webley and he let out a yowl, which couldn't be heard more than ten feet away because of the sirens from the fire engines.

"Easy, Archie," Panzer said. "I'm sure these boys will behave now." They did, allowing themselves to be cuffed. They then got pushed into the Heron.

"Okay, here's how this works," Panzer told them as, side by side, they glowered in the backseat. "We are taking you away, never mind to where, and my friend, here," he gestured toward Cather, "will be riding up front with me but watching you every second. And he's the nervous type, especially when he has a gun in his hand, so you won't want to do anything to upset him. Do you understand me?"

Both brothers were sweating now. "We've got money, lots of it, so … maybe we can work something out, huh?"

"We'll talk about that money a little later," Panzer said, walking away from the auto to talk to us while Cather slid into the front seat with pistol drawn, leering at the Bagleys. "I'm taking these boys to Wolfe's place," Saul told Durkin, Bascom, and me. "Be someplace where I can reach all three of you, okay?"

"How 'bout my office?" Del said, scribbling his phone number on a sheet and handing it to Saul.

"Good. Oh, and call Gore and tell him he can take off from that lawyer's office now. We're going to need all of you later, so tell Bill to go to your place, too."

"What's the plan?" I asked.

"You'll know soon enough, Archie. All of you will, as soon as I know myself, but I think Mr. Wolfe is going to stage one of his shows, probably tonight." With that, he climbed behind the wheel of the

Heron and drove off with two shackled brothers and an itchy-fingered operative glowering at them from the front seat.

I turned to Durkin and Bascom. "What are these shows of Wolfe's that Saul's talking about?"

Both men grinned. "Be prepared for an interesting and unusual evening," was all Durkin would say, and Del just nodded his agreement.

# CHAPTER 27

**W**ilda brewed a late afternoon pot of coffee for the four of us, and we sat in Bascom's office sipping from mugs. For me, it was another educational session about the world of private operatives in New York, as the trio of old hands traded stories.

"So there I was, on the southbound Staten Island Ferry shadowing this weasel who had been lifting the purses of women passengers on the boats," Bill Gore said. "The ferry company had hired me to catch him, because up to then, he'd been so damned sneaky he hadn't been nailed. Also, the guy was good with disguises, so it seemed from victims' reports like he never looked the same twice."

"That being the case, how did you know you were even tailing the right guy?" Bascom asked.

Gore grinned. "Damned good question, Del. I'd been on the case about a week by this time, and I kept seeing somebody wandering all over the ferry, pacing from one end to the other and back again, except that it was always a different man, or so I thought. I got suspicious because all these guys were about the same size, and I finally figured all of them were the same person.

"Anyhow, I felt that I really had him this time. I saw him moving toward a fairly large woman who was standing at the rail with her purse on the deck at her feet. He edged over next to her and bent down to pick up the purse. As he grabbed for it, she turned, screamed, and drove her knee up hard, into his crotch. The next scream was his, louder, and he doubled over as she stamped on his hand with her high-heeled shoe, cursing him with words some sailors might not even know."

"So you earned your money," Durkin said.

"Not quite. They did pay me for my time, all right, but the woman got the money I would have been given for catching him in the act. How could I argue, though? She was on him like a flash. One tough customer."

"Yeah, and you wouldn't have wanted to fight her for the dough," Bascom observed. "Not after what she did to the dip."

"Reminds me of a case I was on a few years back," Durkin said. "There was this forger who had—" He got interrupted by the ringing telephone.

Bascom picked up his instrument before Wilda could answer in the outer office. "Saul! Yeah, we're all here. Yeah, right, Bill left that sleazy lawyer Harding pretty shaken up, worried that the Bagleys will come after him for giving them away. ... No, I guess he doesn't have to worry about that happening, all right. ... When? ... Eight thirty, Wolfe's? ... All of us? ... We'll be there."

He cradled the receiver and swiveled to face us. "All right, the show is on, boys. We are to be at Wolfe's at eight thirty for instructions. The guests will be arriving at nine."

"Guests?" I asked.

"Oh, yes, Archie, quite a few. I'm sure you'll find it an interesting night."

Fritz Brenner swung open the brownstone's door and invited us in. He wore a worried look on his puss. "Everything okay?" Durkin asked.

"Bad business," Fritz said, shaking his head. "Bad men, bad business." I assumed he was talking about the Bagleys, but he may have meant all us trooping in and disturbing the sanctity of the Wolfean abode.

We went down the hall to the office, which was filled with chairs. "Looks like there's going to be a lecture here tonight," I observed.

"In a sense, you're right," Saul Panzer said. He was sitting in one of the yellow chairs making notes on a pad.

"Is it fair to say that Nero Wolfe will be the one doing the lecturing?"

"Absolutely, Archie, and as you can see, he's going to have quite an audience. I'm just figuring out where everyone's going to sit."

"Everyone being …?"

"The Williamsons, for starters, father, mother, son. Then, their entire household staff. And we certainly don't want to forget Inspector Cramer, who will be bringing Sergeant Stebbins with him."

"That's a new name to me."

"Ah, so you haven't met Purley Stebbins yet." Saul turned to Durkin. "Do you think Archie is in for a treat?"

"I wouldn't call it a treat," Fred said. "What do you guys think?" Del Bascom gave the thumbs-down sign and Bill Gore just shook his head.

"That answers that," I said. "Where's Wolfe?"

"Oh, he'll be the last one in," Durkin said. "He likes to make a big entrance."

"Okay. What about Orrie Cather?"

Panzer smiled thinly. "He's down in the basement, with a couple of our other guests. In fact, Bill and Fred, why don't you go down and keep him company? I have the feeling Orrie's not in love with the idea of being the solo jailer for those cretins." The two big men shrugged, indicating their lack of interest, but lumbered out of the office as instructed.

"I've only sat in on a couple of Wolfe's big evenings before," Del Bascom said. "How do you figure this one will go?"

"I'm not about to hazard a guess," Panzer said. "I was in here earlier when Mr. Wolfe called to invite Cramer, and I could hear the inspector yelling through the receiver from ten feet away, so our local homicide chief is not going to arrive here in the best of moods."

Bascom snorted. "When is Cramer ever in a good mood?"

"Nice point, Del. Never in my memory, at least not when he's sitting in this office."

"Why does he even bother coming here?" I asked.

"He feels he can't afford not to," Panzer said. "The two have had their differences to say the least, but Cramer knows damn well how smart Mr. Wolfe is, and how often in the last few years he has helped do the department's work for them. I'm not overly fond of the inspector, but I don't envy him, either."

"How does the guy hold his job?"

"One thing you should know, Archie, is that Cramer is by no means a dummy. As Mr. Wolfe has observed on occasion, including right here the other night, the inspector is brave, honest, and intelligent most of the time. When he's in this room, however, he tends to blow his stack."

"And he may really blow it tonight," Bascom said.

"That wouldn't be a surprise," Panzer agreed. "Okay, I think we're ready for the crowd. As you can see, Fritz has set up the bar cart, and chances are, it will get some customers."

At five before nine, the doorbell rang, and Fritz ushered into the office an already-angry Inspector Cramer, who was accompanied by a shambling, bony-faced guy with big ears, a square jaw, and a glum expression.

"Inspector, Sergeant," Panzer said. "Purley, you know Del Bascom, but I don't believe that you've met Archie Goodwin, who's working with us."

Purley Stebbins nodded grimly at me, saying nothing. I returned the nod and the grim expression, also saying nothing.

"Where's Wolfe, dammit?" Cramer barked. "And why all these chairs? I thought this was to be a meeting with Williamson."

As if in answer to the inspector's question, the doorbell rang again, and Burke Williamson's voice could be heard in the hallway. He did not sound happy.

"All right, where's Wolfe?" he demanded as he strode into the office. "I've brought my wife, my son, and my whole household staff, just as he had insisted. We had to take two cars, and I'm not sure why all this is—oh, it's you," he said, suddenly noticing Cramer.

"Incredible, isn't it?" the inspector observed. "Wolfe snaps his fingers, and we all jump, like a team of trained seals. He even told me to bring a squad car along. This had better be good." As he was talking, the Williamson entourage filed in, led by his wife and son.

"Hi, Archie!" Tommie said, breaking into a wide grin when he saw me. "Are we still going to that football game?"

"A week from Saturday," I answered. "Right, Mr. Williamson?"

"Huh? Oh, yes, yes," Williamson said, momentarily confused. "Yes, the three of us are going. The Princeton game."

"If I can get everyone's attention," Saul Panzer said as the Williamson staff filed in, filling the room. "Would anyone like a drink?" He gestured toward the rolling cart, with its bottles, glasses, and ice.

"Yes, I'll take a scotch, rocks," the hotel baron barked, turning to his wife. "What about you, dear?"

Lillian Williamson declined with a shake of her well-coiffed head, perhaps not wanting to be seen taking a drink in front of her employees.

After handing Williamson his scotch, Saul Panzer efficiently got everyone seated. Cramer took what I now realized was his usual spot, the red leather chair at one end of Wolfe's desk. The Williamsons—father, mother, and son—were given three yellow chairs in the front row, with their staff arrayed in the row behind them, in no particular order that I could see. Closest to me, as I stood in the rear of the room on the left side facing Wolfe's desk, was the staid butler, Waverly, who looked uncomfortable away from his surroundings.

Beside him was my old friend the cook, Mrs. Price, who blew me a kiss and winked as she sat. Next, in order, were a nervous young Mary Trent, the belligerent gardener Lloyd Carstens, a sniffing Emily Stratton, a subdued Sylvia Moore, and a scowling Mark Simons. Miss Stratton, Carstens, and Simons all aimed their most disapproving looks in my direction. Since I did not see Gentry, my successor as chauffeur, I assumed he was out in front keeping watch on the valued Williamson automobiles.

Sergeant Purley Stebbins, having declined Panzer's offer of a chair, stood in the back of the room, with his arms folded across his chest and the bulge formed by the shoulder holster under his suit jacket.

Del Bascom and I found seats on the couch, leaving space for Panzer, who went to Wolfe's desk and reached under the center drawer for the buzzer. "Mr. Wolfe will be with us shortly," he said to a chorus of grumbling. About thirty seconds later, Wolfe entered, acknowledging the crowd with a curt nod.

"Thank you all for coming," he said as he sat. "Has everyone desiring a beverage been served?"

"We're not here to party, Wolfe," Cramer said gruffly, pulling out a cigar and jamming it into his mouth.

"Of course not, but I would be remiss as a host if I failed to make the offer. Does anyone other than Mr. Williamson desire something?" He looked at a sea of impassive faces and silence, shrugged, and started to ring for beer. Fritz must have been waiting just outside the office door, however, because within seconds, he placed two bottles and a glass on the desk in front of Wolfe.

After taking a first sip, Wolfe surveyed his audience, and proceeded to pronounce the names, from left to right, of the members of the Williamson household staff. It seemed to me that he was showing off, given that he had never seen any of them, but far be it for me to question the motives of a purported genius. He took a second drink, dabbed his lips with a handkerchief, and resettled his bulk.

"If I may dispel any misconceptions that exist, you all should be aware that I now have no client," Wolfe said. "Mr. Williamson hired me to safely retrieve his son from kidnappers. Once that task got accomplished, he was satisfied, but I was not.

"I mean no disrespect to my former client," Wolfe continued, "but I found it execrable that any kidnappers, particularly of a child, should remain at large. I determined, with the help of a group of men including those seated on the couch, to find these scapegraces and apprehend them. This I have done." He paused to let his words sink in as the room filled with murmurs and exclamations.

"You had damned well better explain yourself!" Cramer roared, pounding his fist on Wolfe's desktop.

"I shall, sir. Please allow me to continue. From the first, it seemed patently obvious that this was both an outside and an inside operation. Now as to—"

"So you're saying that Charles Bell really was part of the plot," Burke Williamson cut in.

Wolfe held up a palm. "If you please, sir, I would like to continue without interruption. There will be ample time later for discussion. Now, to the outside part of the kidnapping plan: as I said a moment ago, through the very able work of operatives in my employ, the men who held Tommie—and also received the ransom money—have been apprehended and are now under this roof and in custody."

"Not police custody, by God!" Cramer howled. "I want those men, and I want them right now!"

"So you shall have them, Inspector," Wolfe replied calmly. "Saul, if you please." Panzer rose and left the room while Cramer fumed and Purley Stebbins slipped a hand inside his suit jacket.

The next scene is one I will never forget. The two glowering Bagleys, with wrists manacled in front of them, were led into the room by a grinning Orrie Cather, who was followed by Fred Durkin and Bill Gore. Mouths dropped open, gasps broke out, and Mrs. Price leaped to her feet, jabbing a fat finger at one of the Bagleys. "That's him! That's the one who came into my kitchen with those groceries that I hadn't ordered! He's the man, yes he is!" Before Wolfe could introduce the brothers, Stebbins stepped toward them. "I'll take it from here," he barked, drawing his revolver.

"Sergeant, these brothers go by several first and last names," Wolfe said, "although it appears probable that their birth certificates read Chester and Calvin Bagley. It is more than probable that they killed both Barney Haskell and Charles Bell."

"And just how are we supposed to know that?" Cramer said.

"Who has their guns?" Wolfe asked.

"I do, in here." It was Fred Durkin, who held up a paper sack.

"Inspector, these weapons were taken from the Bagleys. If you get that Bureau of Forensic Ballistics to run tests on them, I am confident you will find that one or both of these weapons fired the shots that killed Messrs. Haskell and Bell."

"Don't try to tell me my business," Cramer said.

"Far be it for me to do that," Wolfe said as Stebbins led the Bagleys out, presumably to the waiting squad car. The last we heard from one of them, Chester, I think, was a demand to see his lawyer. ''

"Well, you have meddled in police business yet again," Cramer snarled, getting to his feet.

"If you please, sir," Wolfe said, "I was about to review the inside aspects of the kidnapping and the reasons for the deaths of two men."

The inspector snorted but sat. "It seems to me the 'inside aspects,' as you call them, consist of the chauffeur's cooperation with those brothers."

"In part," Wolfe agreed. "The Bagleys had somehow come to know Mr. Bell. Perhaps your department's investigation will discover the connection. What likely happened is that the Bagleys approached the Williamson chauffeur and inveigled him into being part of the plot to seize Tommie and hold him for ransom. Then, one of two things almost surely occurred: either the brothers reneged on the deal or Mr. Bell demanded a larger share than originally agreed upon. In either case, he became expendable in the eyes of the Bagleys."

"Since you claim to be so smart," Cramer shot back, "why did this Haskell character also find himself on a slab in the morgue?"

"I concede this is conjecture, but it seems likely that Mr. Haskell, a small-time confidence man living on life's margins, somehow learned of the kidnapping plan through underworld channels and pressed the Bagleys for a share of the proceeds, threatening them with exposure if they did not come across with a substantial emolument. As with Mr. Bell, he had to be disposed of."

Cramer gnawed on his stogie, eyeing Wolfe from under bushy eyebrows. "Okay, let us move on to what you term these 'inside aspects' of yours."

Wolfe drank beer and set his glass down. "Let us by all means. There is an individual in this room who must bear some of the responsibility for the kidnapping of Tommie Williamson."

## CHAPTER 28

If Wolfe's intent was to further shock his audience, he hit the jackpot. Members of the household staff tensed up and snuck sidelong glances at one another. Lillian Williamson kneaded her hands, and Tommie looked over at me with a grin. "You had better know what you're talking about," Burke Williamson said sternly.

"I second that," Cramer growled. "There's such a thing as slander, and plenty of witnesses heard you."

"I am familiar with the statutes," Wolfe said, clearly pleased with the stir he had generated. "After I have identified the individual in question, I invite anyone to initiate a lawsuit against me."

I scanned the group, trying to spot someone wearing a guilty or a nervous expression on their mug, but all I saw were shocked faces. We had a very good actor or actress in our midst.

"Not that I necessarily believe you, but who is it?" Williamson demanded, leaning forward and glaring at Wolfe.

"Don't try to rush him," Cramer said. "I've been a party to these melodramas before, and he moves at his own speed, regardless of how hard he gets pushed."

"You, an officer of the law, intimidated by this man!"

"I am *not* intimidated," Cramer flared. "But since we are all here,

I am willing to hear him out, Mr. Williamson. I remember that you praised him not so long ago for helping to get your son freed."

For the moment, that silenced the hotel magnate, who sank back into his chair wearing a scowl.

All eyes focused on Wolfe, who seemed determined to take his time. "The more I learned about the kidnapping, the more I recognized it had to be a complex and well-coordinated operation, one requiring several individuals working in concert," he said. "Two of these persons, at the very least, had to be members of the Williamson staff. It seemed conclusive to me that Mr. Bell was one of them. In an attempt to determine the identity of others involved, I dispatched Mr. Goodwin here to work among them both as Tommie's bodyguard and as a chauffeur."

"He never seemed like a chauffeur to me," Carstens snorted. "Too doggone young, for one thing. And, of course, we all knew he was there as some sort of detective. Pretty young for that, too."

"Perhaps," Wolfe allowed, "although young he has skills, among them a well-developed sense of observation and an ability to repeat extended conversations verbatim. The second of those attributes has been particularly helpful, but more about that later." He paused to drink beer.

"In reviewing the events leading up to the kidnapping, I became intrigued with the alleged telephone call that drew Miss Moore into the house, leaving Tommie alone in the yard."

"Oh, there truly was a call," Waverly attested. "I was in the parlor when I heard the instrument ring. I am prepared to swear to it. Miss Trent answered the instrument and she said something like 'Oh dear, oh my!' and then ran to the terrace doors to call to Miss Moore."

"So noted, sir," Wolfe told the butler, shifting his attention to Sylvia Moore. "I understand your mother in Virginia has been seriously ill, suffering with a heart condition. Is that correct?"

She nodded somberly. "Yes, sir, it is."

"What is her medical condition at present?"

"She is much better, thank you."

"Have you visited her recently?"

Sylvia's cheeks reddened. "No, not for several months now. But I really should."

"Yes, you should indeed. Tell us about the telephone call."

"Mary—Miss Trent here—called out to me from the terrace, saying that a man was on the wire and said he had to talk to me right away, that it was a matter of life and death. Of course I immediately thought of my mother. I became terribly upset, as anyone in that situation would."

"Understandable," Wolfe said, turning to Mary Trent. "Can you recall the exact words spoken by the caller?"

The young woman shifted in her chair, clearly uneasy with the attention now focused on her. "It was just as Miss Moore told you," she said, clearing her throat. "The man sounded very excited and told me that he had to speak to her right away, that it was a matter of life and death. Those are the words he used. I knew about her mother, so I ran onto the terrace and called her to the instrument."

"Did you recognize the voice?"

"At first I thought maybe I did, but now I don't believe so."

"Who did you initially think it was?"

She looked down onto her lap. "I would prefer not to say."

"Come, come, Miss Trent. We are investigating a kidnapping and two murders. This is not a time to become coy."

"He's right," Cramer said. "Answer the question, or you may find it being asked of you in a far less pleasant environment."

She took in air and let it out slowly. "The voice sounded somewhat like, well … like Mr. Simons."

"This is both ridiculous and slanderous!" the stable master snapped, rising. "I don't have to sit here and take this." He started for the door.

"If you like your job, sit back down right now!" Burke Williamson growled at him. Simons sat.

Wolfe turned back to Sylvia Moore. "Tell us exactly what happened when you picked up the receiver."

"Nothing. That is to say, no one was on the other end. I must have yelled into the mouthpiece several times. I became panicked, and I ... I forgot all about Tommie." She looked mournfully at the boy as tears welled up in her eyes. He smiled back at her as if to say "no hard feelings."

"Did it not occur to you, Mr. Waverly, or you, Miss Trent, to look out into the yard to check on Tommie while Miss Moore was at the instrument?"

The butler, obviously embarrassed, shook his head and said nothing. The housemaid continued to stare at her lap.

"That telephone call is, of course, the key to everything that subsequently occurred," Wolfe pronounced.

"I don't believe there was a telephone call at all," Cramer said, fixing an intense gaze on Mary Trent.

"There I must now disagree, sir. Both Mr. Waverly and Miss Trent attest to hearing the ring, and Miss Trent tells us she heard a man's voice through the instrument. I believe a call was made, a call perfectly timed to coincide with the arrival in the yard of a closed truck containing produce—produce that Mrs. Price has said was not requested by her."

"That is correct," the cook declared. "I had never heard of that particular purveyor before, and I even looked them up in our New York telephone directories later. They were not listed."

Wolfe nodded. "Given your reaction moments ago, may I assume you would be willing to identify one of the men who left here in handcuffs?"

"Yes, indeed, sir. That was him, no doubt whatever about it. I will not ever forget that face as long as I live," Mrs. Price asserted dramatically, folding her chubby arms across her chest to underscore her certainty.

"You will be hearing from us," Cramer told her. "Okay, Wolfe, are you now ready to share your conjecture with us?"

"It is not a conjecture, but rather a fact. Early on, I correctly identified those in the Williamson world whom I felt had conspired in the kidnapping. You will have to believe me when I tell you that even before his disappearance and murder, I had marked Mr. Bell as one of the in-house cabal."

Cramer snorted. "And I suppose you're going to take your own sweet time telling us who else was in on the plot."

"Only as long as it takes to explain my reasoning, sir. Back to the telephone call. Given all the outside lines that feed into the Williamson estate, that call could have come from any number of locations: the kitchen, the stables, the greenhouse, the garage, an upstairs bedroom, even Mr. Williamson's own study. Of all these, the telephones with the best view of the driveway that curves around to the back of the house are those in the garage and in Mr. Bell's lodgings over the garage."

"It doesn't take a genius to figure that out," Cramer said sourly.

"No, it does not. Mr. Bell, like everyone else on the staff, could easily have known Tommie would be outside gathering leaves with Miss Moore. I understand that you all discuss household activities when you gather for meals," Wolfe said, looking at each of them in turn.

"Quite often," Mrs. Price piped up. "I can't remember if the leaf project came up. Can anyone else?"

"Oh, I'm almost positive I mentioned something about it," Sylvia Moore said. "I always talk a lot about what Tommie and I are doing. Some of the others on the staff like to hear about his activities." She looked at the boy again and got another smile from him.

"So the call is made, and Miss Moore is drawn into the house in terror, fearful of her mother's condition," Wolfe continued. "The kidnappers must act quickly, and they do. The one brother posing as a purveyor knows he will be rejected in the kitchen and leaves, although he has kept Mrs. Price occupied just long enough for Tommie to get hustled into the windowless rear of the truck by the second brother. Likewise, Miss Moore is fruitlessly occupied on the telephone during the same few minutes.

"Both the butler, Waverly, and Miss Trent presumably are so distracted by Miss Moore's panic in trying to reach someone on the other end of the line that they neglect to look after Tommie. The kidnappers gamble, correctly, that Miss Stratton and Messrs. Carstens and Simons are so busy with their own work elsewhere on the estate that the snatching of the boy will go unnoticed. In all, this was an efficient, well-executed operation."

Burke Williamson cleared his throat. "You appear to have just disproved your own point that someone other than Charles Bell on my staff was involved in this ugly business."

"Such was not my intent, sir. One of those mentioned above played a pivotal role in the event, and several seemingly innocuous occurrences pointed me toward this accomplice. As I said earlier, Mr. Goodwin is precise in recounting conversations, and my realization of this individual's culpability began with the use of a pronoun in a sentence that was spoken in his presence: 'I would never let anything happen to Tommie *myself.*'

"I stressed the final word, which I believe was included to suggest that someone other than the speaker was responsible for Tommie's being seized. Later, the same individual drew Mr. Goodwin aside, telling him a most implausible story about overhearing part of a conversation in the dining room of the Williamson home between Miss Stratton and Mr. Carstens in which they seem to be speaking in a conspiratorial manner about the kidnapping."

"That is ridiculous!" Lloyd Carstens stormed, popping out of his chair. "I have never—repeat never—set foot in the dining room of the house. The only room I've ever been in is Mr. Williamson's study, and then to discuss the maintenance of the grounds. Who told that outlandish story?"

Wolfe held up a hand. "Please be seated, sir. I have stated that the story was implausible, and I would like to move on. The individual in question had suggested to Mr. Goodwin that she tell him her eavesdropping story in his chauffeur's quarters, suggesting that she had spent time there before, perhaps when Mr. Bell occupied those rooms." As he spoke, Wolfe turned to Mary Trent, who, small as she was, seemed to be shrinking in her chair.

"That's, that's … not true," she said in a voice barely above a whisper.

"What is true, Miss Trent, is that you have said consistently that you did not recognize the voice on the telephone—until now," Wolfe remarked. "And tonight you tell us the voice just might be that of Mr. Simons."

"But I just cannot be sure," she said, near tears and holding her head in her hands.

"You do not seem to be sure of anything," Wolfe said sharply as Inspector Cramer moved to stand behind Mary Trent. "You have variously suggested that Miss Stratton, Mr. Carstens, and Mr. Simons have been involved in the kidnapping. Is there anyone else you would like to implicate?"

She was sobbing now, although the expressions of those around her showed no sign of sympathy.

"Miss Trent," Wolfe said, "I am going to imagine a scenario, and I invite you to comment upon it. In your time as an employee in the Williamson household, you and Mr. Bell became extremely good friends, although you both went to lengths to keep the extent of your friendship from your coworkers."

"They certainly didn't do all that good a job of keeping it a secret," Emily Stratton huffed. "You should have seen the way she would look at him across the dinner table. We all knew what was going on. We are not blind. And heaven knows what happened when she went over to the garage to clean his rooms. He used to say he didn't want his rooms cleaned, but little Goody-Two Shoes here often disappeared for certain periods, and I know just where she disappeared to."

"Did you ever share your observations about this relationship with any of my investigators?" Wolfe asked sharply.

"No, I certainly did not," she snapped. "I am not a gossip. I hardly feel that it is my place to comment on or judge the morals, or the lack of morals, of other members of the staff. If people exercised more self-discipline, the world would be a better place. I will say no more than that."

Wolfe glared at the housekeeper, then turned back to Mary Trent. "The two of you made plans to start a new life, but you had big dreams, dreams that would take money. Mr. Bell had come to know the Bagley brothers, and perhaps you are familiar with the circumstances of their meeting. Together, the three of them conceived Tommie Williamson's kidnapping. Mr. Bell quickly realized he would need an accomplice

ARCHIE MEETS NERO WOLFE

within the household to make the plan work, and who better to play that role than his closest friend on the staff?

"You may originally have been conflicted about the plot and your role in it. Only you can know how enthusiastically you took part. In any event, you became the fourth member of the team, if we can so term it.

"The Bagley brothers rented a truck in the Bronx. This we know from the investigative work of Mr. Goodwin and Mr. Bascom. On the morning of the kidnapping, the Bagleys drove to the Williamson estate, timing their arrival to coincide with the period when Tommie would be out in the yard collecting leaves before leaving for school.

"Mr. Bell, stationed either in the garage itself or at a window in one of his rooms above it, dialed the number of the instrument on the first floor the moment the truck pulled around to the back of the house. Expecting the call, you, Miss Trent, were hovering around the telephone and picked it up, probably on the first ring. Mr. Bell likely spoke no more than a word or two, perhaps something like 'They're here!' You made an exclamation of some sort for the benefit of anyone within earshot. You then ran out onto the terrace, frantically calling to Miss Moore and telling her that she had an emergency call.

"As this was transpiring, one of the Bagley brothers, carrying a box of produce, went through a rear basement door to the kitchen, having been told either by you or Mr. Bell of its location. While he talked to Mrs. Price, the second brother got out of the truck the instant Miss Moore ran into the house and lured Tommie over to the truck. Do I have that right?" Wolfe asked, turning to the boy.

Tommie nodded, his expression serious. "Yes, sir, it happened just exactly like you said. Miss Moore was very upset. I watched her run inside, and right after that, this man came over to me saying he wanted my help taking something out of the truck. Then he shoved me inside. He stuffed a cloth in my mouth and tied me up. Then they drove away."

Even though they had surely heard the story before, both of

Tommie's parents tensed up as he recounted his ordeal, but the boy seemed totally self-possessed. I believe he was enjoying the attention.

"And was that man one of the two who just left here?" Wolfe asked.

"Yes, I'm pretty sure," Tommie said. "Except that he had dark glasses on all the time before."

"Well, the brother I met wasn't wearing any dark glasses in the kitchen," Mrs. Price asserted, "and as I told you before, he definitely was the same man who the police just took away. Also as I told you before, I will testify to that in any court if I am asked."

"Thank you," Wolfe said. "Now, Miss Trent, what do you think of my scenario? Do you have anything to add?"

Despite what she had done, I almost—but not quite—felt sorry for the young woman, who now was hunched over, weeping into a handkerchief. "We were in love," she sobbed as if to justify her actions. "When they killed him, I wanted to die, too."

"Did it occur to you that they might have killed Tommie as well?" a red-faced Burke Williamson yelled at Mary Trent as his wife tugged on his sleeve to hush him up.

"You got anything else you want to add, Wolfe?" Cramer snapped.

"No, sir, I have spoken my piece."

"Miss Trent, I am going to request that you come with me," the inspector said grimly, taking her arm and helping her up. She looked at each of her coworkers, finding nothing but hostility in their expressions. She started to speak, then bit her lip and took one last, watery-eyed look at a roomful of people she would never see again—except perhaps in a courtroom.

# CHAPTER 29

Much of what happened to the accused murderers and kidnappers after that night in Wolfe's office I learned from newspaper reports. The Bagleys tried to get Stanley Harding to represent them in court, but the little man begged off, claiming, with justification, that he had no experience as a defense attorney in a murder trial.

The ransom money, less several hundred dollars, got recovered from the apartment of the Bagleys' sister in Brooklyn where they had stashed it, so the brothers had no funds to hire a top-notch lawyer, not that one would have helped them. A public defender was brought in, and although he labored manfully for his clients, according to the newspaper stories, the jury brought in a quick verdict of guilty on two counts of first-degree murder and one of kidnapping. Both men were sentenced to death and were electrocuted on successive nights at the Sing Sing prison up on the Hudson north of the city.

Never before had siblings been sentenced to die in New York in the same case, and the tabloid press turned it into a circus. When the verdict got handed down, the *Daily News* headline screamed DOUBLE BROILER! The rival tabloid, *The Mirror*, which was not to be outdone, countered with ONE FOR THE MONEY, TWO FOR THE CHAIR! The usually staid *Gazette* even got into the act with TIME TO TURN ON THE JUICE.

All but lost in the furor over the executions was the fate of Mary Trent. She was found guilty as an accessory to kidnapping and received a three-year term at what was called "a women's correctional facility." I never read another word about her.

The ransom money got returned to Burke Williamson. Although he earlier had said the cash meant nothing to him, he accepted it, giving a chunk to Wolfe, who divvied some of it up among the six of us, which was a pleasant surprise.

Soon after that last meeting in Wolfe's office, Williamson, his son, and I went to that Columbia University football game. It was a beautiful autumn afternoon, and Tommie entered into the spirit of college football waving a Columbia pennant his father had bought him and yelling "Let's go, Lions!" along with the cheerleaders and the students seated around us. The rooting must have worked, because the home team defeated the Princeton Tigers by scoring a touchdown in the last minute of the game.

As we left the stadium, the hotel magnate pulled me aside and quietly thanked me for having spent time with Tommie during my short stint as his chauffeur.

"Perhaps without intending to, you showed me how to be a better father," Williamson said. "I hadn't tossed a football in years, but now Tommie and I throw it around several times a week, and my arm has even stopped aching. Come spring, we're going to switch to baseball, and I would like you to come to a game with us, Goodwin. Yankees, Giants, Dodgers, whichever team Tommie wants to see."

I told him that I would be honored, assuming I was still living in New York in the spring.

"Why in the world wouldn't you be?" Williamson asked.

"Operatives' jobs are hard to come by these days, and I don't know how long Del Bascom can afford to keep me on. He's having a rough time himself, damned rough."

# CHAPTER 30

In fact, about two weeks after that football game, Del called me into his office. I could tell by his expression that he was about to be the bearer of bad news.

"Close the door, Archie, and sit down." I closed and I sat.

"You read the papers. I don't have to tell you what the times are like," he said, firing up one of his cheap stogies. "Shoot, we haven't had a case of any kind in almost two weeks, and the one we did have barely paid the electrical and the telephone bills, not to mention Wilda's queenly salary."

"You don't have to beat around the bush with me, Del. I'm a big boy now, and I have seen this coming for quite some time."

"I'm really sorry," the old detective said, shaking his head. "I'll tell you what, though. You can keep your office here for as long as you want, and if you happen to dig up some cases on your own, that's jake by me. And if you want to try catching on with another agency, I'll give you a good reference, a very good reference. And I will mean every word of it."

"I appreciate that. Things are bad for everybody in this business right now, aren't they?"

"Pretty much. I know that Durkin, Cather, and Gore all are hurting. About the only thing keeping any of them—and us—

above water is that welcome money that Wolfe spread around after Williamson got the ransom dough back."

"Yeah, that has been damned helpful. What about Panzer?"

"Oh, Saul's okay. His reputation around town is sterling silver. He can hold a tail like a bloodhound and disappear into the woodwork when he doesn't want to be seen. I don't think that he'll ever lack for business, and neither will Nero Wolfe, for that matter. The big difference is that Wolfe needs a lot more money than Saul to live in the manner to which he has grown accustomed. All those orchids, all those books, all those wonderful meals. Almost any good restaurant in Manhattan would hire his man Brenner in an instant if they had the chance."

"Okay, Del, I'll take you up on your offer of me keeping an office for now. But if by some miracle, I do drum up some business, I'll cut you in, which is only fair." I got no argument from him.

A couple more weeks went by without success. One morning, as I was sitting at my desk and reading the want ads, Del came in. "Nero Wolfe wants you to call him," he said.

"What does he want?"

"He didn't say. Here's his number, in case you've forgotten it," Del said, handing me a sheet of paper. I hadn't forgotten it.

"Huh! Maybe he's going to give me an even bigger share of that last payment from Williamson," I said.

"If that's the case, let me know," he said laughing, "because I'm going to demand more, too."

I dialed the number. "Yes?" Wolfe's voice.

"Archie Goodwin. You asked that I give you a telephone call."

"Yes, Mr. Goodwin. Would you be able to come to my office late this afternoon? Say at six o'clock?"

"Sure, I can be there. What's the subject?"

"I would like to discuss something with you, but only in person."

"I'll see you then."

At precisely six by my watch, I rang the doorbell of the brownstone on that quiet block of West Thirty-Fifth Street. Fritz Brenner swung the door open and invited me in. "A pleasure to see you, Mr. Goodwin," he said.

"Nice to get such a warm welcome," I answered. "I believe that I am expected."

"Yes indeed, and you are right on time. Mr. Wolfe just came down from the plant rooms."

I walked down the hall to the office with Fritz and found my host sitting at his desk, about to open one of the two chilled bottles of Canadian beer on a tray before him. "Ah, Mr. Goodwin, thank you for coming. Will you have something to drink?"

I asked for scotch and water, for which I was developing a taste. Fritz scrambled to get it as I parked myself in the red leather chair that Inspector Cramer seemed to like so much.

Wolfe drank beer, licked his lips, and looked at me, saying nothing. I returned his gaze. After a minute or so, he cleared his throat. "Mr. Bascom has spoken highly of your work."

"I'm glad to hear that. I have learned a lot from him these past weeks, and I'm still learning."

"He informs me that he cannot keep you on his payroll any longer, however, for economic reasons."

I nodded. "The business just isn't there now, and nobody knows when it will be."

"You are still relatively new to the city," Wolfe observed, "but your time here has hardly been uneventful."

"I won't argue that, sir," I said, wondering where this conversation was going.

"I am aware that your very first job in New York ended with you shooting two men fatally. How do you feel about that?"

"I'm not in any way proud of it, but you probably are familiar with the circumstances."

"I am. You were under fire yourself, I believe."

"Yes, sir, I definitely was. I feel I came very close to dying right there on that North River pier. If I hadn't thought I was in immediate danger, I would have continued firing in the air."

Wolfe dipped his chin a half inch, which I took to be a nod.

"The reason I bring this incident up, Mr. Goodwin, is that I am not interested in anyone who uses firearms indiscriminately. There are occasions, however, when one has no choice but to act with dispatch, as you did that night."

"Glad to hear you say that. I got fired because the boss of that pier felt I was too quick on the draw. I don't agree with him, and I also don't apologize for what happened that night."

"Nor should you. I am satisfied that you acted properly under the circumstances. Mr. Goodwin, I have a proposition for you."

"My ears are open."

"I would like you to work for me."

"Really? What kind of case is it?"

"You misunderstand. I am seeking a full-time assistant."

That threw me, and I covered my surprise by taking a belt of the scotch. "What exactly would the job entail?" I asked after swallowing.

"A number of things. For one, I need a man who is comfortable moving about in the city. As you can see, I am not mobile, nor am I interested in so being."

"Ah, you want a leg man, is that it?"

"In part, yes."

"Why not hire Saul Panzer? From everything I have seen and heard, he knows this town backward, forward, and sideways. He's smart, he's nervy, and he knows when to keep his mouth shut."

"I agree that Mr. Panzer possesses all those attributes you mentioned, and a good many more as well. However, he prefers to be self-employed, and with his talents and deserved reputation, he is easily able to find a steady succession of clients. I feel fortunate when I am able to retain his services for a case."

"You said my being a leg man would be a part of the job. What else do you have in mind?"

"It takes a lot of money to finance the life I have chosen to lead, which means I must use the talents I have been given. However, I confess that much of the time, I find work distasteful, and I need someone who will spur me to action."

"You mean give you a swift kick?"

He made a face. "If you insist upon putting in that way."

"Well, I tend to be somewhat antsy, so maybe I'm the right guy to—how did you put it?—spur you to action. I like to be busy, all the time. Any other duties?"

"Yes. I assume you can operate a typewriter?"

"Well, I'm by no means the world's fastest, but I know my way around the keyboard. Why?"

"You would be required to answer my correspondence as well as pay the bills and keep the checkbook and other financial records. A man currently comes in two days a week to perform these and other functions, but I have not found him to be satisfactory."

"So there's a good deal to this job besides being a detective," I said. "Have you covered everything?"

"Almost. You also would maintain the germination records for the ten thousand orchids I grow."

"Orchid records? Sorry, but I'm afraid I just struck out. I don't know a damn thing about flowers."

"You don't have to. Theodore Horstmann, who works with me up in the plant rooms, brings down note cards on plant propagation each afternoon. All you have to do is file them in their proper place in the drawers over there." Wolfe indicated a steel cabinet in one corner.

"Okay, regarding salary, what neighborhood are we in?"

Wolfe wrote a figure on a sheet and handed it to me. "I could live in that neighborhood," I said. "Speaking of neighborhoods, my hotel isn't all that far from here. What would the hours be?"

"Ah, there is one more thing, of course," Wolfe said. "I would expect you to live here."

"Here? In this house?"

"I do not think you would find life in the brownstone to be onerous. You would have a commodious bedroom on the second floor—Fritz can show it to you. It is furnished, but if the décor is not to your liking, you may purchase your own fittings.

"As to meals, you are free to eat with me in the dining room each day at lunch and dinner, and Fritz will prepare breakfast for you in the kitchen. I take my morning meal up in my room. It is not braggadocio on my part when I state to you the food served under this roof is superb. America's fourth-richest man and three well-known and highly esteemed Manhattan restaurateurs have attempted to hire Fritz away from me, but, I am happy to say, without success."

"Hmm. I think I would like to see the bedroom."

Wolfe used the buzzer to summon Fritz, and the chef and I climbed to the second floor. "That is Mr. Wolfe's bedroom," he said, gesturing to a door across the hall from the room we entered. The space that I might choose to call home was fair-sized, with its own bathroom and two large windows that looked out on West Thirty-Fifth Street. The bed appeared to be comfortable, and the desk had plenty of drawer space. There were three chairs—more than I would likely ever need. I didn't much like the pictures on the walls, but they were easily replaceable.

"Nice, yes, very nice," I remarked to Fritz as I looked around. "And where is your room?"

"In the basement," he said. "I have everything there that one could possibly need."

"Mr. Wolfe praises your cooking," I said, and the guy actually blushed.

"He is too kind, Mr. Goodwin. Mr. Wolfe is a connoisseur of fine cuisine, and I try hard to please him."

"It sounds like you succeed. Thanks for the tour."

I went back to Wolfe's office, where he was reading a book. He set it down and gave me a look as I entered. "Nice room," I told him. "You have thrown a lot at me tonight, and I would like to think about your offer."

"Very well," he said. "How much time do you feel you would you need to make your decision?"

"Just a couple of days, maybe less."

"Satisfactory. I await word." He went back to his book, and I stepped out into the hall, where Fritz was waiting. His face wore a question mark.

"This is a nice operation you've got here," I said. "Do you think I would fit in?"

"Yes, I do, Mr. Goodwin," he said with a smile.

"Remember, when we first met, I asked you to call me Archie," I told him as he held open the front door.

"And I now remind you to call me Fritz," he said. I told him I would as I said good-bye and walked down the seven steps to the sidewalk.

I stood in the breezy New York evening and looked up at the brownstone, trying to picture it as my home. I liked the picture.

# AUTHOR NOTES

First and foremost, a bow to Barbara Stout and Rebecca Stout Bradbury, to whom this book is warmly dedicated, for their support and approval. My heartfelt thanks goes out to them not only for this volume but also for my seven earlier Nero Wolfe novels, for which they also offered encouragement and wise counsel.

In developing this story, I based some events and characters, albeit loosely, on references in Rex Stout's novels. In the novella "Fourth of July Picnic," from the collection *And Four to Go* (1958), Archie Goodwin describes himself to an audience: "Born in Ohio. Public high school, pretty good at geometry and football, graduated with honor but no honors. Went to college two weeks, decided it was childish, came to New York and got a job guarding a pier, shot and killed two men and was fired ..." In several other stories, Archie mentions his Ohio origins.

In *Fer-de-Lance*, the first Nero Wolfe novel (1934), Archie refers briefly to the kidnapping of Tommie Williamson, the son of Burke Williamson, owner of a chain of hotels, and says that each year on the anniversary of the boy's safe return, Mr. and Mrs. Williamson and their son dine at Wolfe's brownstone to mark the occasion.

All the freelance operatives in this narrative also appear throughout the corpus. Del Bascom plays a far larger role here than in any of the other Wolfe stories and is generally used far less frequently than "regulars" Saul Panzer, Fred Durkin, and Orrie Cather. However, Nero Wolfe respects Bascom, and in Rex Stout's *The Silent Speaker* (1947), Wolfe recommends the old-school private eye to a prospective client, calling him "a good man." Bill Gore, like Bascom, appears only on occasion in Wolfe stories. Overall, I have tried to make all the recurring series characters, including NYPD's Inspector Cramer, Lieutenant Rowcliff, and Sergeant Stebbins, behave and react as they did in Rex Stout's compelling tales.

In addition to Mr. Stout's stories, I found three books most helpful in my research. They are: *Nero Wolfe of West Thirty-fifth Street: The Life and Times of America's Largest Private Detective* by William S. Baring-Gold (The Viking Press, 1969); *The Brownstone House of Nero Wolfe* by Ken Darby as told by Archie Goodwin (Little, Brown & Co., 1983); and the fine biography *Rex Stout* by John McAleer (Little, Brown & Co, 1977), which won a Mystery Writers of America Edgar Award for best critical/autobiographical work in 1978.

This book would not have taken flight without the tireless work of my agent, Erik Simon of the Martha Kaplan Agency, and the enthusiastic support of my publisher, Otto Penzler of Mysterious Press. I am pleased to say my history with Otto goes back quite a while. It was in his Mysterious Bookshop in Manhattan that I had the launch of my first Nero Wolfe book, *Murder in E Minor*, in 1986.

I also want to thank my longtime confidante, the literary agent David Hendin, for his support, as well as the superbly gifted mystery writer and film producer Max Allan Collins, a faithful friend who voluntarily read my manuscript and made invaluable suggestions that have improved the final product.

And the biggest thanks of all go to my wife, Janet, who not only has cheerfully put up with my idiosyncrasies and irascibilities for nearly a half century, but who also is a far better speller and grammarian than I could ever hope to be. Her eagle eye has saved me from embarrassment more times than I can count.

## ABOUT THE AUTHOR

Robert Goldsborough has been a longtime journalist with the *Chicago Tribune* and *Advertising Age* and is the author of seven previous Nero Wolfe novels. He also wrote five Snap Malek Chicago historical mysteries published by Echelon Press. He lives in Illinois.

ISBN 978-1-4532-7096-7

Published in 2012 by MysteriousPress.com/Open Road Integrated Media
180 Varick Street
New York, NY 10014
www.mysteriouspress.com
www.openroadmedia.com

# EBOOKS BY
# ROBERT GOLDSBOROUGH

FROM MYSTERIOUSPRESS.COM
AND OPEN ROAD MEDIA

Available wherever ebooks are sold

MYSTERIOUSPRESS.COM

Otto Penzler, owner of the Mysterious Bookshop in Manhattan, founded the Mysterious Press in 1975. Penzler quickly became known for his outstanding selection of mystery, crime, and suspense books, both from his imprint and in his store. The imprint was devoted to printing the best books in these genres, using fine paper and top dust-jacket artists, as well as offering many limited, signed editions.

Now the Mysterious Press has gone digital, publishing ebooks through **MysteriousPress.com**.

**MysteriousPress.com** offers readers essential noir and suspense fiction, hard-boiled crime novels, and the latest thrillers from both debut authors and mystery masters. Discover classics and new voices, all from one legendary source.

FIND OUT MORE AT
WWW.MYSTERIOUSPRESS.COM

FOLLOW US:
@emysteries and Facebook.com/MysteriousPressCom

MysteriousPress.com is one of a select group of publishing partners of Open Road Integrated Media, Inc.

OPEN ROAD
INTEGRATED MEDIA

**Open Road Integrated Media** is a digital publisher and multimedia content company. Open Road creates connections between authors and their audiences by marketing its ebooks through a new proprietary online platform, which uses premium video content and social media.

CPSIA information can be obtained at www.ICGtesting.com
Printed in the USA
BVOW080019011112

304247BV00001B/8/P